HIGH IRON
A Western Trio

FRANK BONHAM

edited by
BILL PRONZINI

Five Star • Waterville, Maine

First Edition
First Printing: March 2006

Published in 2006 in conjunction with Golden West Literary Agency.

Set in 11 pt. Plantin.

Printed in the United States on permanent paper.

Library of Congress Cataloging-in-Publication Data

Bonham, Frank.
    High iron : a western trio / by Frank Bonham ; edited by Bill Pronzini.—1st ed.
       p. cm.
    "A Five Star Western"—T.p. verso.
    "Published in conjunction with Golden West Literary Agency"—T.p. verso.
    ISBN 1-59414-334-X (hc : alk. paper)
    1. Western stories.   I. Pronzini, Bill. II. Title.
PS3503.O4315H54 2006
  813'.54—dc22   2005030479

HIGH IRON

Table of Contents

Foreword

Among Frank Bonham's abundant gifts was the ability to pack a wealth of story material into a tight fictional framework. His short fiction has greater scope than many full-length novels, and his long novelettes are essentially mini-novels loaded with twists and turns of plot, historical incident, breadth and depth of character, action, romance, evocatively described backgrounds, and rich period detail.

Each story in the Western trio presented here reflects this talent, as well as Bonham's wide-ranging interests and knowledge of frontier lore. "The Sin of Wiley Brogan" is the good-humored tale of a young horse-breaker fed up with his lot in life, whose chance meeting with an entrepreneurial postal official leads him into a riotous new profession involving stagecoach competition for the delivery of mail in eastern Oregon. "Texicans Die Hard" has a south of the border locale and an intricate plot in which Texas cowhand Charlie Drake inherits an old Chihuahuan *rancho* from a *hacendado* whose life he once saved. His decision to work the ranch with his sidekick, Cort Carraday, leads him into a series of conflicts with the *hacendado*'s scheming brother, range saboteurs, tax collectors, border renegades, *rurales* on the trail of border smugglers, a fiery *latina,* and the vengeful, Mexican-hating daughter of a wounded American trader. A saga of epic proportions, "High Iron" tells of the men who built the Central Pacific Railroad through the High Sierras, and of the multiple hazards, both natural and man-made, that they faced and overcame. It is also the story of the personal and professional relationship between Johnny Duff, assistant superintendent in charge of construction, and Babbie Carney, the tempestuous daughter of an Irish railroad engineer.

High Iron, like all of Frank Bonham's collected works, is satisfying and rewarding Western entertainment.

Bill Pronzini
Petaluma, California

The Sin of Wiley Brogan

I

Temptation came to Wiley Brogan on the stage to Cañon City. His seducer may have been sent by the devil, but he wore the guise of a backwoods post office official with a look of raw country honesty about him. Two years before, Brogan would have been too young in spirit, too possessed of impossible ideals to be capable of seduction. Two months earlier, even—sweating in a stage company corral on the Columbia River—he would have been too busy to notice that the card of introduction he had been handed spelled success. But that October his defenses were down. Like the apples of this untamed state of Oregon, he was ripe for picking—ripened by heat and discouragement and hard luck.

All summer he had trained horses for a stage company at The Dalles. He was a horse-breaker by trade. He had trained horses until there was nothing left to tame but the drivers, and with enough whiskey in him he had even been known to try that. It was a tough summer. Unreasonably hot. $50 skates to work with, from which the corral boss expected $400 stage animals. At $10 a head.

In October, they discharged him with a pass and $20 for the last two horses he had broken. The superintendent said there were two small outfits over east in Cañon City that might have something for him. He packed his grip, bought a handful of nickel cigars, and swung onto a Cañon City stage.

Riding on a company pass, he took what was left in the way of accommodations. What was left was a seat up on the hurricane deck behind the driver and messenger, in a rattling snow as gritty as salt. By the time they reached John Day River, his

13

face was stiffer than a coyote pelt on a pasture fence. He would have liked a cigar, but the wind snatched the flame right off a matchstick. Up there on the hard leather seat with his coat collar turned up and his hat tipped down, he became gloomy and introspective. This was out of character for Brogan. Normally he was a good-humored man whose fault seemed to be lack of ambition, an affable and competent man about stables.

But he brooded over the fact that he was nearly thirty, that his education was mainly physical, that horses were so mor- tally stupid. He was getting tired of being a stable hand. At Fossil Spring station, another passenger got on. Brogan was glad of the company. He moved over to make room for the man on the frosty, hard seat.

The newcomer was a short, tight-built man with a firm brown face full of creases. He had alert little black eyes, and there was something Indian about his mouth, hard and thin, yet not ungenerous. He sank right down in his black short coat and tipped his chin onto his chest. The fine snow rattled off his black stovepipe.

They walloped across a dry creek on squealing leather springs. They were now within a few miles of Cañon City. The snow pulled back into the mountains, leaving white rinds of frost on the gullied red valley. They had bored into the very hip pockets of the John Day valley, into a little corner half mountain, half prairie.

Wiley thought of a cigar, but knew he'd never get it fired up in this wind. About the same time, his companion roused up with a grunt and dug two cigars from his coat. "Smoke?" he asked.

"Why, thanks." Brogan figured he meant later.

The small man with the hard mouth and the scratch-owl eyes offered his hand. "Harry Skidmore," he said.

14

"Wiley Brogan." Skidmore's palm was hard as a board, the hand, perhaps, of a businessman who had once worked physically.

He struck three matches and lost them all. Impatiently he said: "Driver, stop this thing."

Brogan caught his breath. Stop the sun, stop the moon, but never ask a mail driver to stop his coach! All drivers were independent, but this particular one was as unsociable as a pint of tobacco juice. Brogan quickly laid a hand on Skidmore's knee and was going to square things somehow when Farrish, the driver, sang out:

"You bet!"

The coach stopped.

Skidmore got his cigar going. Brogan recovered in time to light his own.

"All set?" Farrish asked.

Skidmore took a prolonged puff. "Thanks."

The horses hit the collars. The mud wagon rocked like a baby buggy before settling back into its lurching roll.

"Whereat you heading?" asked Skidmore.

"Cañon City. End of the line."

"Likewise." Skidmore brought his lips close to Brogan's ear. "Tell you a joke on old Farrish. He'd have thrown me into a lava bed if I'd asked that a year ago! I'm a postal inspector now. I could bust him or this line any time I want." He slapped Wiley's leg and laughed silently.

Wiley understood now, and laughed with him. Skidmore smoked up half the cigar. The cold seemed to draw them together. The post office man spoke reflectively.

"It's a good job, as jobs go. Up and down, day after day, all across the state from the Cascades east. Checkin' receipts, rubbing the insides of boxes to find dust. Simple as one, two, three. Most of the postmasters do pretty good. But you'd

15

think they were all eating the glue off stamps, the way they howdy and civilize me." There came a pause. Then Skidmore's easy: "What's your line, friend?"

"Horse-breaking."

Skidmore's brown eyes faltered an instant, as if he had said he dug graves. "Good enough," he said without conviction.

Brogan was not unused to the reaction. Between jobs, wearing his gray check suit, black derby, and a clean shirt, he was often taken for a bank clerk, a saloon proprietor, or someone of similarly respected station. He had a fresh Irish face with a snub, broad nose and cleft chin. A scar showed in the dark bar of his right eyebrow, but the broncos had not succeeded in kicking his teeth out yet, or in breaking his nose. He had the manner and all the appurtenances of the successful, except success.

The stage lunged into a winding grade through a wistful grove of poplars still clinging to their summer leaves like an old floozy to a feather boa.

"That's terribly hard work for a man with any education," Skidmore grunted.

"That's it," agreed Brogan. "The education."

The inspector frowned. "Read and write, don't you? That's education."

"Not the kind the business houses pay for, nor the banks and such. Hell"—he shrugged—"I'm doing all right. It's a good trade. Maybe I'll buy a livery stable someday. Run it into a stage line. I've got a lot of ideas, if I ever get a stake."

"If it's a good trade, why buy a livery stable?" Skidmore snapped his cigar from his mouth. He seemed right on the point of being mad about something.

This was a tender point with Brogan, a blackhead on his ego fast becoming a boil, because his ambition was a thorn that never stopped deviling him, and he, too, was warming.

"If you're too holy to sit by a horse-breaker," he said, "there's other seats in back."

Immediately Skidmore softened. "Excuse me, son," he said. "I was brought up frugal. I hate to see a good saddle wasted on a bad horse, or a good man on a poor job." They were silent a while, letting the breach close, but Skidmore said finally: "I was doing the same kind of jackass figuring myself at your age. Cutting wood outside Portland. Day wages. But someday I was going to own a wood yard. Like hell I was! I'd still be felling trees and going to own a wood yard, if I hadn't had a jolt."

Brogan drew on his cigar. "What was it?" Did he sound as hound hungry as he felt? He was bone-tired of breaking horses; his concept of hell was a vast stable full of horses to break, and all of them without a brain. But a father trying to raise wheat on rock, on a rainless prairie, cannot send out sons equipped for much bookwork, and Wiley's father had sent him out with a minimum. A little reckoning, penmanship, reading—a whole trunk full of moldy paperbacked classics of his mother's—a buckshot charge of education fired at a distant target. Not enough to put a boiled collar between him and a horse—just enough to breed an ambition that must feed on itself and end by devouring the man.

"Well, I broke an arm," said Skidmore.

Wiley's face fell. There was no golden key in that.

"I was laid up for two months. I like to starved. I got so hungry I had to think. And what I thought about was how to get out of wood chopping. I heard about a mail contract open between a couple of camps nobody ever heard of. A jackass could pack it. I bid low and got it. I made less than I did cutting wood. But I was in gov'ment work."

"You still weren't using your head so's you could notice it, were you? A packer."

Skidmore winked. "Between runs, Wiley, between them! I had pretty high expenses on that contract. Most of it was for whiskey. Drinks for people. I always did like people, and I just loved them on that job. They loved me, too. Postal inspectors and such. I got other contracts, and then I landed a post office. Pretty good-size one. When this job opened up, I went after it. How do you like that cigar, Wiley?" he asked. "They cost two bits. Have another." He was like a man new to prosperity, still in the oysters-and-champagne stage, but not offensive about it.

Up ahead, Brogan could see the houses and mine stopes of Cañon City. Suddenly a panic seized him; he had an urge to squeeze this little man dry of all the advice he had, to turn him upside-down like a sack and shake him empty of all the tricks he knew. But the stage was almost there; a golden conversation had opened too late. He just sat there with his eyes hungering, and the buzzard beak of regret tearing at him.

Skidmore laughed softly. "Like taw it's a good trade!" Then he said something revealing; the kind of remark a man made who knew you would find out about him sooner or later, anyway. "Some of the boys I left behind would tell you Harry Skidmore was a back-slapper who hoorawed his way up. Or that I was a plain crook. Or I chested my authority over the ones under me to work their behinds off and get me my promotions. Maybe they're all true. Maybe none of them. I've been too busy to notice. I've gone after the things I wanted, and I've got 'em. They still lay down the carpet for me, and old Bob Farrish stops his stage when I want to light a cigar."

Wiley dropped all these remarks in a mental clasp purse for examining later. "I've heard it said," he reflected, trying to recall where, "that success was virtue. Or something like that."

Skidmore squinted. He ground down on that remark as if to wring it dry of all its juice. "That's deep," he said. "That's a damn' sight deeper than you think! Even a bank robber will be looked up to if he makes a success of it. Look at the James boys! But, by grabs, he'll be a better man for having the money, too. *There's* the deep part. He'll be kinder and pleasanter, and you can bet he'll help his wife with the dishes oftener than if he was scrounging around for a dollar a day."

They were bursting onto the main street then, with a vista of turn-outs on the gullied road, sprinkled with snow, of lank dogs and horses tailed against the wind at hitch racks. Tan stone buildings shared the streets with wooden false fronts and vacant lots. High hills wedged the town into the wide cañon. Distantly tall blue ridges diked across the southern sky. This was a cattle and mining town, and prosperous, to the first glance.

"Well," said Skidmore, "have I given you anything to chew on?"

"Lots," Brogan admitted. "But I reckon it will only make me hungrier. I wish . . . oh, hell. . . ." He shrugged.

For an instant Skidmore hesitated, like a man looking the road over before he attempted it. "Listen. You sober, don't gamble? Can you get me a couple of references? Maybe you'd like a jackass contract or a little P.O. somewhere. I don't know why I give a damn whether you break horses or lick stamps," he added ruefully. "But you've got more up there than most men running a dry-goods store and getting rich. I can see it, and I can see it's eating you up, too."

Something flagged Wiley off. "Reckon I'm not the type for licking stamps."

"OK, let's try it this way. . . ." Skidmore pulled a card from his billfold and wrote with a pencil under his name. **This will introduce Mr. Wiley Brogan.** "This might help

19

you get a job around the stage stables. I'm down here to let a new mail contract to one of their baling-wire stage outfits. We're opening up some new offices in the mining camps. It might even help some other people. Use it," he said tersely, "and then get rid of it. People get the damnedest ideas. And don't let me run into you a year from now unless you're wearing a suit that ain't out at the elbows."

They swung into the stage yard. Brogan slowly tucked the card under the sweatband of his hat. He had a queer, intuitive notion that he must get rid of it the first chance he had.

The brake shoes scraped rustily, the horses stood impatiently while hostlers threw off the chains. From the warmth of the depot came two men and a girl. Brogan's eyes passed studyingly over the girl, a dainty, coppery-haired little trick without a straight line in her body. She was with an older man. The other man stood apart from them, staring up at the pair on the deck of the stagecoach. He was tall and narrow as a hall door, a homely man with a heavy, dark mustache.

"There they are!" Skidmore chuckled. "Let a P.O. man open the front door of a county and they know about it at the back. Them are the stage people I'm to see."

He stood up and plunged his hands into the pockets of his coat. Wiley sat there, disconsolately feeling that opportunity had departed his life forever; there was, unhappily, no lock in his life that Skidmore's key would fit.

Skidmore said nasally: "Another thing I hate to see wasted is good advice on a damned fool." He stepped across the rail at the back of the driver's seat and descended to the ground.

II

When Brogan dismounted, the long-shanked man was pumping Harry Skidmore's hand lustily. He had a rich bass voice and used it to dominate the pipings of the older man.

"I've got a couple of antelope steaks spoke for at the hotel, Mister Skidmore. I'll have your bag sent over. Say, this is real nice, Mister Skidmore, real nice!"

The other man had a foot between them and was prying into the conversation. He captured Skidmore's hand. "Or how about some Oregon fried chicken? The missus has the tockwallopin'est feed laid you ever set down to. Mister Skidmore, meet my daughter, Drusilla."

He played his daughter like an ace, and she was one to take the pot. Small and grateful, with just the right amount of warmth in her eyes as she gave the inspector her hand.

Skidmore bustled right on through them. "Pleased, Miss Pennoyer. Sorry, Thoss. That steak sounds good, Pete . . . already got plans." He took his bag from the small collection under the rear boot. Then he turned to fire a direct glance at Wiley. "I'll be around till tomorrow afternoon, son. Meet me here at stage time."

Wiley waved, collected his India rubber bag, and started for the street. As he passed behind the Pennoyers, the girl stepped back. The suitcase banged against her, and Brogan experienced a soft and fragrant collision with her back. It cast her off balance; he caught her arm, and she threw him a glance of surprise.

"I guess there's another way to do that, ain't there?" he said.

"There must be." She smiled. Her lips were smooth and full and her teeth were matched like a $500 string of pearls. Her hair, brushed back and then curled like so many small sausages, was the shade of new copper wire. Standing so close, he could not look her up and down, but he had the feeling everything was in place. She stood about to his nose.

"Are you Mister Skidmore's assistant?" she asked him.

"Just a friend."

She looked disappointed.

Wiley did not move on; these were, after all, the people he had come to Cañon City to see—the small stage operators. It might be that the factor of his friendship with Skidmore would serve as a lever to remove their inertia against hiring help. As yet, the card of introduction had no importance for him.

"By the way," he said, "I'm down here to break horses. Stage stock or pack. That's one of my teams right there. Ask Bob Farrish what he thinks of it."

An ascetic-looking man with pale eyes and a dyed, dead-black soup-strainer mustache, Pennoyer shook his head. His shallow blue eyes were focused beyond Wiley, if they were focused at all. They looked like the eyes of a man staring into a fog. Nearly bald, he let his side hair grow long and whipped it back above his ears.

"I've got more horses than I can use," he said.

"What if you have to expand? Somebody's going to get a mail contract, I hear."

"We might as well go back," Pennoyer said to his daughter.

She paused to say pleasantly: "I'm afraid there won't be anything. But if there should, where can we find you?"

"I'll be in town a few days. I'll drop around. What company?"

"Oregon Mail."

He caught the other man, who shook his head. "See my super. Jim Shaniko." His mind was away somewhere, too. Not snuffling over its miseries, like Pennoyer's, but baying after a new scent. His dead-black eyes, above the yellowish smudges of slack skin, were indrawn and busy. Brogan sensed that he would be fighting for that contract until the last trick in his bag was exhausted.

Two days of clattering around on top of a stagecoach in wind and snow and rain had left Wiley foggy-headed and fatigued. He lugged his suitcase up the street to the Western Hotel.

The town lay in a bare valley on Cañon Creek. Marsh slopes, scarred with old placers and sprinkled with juniper, climbed high above the settlement. Volcanic cliffs staked the distant edges of the cañon. Along the street, poplars scattered their yellow leaves in the half-frozen ruts; a mountain ash, laden with orange berries, half dominated the roadway. Most of the buildings looked solid, many of them constructed of blocks of yellow volcanic tuff. Back from the main street were winding avenues of unpainted shacks, each shack clutching its clothesline, privy, and shed. Cañon City pulled a mixed trade. Mining was still the mainstay, but ranchers were edging out into the Indian country, and a few farms lay along the rivers.

Brogan got a cheap room at the Western Hotel. He had found that the cheapest room at a good hotel was generally better than the best room at a cheaper one. This time he was wrong. He landed in a sort of kennel under an outside stairway with a rear door to the back house and an inside door on a dim hall. It was furnished with a cot, a graniteware wash pan, a wooden bucket of cold water, and a baking powder can full of soft soap made of wood-ash lye and lard. A damp cold came from the walls like fog.

He lay down. Fatigue retreated slowly from his muscles. He found his thoughts swinging back to Harry Skidmore. He got out the golden key the inspector had given him. It was not twenty-four carat gold, maybe not even good plate. It might turn out to be brass, by ordinary ethical standards. But it had opened the door for Skidmore.

Brogan perceived definitely something he had always suspected—that morals were blood brother to economics. Had he met Skidmore at a time when he was flush, he would have considered him a rather shabby character. He would have been offended by the implications of the card of introduction. But tonight he was low enough to realize two things: that if he got just a little broker, he would pass the card as readily as he would a sawbuck; and that he was nearing a fork in his life.

Skidmore had put the curse on his dreams of owning a livery stable. He was a completely cynical man. What the little post office inspector had got across was that, unless he made some radical change in his life, he would never be more than a common bronc'-stomper. In a few more years, ambition would become a crackling cinder. The habit of deference would incline him more to tipping his hat than to settling it over his eye. But he balked at the notion of using the card. He did not like to look too closely at Skidmore's formula for success in government work. There was a whang of shadiness about it, a hint of winks and nudges, and appointments over the heads of worthier candidates.

He decided to forget about Harry Skidmore and concentrate on that stable he was going to own someday. But the last thing he thought about was the girl he had bumped into at the stage station. A thought stole back over the rubble of worn-out important thinking that had displaced it at the time. *She backed into me a-purpose! Why? To meet a friend of Harry Skidmore's? To get a toe-hold on that mail contract?* But that seemed to lap over into his heavyweight speculations about integrity again, and he shied away from it. Instead, he thought of her hair, and the provocative turn of her lips, and the figure he had not been able to look over to his satisfaction.

III

In mid-afternoon, when he had finished sleeping, he went out and poked around town, critical as a horse trader. You could tell a lot about towns by small things. The way the men dressed their women, for instance. You'd know by that if they'd pay to have a horse broke. Shabby dresses and scuffed shoes meant they probably knocked their own horses in the head with a singletree, tied a sack of grain in the saddle, and figured they were broke when they quit pitching. Contrariwise, a livery stable where the manure was shoveled out before it got hock deep meant the citizens were considerate of their animals. All these phenomena hauled back to money. Cañon City was well dowered with mines, farms and ranches, and there were the mountain mining camps, fifteen to fifty miles distant. Wiley's personal well-being revolved about the stage companies feeding these remote camps. There was a pack-train outfit supplying the camps beyond the roads, an express company, and there were the two stage lines.

He hiked first down to Pete LeeMaster's Mountain Stage Line corrals. LeeMaster was the dour, coffin-jawed man who had told him to look up Jim Shaniko. At a livery stable, he learned a lot about LeeMaster without learning anything for sure. "Sure, Pete's all right," a man forking hay told him. And then he explained that LeeMaster was all right except— except that he worked his men an hour longer than anybody else. Except that he pounded the seed heads out of the hay he bought to feed his own stock and gave the straw to animals he boarded. He was really a generous man, unless you were trying to make a living out of doing business with him.

Brogan was feeling good after his sleep, and took a whiskey to put the final edge on his gusto. Then he went down and asked for Jim Shaniko. A workman told him he was out back somewhere.

Wiley found him standing by a dusty Concord stage with another man. You couldn't tell which was Shaniko, but you could tell which was not. The man in overalls, who listened while the other talked, was not Shaniko. Shaniko was a tremendous man with a chest deep as a vinegar barrel. He wore a striped jersey with long sleeves, and trousers held up by suspenders from which the elastic had gone, so that the waistband was about where the hip pockets should have been. He was talking earnestly and gesturing with a hand that held a cigar; the other hand, rammed into his pocket, jingled coins.

"I don't see why you've always got to make a major job out of something piddling," he was complaining. "I used to keep all the wagons in this outfit running single-handed, before LeeMaster doubled his crew and his grief, and I can tell you I didn't have a junk pile full of first-class machinery like you have. You could dust off half of that corruption out back, throw a little paint at it, and sell it for new. Now, why have we got to install new thorough braces in this thing instead of taking up on the old ones?"

"Because I've took up on them so many times they ain't got any more snap than them suspenders you're wearin', Mister Shaniko. I can take up on them again, but what happens? The coach hits a pothole and the reaches come down on the axles like the devil splittin' kindling. And they don't come back up. They lay there a-jouncin' and a-shakin' all the glue loose, and pretty soon we're buying a new coach instead of a new set of braces."

Shaniko spat and walked around to take a better look at the dusty leather springs, muttering to himself, and gave a wheel a kick. Wiley could see his face. It was red, as he had known it would be from the back of his neck. He had a mouth like a black bass, thin blond brows, and shallow blue eyes. His hair was parted in the middle and ostentatiously brought aside in twin bartender's curls.

The workman was not unskillful at handling employers. "I'll tell you what I think," he said darkly. "It's them infernal freight wagons. They're kicking hell out of that road, but do you think they'd ever get out and fill a hole? Not if they lost their load six days a week in it! They're ruining the road, and *we* pay for it!"

"That's about the size of it," the superintendent agreed. "Well, if you've got to, you've got to. But hold these repairs down. I'd hate to have to can you over a set of carriage lamps."

He saw Brogan then. Brogan was of half a mind to turn around and go back. This was a scrounging outfit, and no mistake. But Shaniko was coming over to growl at him. He stood about four inches taller than Wiley, a big man a little gone to fat but still hard.

"LeeMaster told me to look you up," Brogan said. "I'm a horse-breaker."

"He told me you'd hit him. I've got enough horses around here to outfit a cavalry troop. How much do you work for?"

"Ten dollars a head. That's fully trained. No foolishness about any horse I break."

Shaniko looked as though he had been hit in the face with a wet fish. "Ten dollars! I can get Siwash Indians over yonder across the hills to break for three."

"You'd better do it, then," Wiley said curtly. He gave him the barest nod and started back, but waited when Shaniko said, staring after him: "What's your experience?"

"What's the difference? You can't afford me anyway."

The corral boss frowned over this, trying to decide whether he was offended. "I can tell you right now, brother, you won't get ten in this town. If you want to work for eight, I'll take it up with the boss."

Wiley said: "I'd get a tin bill and pick manure with the birds before I'd train a horse for eight dollars. So long."

Jim Shaniko was sure now; he was angry. He threw away his cigar. The hand in his pocket ceased jingling coins. "Maybe you'd better get started right now. We've got plenty of it right here. Maybe I'll help you start."

Wiley laughed in his face. When a big man angered this easily, it showed he was less sure of himself than he should have been. "I wouldn't be selfish," he said. "You can be my guest."

What Shaniko meant to do was not clear, but at that moment the cold breeze brought the bronze cry of a stage horn. A Concord stagecoach behind six horses brawled into the yard. Up on the box, the driver was geeing and hawing and muling away on the lines as though he were managing a gang plow.

"Whoa, Sam! Dad-blame you, Belle! Haw it over!"

The horses were lathered from bit to breeching. They responded to the driver's hands the way a bull reacted to the buzzing of a fly. They wrestled around until they were ready to stop, then the hostlers jumped on them as though they might decide to turn around and run back up to Garnet all of a sudden. Brogan's eyes picked at the Roman-nosed bay on the off leader's tree. There was a jade that wouldn't have made wheeler on any of his teams.

Shaniko said ominously: "I'll see *you* later, fella." He hurried to receive the express box and waybill and welcome the passengers with chesty cordiality. Pete LeeMaster came from the office and began snooping about the coach as though he

29

expected a wheel to have been stolen.

The passengers were crippling out, stretching in the yard before they claimed their baggage. They looked as if they had been dragged across the lava beds in a gunny sack. A poor team could do that, just as a poor road could. A poor team instinctively knew where to find the broadest and deepest chuckholes. Shaniko and LeeMaster stood together studying the waybill. Brogan had seen all he wanted of this cheap-jack outfit; he started out, but, as he passed, Pete LeeMaster's eyes came up and pinched with slow recollection.

"Wait a minute!" he said. Something surprising happened to his face; it became cordial. He handed the papers to Shaniko and got between Brogan and the gate to take his hand and clap him on the other shoulder. "What happened to you? I looked around for you after you left but nobody'd ever heard of you."

Wiley said he'd probably been asleep in his suite at the Western Hotel. "I generally check in and then wait for the offers. I had one for eight dollars, just now. I guess I'm still a little green."

LeeMaster laughed, that rich mahogany voice of his keyed down around his belt buckle. "Jim would offer you a dollar and six-bits, if he thought you looked like you'd take it."

"Do I look like eight dollars?" Wiley asked.

Shaniko's mouth opened with some sour witticism, but he saw that LeeMaster was laughing with Brogan just now and contained it. "As a matter of fact," LeeMaster admitted, "I may be having a lot of horses broke before long. If a certain piece of business goes through."

The stagecoach had been rolled into the barn, where men attacked it with buckets and slop rags. Wiley observed the cautious manner of the hostlers unharnessing the team in the big corral. "I can see six horses that need breaking, right now," he said.

LeeMaster smiled. "They get the wagons through." He found cigars, snipped the ends with a gold cigar cutter, and struck a match for Wiley. It seemed to Wiley that he was being cigared all over the lot today. "I was thinking, after I saw you with Harry this morning, that I'd get my bid in before you got tied up with someone else."

Shaniko could not watch. He turned his back.

"Harry?"

"Harry Skidmore."

"Oh, yeah, well, I'm still available. Eleven dollars a head, with a minimum of twelve horses."

The corral boss turned. "Eleven! Damn it . . . Pete . . . !"

LeeMaster arched an eye at him. "We can dicker over it later." He turned the cigar between his fingers and glanced at Wiley. "Know Harry pretty well?"

"Never met him before today."

Cordiality began to ease out of LeeMaster's face, like a friendly hound with dirty feet being cuffed back. "But I heard him tell you to see him off tomorrow. . . . ?"

"Why not? We got to talking. He wanted to finish it up, I guess. I'd never seen him before today."

He knew what was wrong with the stage man, had known all along. He had taken him for a doormat to wipe his boots on before he went in to submit his bid. A little favor done for a friend of somebody who had big favors to pass out. Skidmore's strategy was in operation.

"Eleven dollars isn't what I like to get," he said, "but maybe it's the best this town can offer. I'll start tomorrow on that team that just came in."

LeeMaster frowned at the tip of his cigar. "I'll let you know if I need you."

Into Wiley Brogan's head came the picture of a small, rectangular card on which was written: **This will introduce Mr. Wiley Brogan.** A golden communion wafer to make him and Pete LeeMaster friends in the spirit. And because LeeMaster could even make him think of something dishonest, he wanted to take him by the shirt and smash him in the face.

He dropped the cigar in the dust and gave it a boost with the toe of his boot to roll it away from him. "If you only knew it," he said, "you haven't got a horse in your corral fit to pull a Concord! Why, that team over there. . . ."

Jim Shaniko saw that he had been released from his vow of silence. He took a deep breath and hitched up his slack-suspendered pants three inches. "You can start work tonight at Big Annie's as far as we're concerned."

Wiley regarded him with gentle contempt. "Lemme show you something about that team of yours they just brought in. Why it ain't safe on a mountain grade! I'll bet you a brass bedpan the bay boogers. . . ." He ducked under the corral bars and advanced on the team, still under collars.

Shaniko yelled: "Keep away from that team, you fool!"

Wiley went on, not slowing, not hurrying, walking straight up to the Roman-nosed bay leader he had taken a dislike to. The mare shied and began toe-dancing. He raised his hand to pat her on the neck and she threw over against the near leader, rearing. Shaniko was roaring like a bull elk.

One of the handlers came toward Wiley; he waved him off. He made a pass at the horse with his derby, casually, as a passenger might remove his hat as he stood by the road on a warm day. The mare lunged back into the breeching and the swing horse behind her started to sashay about. In a moment the whole team was backing and kicking out at each other.

Wiley turned away, grinning. Shaniko had come on the run. "That's no team, brother. That's a horse herd. There's only one way to straighten out a horse like that bay mare. Shoot a gun off in her ear, take off an inch of the tip. She'll lose a lot of foolish notions. If I had my Colt. . . ."

The superintendent was tomato-red. He stood close to Wiley, six-feet-four and smelling of sweat, his face turgid with anger. "Get out of here!"

"What are you going to do? Shoot me full of hard bullets?"

Shaniko grabbed him by the shoulder and hauled him back to the gate. He was in mid-stride when Wiley's fist came around from the side, smoking hot, and landed in the middle of his face. It made a splattering sound and the corral boss stumbled back with a bellow like an injured elk. He covered half his face with his hand for a moment, closing his eyes, then pulled his hand down and looked for Wiley. He said a word that had touched off the demolition of many a saloon. He lunged back, enormously strong and monstrously angry.

Wiley lacked an inch of six feet. He did not weigh over 170. All he had was a conviction that he could lick any man he had to, if he stayed with it long enough. That didn't make the corral boss any smaller, but it made Wiley larger. He came in as though to swap punches with the big man, but ducked the first swing, let the second bruise his shoulder, and then slammed him on the ear with a good roundhouse blow, and stepped aside. Shaniko made a grimace and pivoted. He shot a long, reaching blow that caught Wiley on the cheek bone. It was unbelievable. The man had a reach like a pine tree.

Wiley felt blood oozing from the split skin. He was pedaling around groggily and Shaniko was crowding him, slinging punches from both sides. He caught one on his forearm and it felt as though it were broken. But when the corral boss stepped in to grapple, he clipped him on the chin with his elbow. Then he rammed an uppercut, but Shaniko clubbed it aside and slugged him on the side of the head.

Wiley rolled away from him, staggered. Shaniko was momentarily too punchy to finish it up, or the fight would have been over.

The horses were cavvying around wildly, fighting the handlers. LeeMaster stood by the gate impassively viewing the battle. Wiley was wondering why he had started this, but he knew the answer. He needed a scrap right now to remind himself he was as tough as they come. He couldn't prove it by the contents of his poke. Shaniko had made himself a logical candidate.

Shaniko quartered in. He felt for Wiley's head with a couple of long stabs of his left arm. Brogan swung and missed him a foot. Then Shaniko snapped into it. He smashed out with that murderous right hand of his. It connected, grazingly but with stunning power. Wiley went down.

He knew he could not stand up to it much longer, and he had the feeling that Jim Shaniko could keep right on giving better than he took for some time. Shaniko looked as though he knew it, too; he was feeling better about things. The big man reached down to haul Wiley up for the snapper. Wiley grabbed his arm, tilted his head, and let Shaniko's face collide with it as he came down. There was a pained grunt. Brogan lurched to his knees and began to slam blows into Shaniko as though this were the last fight he would ever be in and he must unload all his Sunday punches at once. He caught Shaniko by surprise. His eyebrow was cut and bleeding, his mouth was smashed but the blows kept piling in savagely.

Wiley got to his feet, making feinting motions at the corral boss as he started to lumber up. Shaniko was so foggy that all he knew was to get up and wade in for more. Wiley ripped loose. He hit Shaniko on the point of the chin with a long upswing clout. Then he watched the huge shoulders cave and the long arms reach toward the ground, and saw Shaniko, his face still resisting the proposition that he was whipped, fall to his knees and lunge forward against the earth.

IV

LeeMaster had taken the whole thing impersonally. Standing with some other men at the gate, he watched Wiley leave the corral. Spiritually Wiley felt cleaned out; physically he was about to collapse.

"First time that's ever happened to Jim," LeeMaster said. "Look out, Brogan."

"Why don't you fire that big clown and get yourself a good corral boss?" Brogan asked. "I know horses, and I've got some ideas about how to run a stage line to make a profit."

"Everybody," said LeeMaster, "has an idea about how to run somebody else's business." He left the group and went inside.

Pride kept Wiley on his feet until he reached a vacant lot. Here he stepped off the boardwalk, planted his back against a wall, and slid down. For about five minutes he was cold sick. A man leaned over him and said: "All right, fella?"

"I'll make it. Where's a barbershop?"

"Next to the hotel. I'll give you a hand."

"Never mind."

After a while he moved on up the street toward the barbershop, advancing with the grave and uncertain progress of a drunk. The barber, a mustachioed little man who looked like a German bandmaster, worked on him for an hour. He reduced the swelling under his eye and pulled the cuts together with plaster, pickled his skinned knuckles in alum water, and tried to sell him a hair singe and tonic. Wiley resisted the flourishes, but paid another quarter to have his clothes brushed.

He went out. A wind was darting up the street. The day was ending in melancholy grays and a dishwater sky. There was more snow in the sagging belly of the gray clouds massing over the town. He had a steak at a small café, and this, and three cups of coffee, did much to iron out the kinks. But all through it that key of Skidmore's kept rattling about a lock just too small to admit it. *Now, why?* he thought. *Why didn't I use the card? A lot of preachers wouldn't have thought twice about using it.* It was the way business was run. You did something for a friend; the friend did something for you. But the matter of a federal mail contract made it just a little more serious than that.

When he felt like it, he hiked up the road to the barn which was headquarters of the pack-train outfit. He was self-conscious about his battered face, but the barber had done a masterful job. People hardly grinned at him. It developed that the packer broke his own stock. Wiley went on to the freight depot and asked around. They were pretty well fixed up, too. He wondered about the mines. No use, they told him. They used mules, and mules just didn't wear out.

He walked back to town. It was cold and he missed his hat, which he had left at LeeMaster's. He felt singularly annoyed with God, or somebody. He was doing his gad-blamedest to stay honest, but they were not doing their part. He had recited to Skidmore the saying about success being virtue. Now he recollected another proverb about that sterling quality. That virtue was its own reward. There was sour humor in it.

He was sauntering down the road, chewing on his dislike for Shaniko's big face and bass-like mouth when he saw the Pennoyer girl walking ahead of him. She was moving along with pert strides that advanced her nearly as fast as Wiley's saunter. There was a vitality about the girl that aroused him. He amused himself by watching the brisk sway of the long skirt flowing down her hips, gay as a schoolgirl's chatter. He stepped up his walk and moved in beside her. She gave him that swift blue-eyed glance.

"Well, hello," he said "This is a surprise. I just happened to be running down the street full tilt and danged if I didn't run into you!"

"Isn't it wonderful, how things happen?" she said. She had an unflinching way of looking at a man. Nothing coy about her. Her face was swift and alert, delicately cast but far from having any Dresden-doll look about it. She was taking his measure as frankly as he took hers, not brazenly, but reading all she could about him in his face. The first thing she saw was that it had lost some hide and gained some bruises in the last few hours.

"I said to myself when I saw you," she said, " 'he's a brawler.' Who was it?"

Wiley sadly shook his head. "Ah, it's a rough trade! I was in a stall with these three horses when a mule walked in. You never saw such a brawl! I was lucky to come out alive."

"It's the people in a trade who make it rough."

"Speaking of that," Wiley said, "have you managed to gouge LeeMaster's eye out yet? In the way of getting the contract away from him?"

"There are some details to be worked cut. Mister Skidmore's name on the paper, for one."

"I've been wondering," he said, "who ate Skidmore's Oregon fried chicken?"

"The Pennoyers. We didn't really expect him to eat with us. But we knew LeeMaster was out to grab him and we certainly weren't going to sit back."

Am I wrong about something? Wiley mused. *I get the notion that Miss Drusilla is the shove in that outfit.*

She smiled and modestly kept her eyes on the walk. "I

keep books for Father, that's all. But I'm going to land that contract somehow, if I have to give Skidmore dope and guide his hand on the paper. I've been wondering something, too. Would you be interested in breaking horses for fifteen dollars a head?"

Wiley closed his eyes. "For twelve dollars," he said, "I teach the horse to say excuse me when he belches. For fifteen, I train him to eat with a knife and fork, salute the flag, and blow the horn when approaching a station. I'm so interested in busting bronc's for fifteen dollars," he said, "that you'll have to excuse me while I dash away a few tears."

She reached over and patted his arm. "My poor man," she said, "you've had a hard time, haven't you? I thought that was lace at your wrists, but now I see it's your cuffs. Wiley, you're a fool . . . nobody but a fool would break horses, anyway . . . but you're a likeable fool and I want you to work for us . . . after we're packing the mail."

Brogan had the impression that he had been in this conversation before. LeeMaster, however, had been a little more direct about it. Perhaps she did not see the real motive behind her interest in him: the hope that Harry Skidmore would hear that she had given a friend of his a job and his heart would be warmed toward her. He was not exactly shocked, but he faltered over answering.

The girl, suddenly noting his silence and glancing at him, said with a catch of her breath: "Wiley, for heaven's sake! What did you think I meant?"

"I thought you might like me to deliver that contract in person."

She stopped, annoyed and angry. "If you think I was trying to bribe you. . . ."

Her color was fine when she was angry, paling her cheeks a trifle but darkening her eyes and lips. Her reaction was reas-

suring and enhancingly feminine; she hadn't known herself
what was in her mind.

"I've been philosophizing too much," he said. "I'm close
to thirty years old, Drusilla, and all I know is horses. I know
they're a dang' poor living, and I'd like to get out of it. Maybe
I just *wish* somebody would bribe me."

"If somebody does," she said, "it won't be me." She stared
at him a while, studying over it, looking deeply into him and
perhaps seeing as much of him as he had seen of her. She said:
"You can call me Dru, since you won't be an employee of
mine. Why don't you get out of it, if you don't like it? If a
person really wants something, he ought to be able to manage
it. I haven't any patience with people who are always wanting
to do things, but never find the time to do them. Dad wanted
to get out of being a timekeeper in an iron foundry, and he
just naturally made up his mind and did it."

"How long did it take him?"

She hesitated, then laughed. "Thirty years. But he did it!
He is a transportation man, now . . . an honest to heaven
transportation man."

"How is he making out?"

"You've got a mind like an auditor. It's none of your business how we're making out. We're in business, aren't we?"

She was as capricious as mountain weather. "What I was
thinking," he said, "was that whoever gets to pack the mail is
going to be the only one left in business in a year's time. I hear
they pay about a hundred and fifty dollars a mile for a corner
of the boot to throw their mailbags in. You could cut rates on
LeeMaster till he couldn't afford to ride his own stages. Or he
could cut them on you."

They were before the lava-brick office of the Oregon Mail
Company—*an optimistic title,* thought Brogan. She turned to
stand in the doorway, facing the street. "It would be the only

trick he hasn't used against us," she said. "He's cornered all the grain in town and half starved us, crowded our coaches into the bank, and tried to buy up our notes to put the squeeze on us. But rates are already so low a person would be cutting his own throat if he lowered them any more without a subsidy of some kind."

"Well, I hope you swing it," he said. "And I hope LeeMaster's horses all come down with the swinney. But not if I'm working for him. Can I still call you Dru if I do?"

"You'll call me Miss Pennoyer . . . but I probably won't answer." She said it severely, but her eyes laughed. She turned and was swallowed by the gloom of the office.

Leaving her, he felt good. He felt as though he had just been sliding down a rainbow, or holding hands with spring-time. Everything he looked at had a soap-bubble shimmer. The whole interview was colored with an irrational charm. Realizing it was totally illogical did not lessen the magic of it; she was pretty, and the world was fair, and he was Wiley Brogan, success, instead of Wiley Brogan, failure. She liked him. Would she have given him her nickname to carry, like a lock of hair, if she did not? She was frank about her feelings, so frank that it was like walking through light and shadow to be with her. But she was not quite frank with herself, if she did not know there was design in her offer to him. Feminine as she was, a little hairspring of merchandising vibrated inside her. No doubt there were some hard times and flour-sack underwear in her background, which tended to rise up and shoo her along any time she felt them getting too close.

He tried to take a little corner of the rainbow back into the hotel room with him, but failed. He had to check it at the desk, as he checked his key when he went out, and he knew that, when he went back for it later, there would be nothing left of it but a damp little puddle in his heart.

41

V

Brogan's descent to sin occurred, fittingly, in the dingy hotel room. He had removed his boots, trousers, and shirt, and crawled into the blankets. They smelled of perspiration and dampness. There were cracks in the plank walls through which he could have shoved a saddle blanket. Wind hissed through them and he heard the fingers of the snow secretly trying the walls. He slept for a while but was wakened by slots of light and low voices from the next room. A young couple was talking, the girl apparently consoling the man over something.

It depressed him. Only a woman could do that for a man—heal his splintered ego so that in the morning he could go out, and come back to her that night a little more than before. It bore upon him with the suffocating finality of a cave-in that it was all wrong—that any way you could fight your way out of it was legitimate. Success, by God, *was* virtue! Was there any particular virtue in failure?

This was when he knew how he was going to use the card; it was after he realized that he had left it under the sweatband of his hat, which he had left in the Mountain Stage Line corral. He reared up in bed, intending to go after it. He was as hot to use it now, as he had been not to use it before. But he sank back, reflecting that, if it were lost, he could replace it when he saw Skidmore.

With all his soul-searching behind him, he felt better than he had in years. Born to hang, perhaps. At any rate, he slept, and knew the stories about criminals sitting on the edge of their beds with their faces in their hands was unadulterated hokum.

He slept late, rising at ten to wash his face in icy water and don his other clean shirt. In the soapy steel mirror, he examined his battle scars. He ran a comb industriously through his stiff, dark hair, without taming it much. Then, in his gray suit, a cigar in his mouth, he inspected himself again, and grinned.

Brogan, he thought, *you're a hell of a boy. As a stage man you'll knock 'em over.*

He had no intention of going after a job breaking horses. If he had to sin, it was going to be a blue-chip sin. He was going to be manager, vice-president, or some damned thing. When he said frog, people were going to jump. Wiley Brogan was going to test out some of these theories of his.

The desk clerk had been watching for him. "Mister Brogan!"

"I'm not checking out for a couple of days. I'll pay later."

The clerk was a pot-bellied little man wearing a sweater coat and tight trousers. "This ain't about your bill. Ain't you the fellow that had a mill with Jim Shaniko?"

"Do you have to ask that?"

"Have you got a gun?"

"Why?"

"Shaniko has and he's wearing it. He's never been licked before. He ain't the type to eat a lickin'. He was drunk last night and looking all over town for you. I'd wear a gun, if I was you, if only to call his bluff. Keep out of his way a couple of days and he'll simmer down."

Wiley considered. "The way I handle a gun, I'd be safer without one. Shaniko's a lot of wind, anyway."

But while he ate breakfast at a counter next to the bank, he pondered how to go back for his hat without running afoul of Shaniko, perhaps still half drunk. He was sitting there, drinking a last cup of coffee and staring into the street, where

43

horses and wagons were grinding into mud the four inches of snow that had fallen during the night, when he saw Pete LeeMaster walk by with a bankbook in his hand, studying over it. LeeMaster suddenly glanced around and saw him. He came inside.

He sat down by Brogan, winked at the waitress, and raised one finger, which meant he wanted coffee. While she poured it from a blue enamel coffee pot encysted in soot, he looked Wiley over.

"You don't look so bad. You ought to see Jim. See him first, though, if you do."

"I hear he's going to saw me into stove wood."

LeeMaster looked uneasy. "I'm going to have to let Jim go. He can't get along with anybody. Not even me."

"As easy as you are to get along with?"

"I'm not so hard. Only if you're trying to run a whizzer on me. These Pennoyers. They think I'm the original ring-tailed roarer, just because I don't laugh when they corner all the grain in sight."

"I heard you cornered it on them."

"This year. Last year it was them. They had me feeding my stock so much bran I was afraid they'd begin giving milk. Don't sell that girl short! Don't sell any woman short, in business. They figure anything's fair they don't get caught at. When they hew to a line at all, half of it comes away on the axe."

"Maybe so. But she offered me fifteen a head to break stock for her."

When LeeMaster smiled, his teeth were white and even under the thick, square-cut mustache. "Was that after you showed her the card?"

Brogan's instinctive reaction was to glance up to see if the waitress had heard. She had not. Neither had the only other customer, at the far end of the counter.

"Why don't you come down to the office?" LeeMaster suggested. "The stage for The Dalles leaves in a couple of hours. We can have a talk before you go over."

"Sure," Wiley said.

On the way up, the stage man explained that he had sent Shaniko out that morning to bid on some rye hay that was advertised up near John Day. They went through the cold, untidy waiting room into the rear office. It was small and musty with bare walls and a flowered cotton carpet. Beside a roll-top desk stood a revolving bookcase and a waste basket of woven reeds. There was a calendar on the wall above the desk and an ambrotype of a bearded man with a horse-trader look about him.

LeeMaster sat in the swivel chair and with his toe moved a cuspidor between them. He opened a box of cigars. "What I want to know," he said, "is why you didn't show me that thing yesterday?"

"I thought I'd try to sell myself, first. If that didn't pan out, I knew I could sell Skidmore."

"How much do you think you ought to have out of this?"

"You mean how much per head?"

"That, or a flat rate."

"A flat rate would be a bribe. I want a job. If I've got to get it this way, I suppose I've got to. But it won't be per head, either, because I'm all done breaking horses."

LeeMaster's eyes got that curtained look again. "Then what are we talking about?"

"A position. I've been in this game a long time. Even the boys who shovel out the manure get some ideas about how a stage business ought to be run in fifteen years. I'm practically foundering on ideas."

"What do you want to be? My pardner?" LeeMaster's face

was austerely amused.

"Not exactly. I want to manage the outfit for you. I'll take twenty-five percent of the gross."

"Why, you damned fool!"

Wiley wagged his cigar. "Pardners," he said, "shouldn't talk that way to each other."

"Twenty-five percent of the *gross!* Why, good God! What do you think I'm making here . . . a million dollars a year? Twenty-five percent of the gross is about all I make."

"Don't break down," Brogan said. "If I'm not worth it, don't pay it. But if I am, I'll take a contract that will last as long as the mail contract. Probably four years. We'll adjust at the end of that time. But you'll be the only one in business by then, and we'll both be making so much money we probably won't want to upset the apple cart by making any changes."

LeeMaster got up and toured the office. He appeared to be utterly confounded. "Twenty-five *percent!* Brogan, you must be crazy. What are you? A horse-breaker, all right, that's good, honest work, but what do you know about managing a stage line?"

Brogan got up. He dropped the cigar in the spittoon. "I know Harry Skidmore," he said. "If I still can't sell myself, I can always fall back on him." He glanced about and found his hat on the prong of an antelope head on the wall. He took it and blew off the dust. "Well, you think it over. I'm going on up to the Pennoyers' and talk to them."

LeeMaster impatiently waved his hand at him. "Sit down, sit down! We can work this out, but not in five minutes."

Wiley was staring into the greasy, silk-lined bowl of his derby. "Where's the card?"

LeeMaster waived his hand again. Look," he said, "what about ten percent of the net?"

"What about giving me that card? I didn't expect to be

able to do business with you anyway. Even at twenty-five percent of the gross, you'd be killing yourself to figure out ways to make the gross run smaller than the net. Where's the card?"

Pete LeeMaster drew on the cigar. His face was both apprehensive and stubborn. "I misput it."

Wiley started across the room. "That card," he said, "leaves when I do. You cheap scrounger!"

LeeMaster pulled back the square skirts of his coat as if to hook his thumbs over the snakeskin belt. The left thumb did find the belt, but his right hand drew a bone-handled Colt from the holster at his hip. It was a heavy-caliber Bisley with the bluing worn off the highlights and no front leaf at all. LeeMaster shifted his cigar around in his mouth and handled the gun with no show of excitement.

"Someday," he said, "that pepper pot you call a brain is going to get you in trouble. Sit down. Let's hash this over. I don't know exactly where the card is, but, if I ever need it, I think I can find it."

"If I went to the Pennoyers, I suppose you'd think you needed it then?"

"I suppose so."

"What's the matter with that gaboon you call a brain? It's got my name on it, but it hasn't got the Pennoyers', and it's in your possession. People will want to know how come you to have it."

"It may have the Pennoyers' name on it by then."

Wiley turned and went to the door, angry enough to throw the wall at him if it had not been nailed down. He opened the door and stood there making and unmaking his right fist. "You can do what you want with the damned thing," he said. "But if this ever gets to court, you and I will have our whereases and wherefores out behind the courthouse. You wouldn't look so big without that cannon. You'd look just about right to fit under a cow chip."

LeeMaster laughed at his fury, but the last thing he said had more significance than all the other declarations put together. "There's no way I can keep you from trying to do business against me, Brogan, but I can do one thing. I can promise you it will be the most profitless work you ever got into."

VI

Wiley had been cautious too long, and he was too angry with LeeMaster to be bluffed out this early. He went first to the saloon, had a shot, and slogged on up the hill to the Oregon Mail Company. Some passengers were waiting on benches in the yard for the afternoon stage to Garnet. Inside, in an office too prim, too tricked out with things like clean pen wipers to be thoroughly masculine, he found the Pennoyers, Thoss D. and Drusilla. Near a small post-office cage with one wicket, Drusilla sat on a high stool, making small figures in a ledger. She wore paper cuffs and a starched white blouse and dark skirt.

Pennoyer was tilted back in his chair, stabbing a sharp letter opener at his desk. His wispy Robert Louis Stevenson-patterned mustache looked as dark as serge, but his hair was frankly white. He glanced up at Brogan and said nothing. Dru smiled curiously and swung to face him.

"All right if I close the door?" Brogan asked.

"I wouldn't blame you. Shaniko's on the warpath."

"This isn't for Shaniko."

Women have an insight that makes the average man appear to be wearing mental smoked glasses. They can smell intrigue two counties away. So it was no surprise to Wiley to see small, blue glints of light appear in Dru's eyes. She knew what was coming and he felt she already knew how it was going to work out.

"If I had time, I'd be clever about this," he said. "But Skidmore leaves in forty-five minutes, and I've got to be down at the depot. I had a card from him that said . . . 'This will introduce Mister Wiley Brogan.' He told me it would get me a job. He also told me to burn it after I got my job."

Pennoyer's stiff features refused to react.

"Where is it now?" Dru asked quickly.

"It was in my hat. I lost it in LeeMaster's corral during the fight. He's got the card now."

She shook her head slowly.

"So this is all kind of chancy," he said. "A card like that doesn't prove a thing. I just want you to know about it before we go any further. Shall we?"

Drusilla clasped her hands. "I know," she said. "You've come to deliver the contract in person."

"I'll try, if you want me to." He looked over at Thoss Pennoyer. The old man had not moved yet, but he had pulled his pallid brows together in thought. Wiley stepped over and gripped his hand. "Mister Pennoyer, I'm glad to know you."

"We . . . we've met." Pennoyer straightened up.

"Not exactly. I asked for a job, and you turned me down. Before I go on, I want to be sure we're acquainted. I want to say that you've got a mighty fine daughter, and the raw materials of a fair stage line. I couldn't improve much on the daughter, but I could do wonders for this fleet of mud wagons. If I did, naturally I'd want to be paid for it."

Pennoyer knew the answer to that. His face sharpened. "How much?"

"A third of the net. That may sound pretty rough, but it doesn't mean I own any part of the business. I'll be your manager. I share in the profits while the contract is in effect."

"This," Dru said thoughtfully, "sounds like bribery."

"Then don't have anything to do with it. The way I look at it, either you or LeeMaster is going to carry the mail. The other one won't be in business a year from now. I know LeeMaster, and I wouldn't do business with him for a hundred a week. I let him think I would, just to see his face fall when I turned him down. This isn't a bribe. It's a proposal. I'd like to marry the Oregon Mail Company, and I'll bring a fat dowry if I do."

Pennoyer rose. He walked to a rear door, opened it, and went into a dim parlor. "Will you both come in?" He sat at a small reed organ. When Wiley entered, he was pumping it with a rolling motion of his whole body and tootling a few trial notes to test the pressure.

"I like to clear every move I make in business with the Lord," he said. "We'll sing a hymn or two."

Wiley shivered. "Maybe we'd better leave the Lord out of this, unless there's a lightning rod on the building. When I feel like getting on the right side of Him, I give some old whiskey fighter four-bits for a shot of booze. It keeps him from robbing some honest citizen."

Pennoyer did not hear. He sang a hymn. Brogan noticed that Dru did not join him. She sat in an antimacassared chair, frowning at her linked fingers. Through a small window, he saw into the old man's pious soul. He perceived that he would grab anything he could, but would kid himself about the morality of it. He was as guilty as Wiley, right now, but he would strive desperately to whitewash it for himself.

He finished, and turned. "Drusilla?"

"Why, we're going to do it, of course. Only a third seems pretty stiff. I think twenty-five percent would be more like it."

"Fine." Brogan rose, feeling no different now that he had put a first lien on his soul. "We won't have anything in writing, just as a precaution. I'll come to work after we know it's going through. I could be wrong, of course."

"You'll come to work tomorrow. And try not to have any liquor on your breath. I'm not a prude, but I've only met you a few times now, and I don't think you've failed to have something on your breath every time."

Wiley winked at Pennoyer. "Is she always this hard to get along with?"

Pennoyer for the first time smiled. It changed his whole countenance. There was something ruttish about it, something of the good-humored villainy of a country horse trader who has just taken his prize quarter miler out of the shafts of his buggy for a match with a neighborhood plug. "As a rule," he said.

Dru sniffed, and the reddish-gold sausage ringlets danced as she went back into the front office. She climbed onto her high stool. "Now, then, why don't you get down there and give Mister Skidmore the news? And when you finish that, you might start figuring how you're going to get that card back from LeeMaster."

When The Dalles stage was loaded a short time later, Wiley Brogan was there to shake hands with the overcoated little man who came hustling into the yard at the last moment. The black short coat was buttoned tightly and he wore the stovepipe at a light-hearted list to starboard.

"How are you, my boy?" he exclaimed. "I was worried that you wouldn't be able to make it"

"Wouldn't have missed it for anything." They gripped hands, and Wiley said quietly, "I'm working with the Pennoyers . . . Oregon Mail Company. We worked out something pretty nice. A percentage."

"That's good," said Skidmore. "That's fine." He hung back a moment. "I might have known the girl would carry the day. Enjoy her, my boy, enjoy her!" And so saying, with a worldly chuckle, Harry Skidmore ducked into the stage and out of Wiley Brogan's life.

It seemed to call for a drink, for something to dispel the uneasiness that suddenly engulfed him. Since he already had liquor on his breath, Wiley discerned no harm in a whiskey. In fact, he saw a lot of possible good in it.

At the Emigrant Bar, he sipped the raw fury of a half-aged whiskey, mulling over the purely philosophical question of who was the greater sinner, the briber or the bribee. Since he was both, it offered him a purely academic interest. The Pennoyers bribed him; he, morally, at least, bribed Skidmore. There was a melancholy satisfaction in being the chief of sinners.

Brogan was a unique drunk, in that, when he drank, his eardrums thickened so that he heard nothing until it was shouted at him. For some time he was not aware that Jim Shaniko, LeeMaster's thick-witted giant, had entered the saloon. A dull silence had settled down. Brogan did not notice this. But his eyes were still good, and, when he glanced up at the mirror behind the bar, with its soaped suggestions to drinkers, he saw the superintendent moving slowly through the tables. He could have been the proprietor circulating amiably to see how things were going. But he had more the look of a man looking for someone in particular—hesitating once when he saw the back of a man in a keno game. The man wore a gray suit, had thick, dark hair growing low on his neck, and looked not unlike Wiley Brogan.

Shaniko moved along. Brogan's eyes trailed him. He knew that the thing for him to do was to get out. He was unarmed. Shaniko wore a gun on his right hip, butt foremost. Suddenly Wiley wished he could order a drink that would nullify all the whiskies he had drunk. He wanted all his wits to deal with this, but all he could do was to watch the superintendent's progress through the tables and hold his empty glass between his thumb and forefinger. He stayed there as though the soles of his boots were nailed to the floor.

The men in the saloon must have known about Shaniko

and Brogan. They watched Shaniko closely, except when he was watching them. When he paused at a table, no one commented on his battle scars but made a pleasantry about the stage business or invited him to sit down and have a look at a bottle.

Reaching the back of the room, he turned. Brogan's neck hairs stiffened. Shaniko brought his eyes down the bar without missing a man, like a boy out to hit every picket in a fence with his stick. They reached Brogan, passed on, halted, and came back.

He said: "Ah!" Yet he did not hurry as he walked back through the room. Wiley put his back to the bar, hooked his elbows onto the curled lip of it, and watched Shaniko come on. Shaniko stopped six feet away. "*Mister* Brogan!"

He was grinning in rapt and evil contemplation of the blunt Irish face before him. Brogan was glad he was drunk now. It was easier to look at that blurred red face with all its grossness, its pore-like pox marks, and its grayish under color, without spitting in it. He decided to go along with it as long as he could.

"*Mister* Shaniko!" he said. "I was told you were out buying rye hay. 'What a mistake,' I told m'self, 'when there's rye whiskey to be bought.' I'm glad to see you've reconsidered. I'm drinking bourbon myself."

Shaniko was drunker than he was. That seemed to give Wiley a slight bulge. He was not sure, though. Shaniko was too far away to tag.

The bartender set out a bottle with a thump. "Here's your bottle, Jim. Will you want a glass, or is this a holiday?"

"This is a holiday." Shaniko reached over to pull his gun, watching for the impact on the other's face. Wiley blinked.

"Jim!" the bartender snapped.

"Turn around," Shaniko said.

"Haven't you the guts to do it looking a man in the eye?" Wiley asked him. Brave words, for a man whose knees rattled.

"I've got the guts to do it any way I want. Have you the guts to take it?"

"If I was sure what you were going to do."

"Why don't you turn around and find out?"

"Turn around, mister," the bartender advised hastily.

Brogan figured the man must know Shaniko better than he did. He turned around and watched him in the backbar mirror.

Shaniko sounded like a man steeling himself to something, flexing down to a job he was not sure he could bring off, speaking slowly and without much thought to his words. "We've got a trick we use on bad horses. Just the worst of 'em. The hard-mouthed hell-fires that eat a bit up. It cures some of them, and some it kills. It's kind of like gelding, only you geld them in the head. I learned it from a hoss-breaker named Brogan."

Brogan knew. He had never been closer to sinking to his knees and begging. He could thank the fact that he was partly drunk for having the courage to stand up to it. He said quietly, to the bartender "He'll kill me. He's going to try to shoot off the tip of my ear."

The barkeeper kept both palms flat on the mahogany. "If you shoot, Jim, by God I'll see you hung and I'll buy the rope!"

The hammer of the Colt was back and Shaniko was taking finger-point aim, squeezing his forearm against his ribs and looking squarely at the back of Brogan's head. Brogan fell back on horse training, too, trying a rough Spanish bit.

"You're all I figured you were, Shaniko, yellow and thick-headed. I licked you fairly. I could lick you again. But if you try this, I'll kill you. I'm telling you to put. . . ."

The gun leaped in Shaniko's hand.

VII

The pain, the roar, the flash were a three-tongued flame, insepa-
rable. The explosion was a thunderclap that cut him off from all
but the golden, searing pain. Shaniko's face disappeared as the
mirror was shattered. Wiley stumbled, felt a man clutching at
him, but a moment later sensed that he had fallen. Something
was fluttering against the back of his head like a bat's wings. He
did not understand until after, when he learned that it was
someone beating his burning hair with his hat.

He did not feel the pain, then, but he was numb, brain and
body. On the theory that a man should remain vertical until
proved dead, they stood him up, and had him buckling about
with his head rolling, a man grasping each arm. He saw Jim
Shaniko standing there with his face stubbornly refusing to
confess that he was scared. He was holstering his gun and
saying: "He had it coming, by God! He had it coming, the
little whelp! Didn't he, boys?"

Nobody answered him, and he went outside. About this
time a man said: "My God, look at his ear!"

Brogan passed out.

When he came around, they had moved him up to the
Pennoyers' station and carried him into the parlor. The red
plush of the sofa pricked through his shirt and he was attempting to scratch when he regained awareness. His ear still
rang like a church bell. His nerves were pulled out to harpsi-
chord tautness and pain was plucking them. He sat up wildly
and put his hand to his ear.

A thick bandage, like an earmuff, covered it. He saw
Pennoyer standing sternly by a window, and Dru with a

sweet, inconsequential-looking little woman who, he supposed, was her mother. The frantic fear in his eyes conveyed the question in his mind. The thought of death alarms the average man less than the loss of any part of him.

Dru knelt beside him. "Just the tip," she said. "Oh, Wiley, Wiley!" She shook her head as though there had never been another like him to drink and to brawl.

"How much of the tip?"

"Only enough to be distinguishing." She had a small, folded paper in her hand and quickly opened it. "The doctor left you in my charge. You'll stay in bed until tomorrow night and take these pills if your ear gets to hurting."

"Give me the pills," Brogan groaned.

The little gray-haired woman, who was like something out of Dickens, came timidly to his side. "Would you like some broth?"

"What do I want with broth?" It was a ridiculous question, but he recollected that she was his hostess and said, no, thanks, no broth. Just give him the pills and let him out of here.

Dru stared. "What for? To do what?"

"To go to bed!" he snarled. "I've got a bed at the hotel."

He got up and reeled into a table and leaned on it with both hands until he had his senses again. He remembered Shaniko.

"You'll go to bed right here!" Dru was tugging at him.

"I'd scratch myself to death on that thing before morning." He would not argue it; he procured his hat and the pills and went out. They followed to watch him reel across the street to the Western Hotel. In the dank comfort of his room, he rested for a half hour. It was growing dusk when he came out. The gun on his hip made a large bulge under the tight coat. It was an old Peacemaker he had traded a saddle for. He tramped east out of town until he found a dump among the junipers and sage. A strong, cold wind was blowing. He found a bottle among the offal of the town, set it on a rock, and loaded the gun.

Brogan had never needed to know how to shoot, had little talent for it. He had worked too hard to be off wasting shells on tin cans. He wished now that he had gone in more for those shooting matches they were forever getting up around a stable.

He faced the bottle belligerently at a distance of about fifty feet. He stood the way he had seen gunmen stand, feet set stolidly, arms hanging, head jutting forward a trifle. Then his right hand swept up to the gun. He drew it smoothly but dropped it on the ground. He swore and picked it up. His head pounded when he bent over. Holstering it, he resumed his stance.

The second time he drew, his front leaf caught on the holster. He fought it clear and blazed away. Mud kicked up twenty feet in front of the bottle. The roar set his ear to ringing worse. He blew smoke out of the barrel and holstered the gun. But in sudden lack of spirit he sat down.

"Damn it," he said.

He knew what he wanted to do: kill Shaniko. Obviously a gun was not the weapon for it. Fists, then. But it would be a matter of many hours before he was in shape, perhaps, and by that time his urge to slay might have cooled.

A strong seam of practicality ran through Brogan. If he killed Shaniko, he knew for a certainty they would hang him, if they could catch him. And he did not yearn to spend his life on the dodge. He thought of an alternative that did not offend his pride or his logic. He would wear the gun, and let it be known that he did not generally wear it because he was afraid—of what he might do in a fight. There had been a scrape down in Grass Valley. Shaniko would sweat every time he saw him, but someday Wiley would catch him without his gun and beat the living daylights out of him. He would whip him, put him on a horse, and Jim Shaniko would never come back to Cañon City. With that settled, his conscience clear, he went back to town.

In a week there was only a heavy scab along the top of his ear. A scallop like a rear gunsight notched it. Brogan got used to himself in this form, accepted the fact that some men would feel it necessary to call him Gotch-Ear, and settled down to work.

He heard that all was spit and polish down at LeeMaster's. Shaniko was overhauling the rolling stock, a horse trainer was on the job, and several wagon loads of food had gone up to LeeMaster's meal station at Swamp Creek. Something was getting ready to break.

Brogan's career with the Oregon Mail began with the purchase of a box of cigars. Loading the breast pocket of his tight gray coat with a dozen of them the first morning he was able to work, he started his tour of inspection. Pennoyer introduced him to Press Malloy, a shouting, cavalierly old man who acted as his corral boss. He dressed like a miner in red flannel shirt, knitted silk suspenders, and black pants stuffed into knee-length boots. He may have had a miner's knowledge of rocks, but he was a fool around a stage station, Wiley decided. Yet, having taken orders all his life, he knew how not to give them, and he was slow going about how to tell the old man he wasn't worth powder to blow him to hell.

They started in the stage barn. Malloy had a way of cocking his hip, recklessly flinging his leg out to the side, and shaking the ash off his cigar when he had something to say.

"Gennawine Abbot and Downing stagecoaches, Brogan!"

he shouted. "The real Concord! Treat' em rough. They love it. Ain't had to lay a varnish brush to ary of 'em since I come here."

Wiley said was that right, and spat on a double-tree. He rubbed; beneath the mud, he turned up a red rose on the yellow paint, entwined in a black vine. "Looks sound. Say"— he chuckled—"I'll bet, if we were to keep these washed and varnished, LeeMaster's wagons would look like vegetable carts alongside 'em, eh?"

Malloy squinted. Then he threw out his leg and laughed wildly. "God 'n' wouldn't they? We'll work the butts off them lazy swampers and give 'er a try!"

Wiley laughed with him. "Here, have one of mine," he said, offering a cigar. "They cost two bits."

Malloy sniffed it, and put it away. "Well, let's chase the horses around and see if they can go two laps without wheezing."

Brogan mourned over the raw, ill-matched stock and said they definitely had possibilities, and it must keep Malloy jumping to have such hard-working stock looking so thrifty.

"Well, God 'n' it does!" Malloy admitted.

It ended with his accepting another cigar and the suggestion that they buy some new horses for the express runs, take all the extra stock off expensive grain, and pasture them at the swing stations.

For a week, Brogan's eye went over every entry in the books, half understanding. His hands tried each horse and scrap of equipment, comprehending fully. He compiled a list two feet long of the necessaries of an operating stage line, a line capable of carrying the mail on a daily run. But somehow, despite his industry, he could not get his hands on the satisfaction he had looked for out of being the Big Boss. Fulfillment eluded him. He decided it was the uncertainty of knowing whether or not they were actually going to carry the mail.

That ended when something called a *pro tem* contract came through a month after Skidmore's visit. It was perfectly official, however, and would serve until Washington got around to approving the genuine four-year paper. In heaven, Wiley thought ironically, a notary's stamp a mile wide must by now have come down at the foot of his sinner's papers. Without ostentation, a few days later, the first mail coach went out. That same day, the wrappings came off at LeeMaster's Mountain Stage Line, with a pennant across the street: **LeeMaster's, the Line of Service!** His claim to the title was that passenger rates had been cut, that the food was the best in eastern Oregon, and that the stage did not roll that would take a man to Garnet or any of the way points faster than a Mountain Stage. His strategy was plain—he was out to corral all the passenger traffic until he could do something about the mail.

Wiley talked it over with the Pennoyers and matched LeeMaster's rate. Then he set out to do something about his brag of getting there first. He advertised for horses, sat on a nail keg, and watched horse ranchers lead their horses by at a rapid walk. He was buying for himself this time, classifying and teaming as they passed.

In thickening weather, he broke a team and took it up and down the road. He taught the horses their names by calling them out and hitting them on the rump with a pebble. He had the first team about ready for the road when they heard about a livery stable being auctioned in Garnet. They had nothing much up there by way of a station but a roof, four poles, and a haystack, and Wiley determined to have a crack at it.

The day before the auction, he rode shotgun messenger with Horse Elkins, one of their two drivers. Up one day, down the next. Horse Elkins was a fox-eyed little driver, tough, vain of his black sideburns and tattooed forearms. He was a villainous-looking man who drove like a saint, and could pop a single hair out of a horse's head, it was told, without drawing dandruff.

They larruped over the bridge across Cañon Creek, mounted along a stony hillside to a low pass, and entered a country of tamarack and serviceberry. It had snowed lightly the night before, and the road bore the clean iron print of LeeMaster's stage. He had gone out on the stage a half hour before on the regular daily run. Neither of them mentioned him, but Elkins said once: "Fastest coaches on the road. Hogwash!" Ten miles later, near the first swing station, he said: "This here is a good team."

"Thanks," Wiley said.

Elkins tooled the coach into the yard and sat teetering his foot on the brake while he watched the team led off to roll, be washed, fed, and blanketed. "That there," he said, "is a damn' good team."

They swung back into the road. They climbed and turned and switched higher into the mountains. From the road, trails led here and there to the smaller camps, the placers and coyote holes. A sticky laurel grove filled the air with a strong spice scent. At one point, they could see where LeeMaster's stage had stopped for some minor repair. Boots had trampled the thin snow on the nigh side of the wheel tracks. Coming out on the shoulder of a mountain, they had a view of LeeMaster's stage below them, working down Two-Mile Grade to Sheep Creek ford. Patches of snow glared on the hillside, pierced by the splinter-like spears of starved sedge.

"If we'd have left ten minutes earlier," Wiley said, "we could have passed him yonder in the cañon before we crossed the creek. But it's all one way after that."

"Why, hell's fire," Elkins protested, "we can still pass! That's his first team, and the last two miles of it. So tight he spaces his stations like a drunken printer leadin' obituaries."

Wiley shifted and crossed his knees. "Why don't we?"

Elkins leaned forward, gloved hands' backs up, arms stretching as he let the lines slide through his fingers. The horses came into full gallop down the grade. It was straight-away, with a gentle drop and easy curves. They came down into a motte of mountain ash ablaze with berries, leveled off in a meadow, and whipped off left to drive straight at the ford. Sheep Creek had carved itself a wide granite trough through the mountains, too wide for a country stage road to bridge. At this one point, the banks let down for a few hundred feet to permit a fording.

Someone on LeeMaster's stage sighted them. There was a general straining of necks and a quickening of the clatter of mud flying from the horses' hoofs. The road was a little wider here than anywhere, but there were no bar pits and the terrain favored passing. Tatters of wild cherry slapped at the olive-green coach panels as Horse Elkins began working left to pass. He was on his second team, still cussing the orneriness out of them, whereas LeeMaster, who figured a tired team might as well come on down the Two-Mile Grade since it was really resting anyway, was squeezing out the last of his first team's strength.

Elkins had his leaders reaching past the big yellow rear wheels of the Mountain Stage for the step plate. They could see Shively, the driver, popping his whip like a fool. They could see and hear Jim Shaniko, enormous in a deep sheepskin coat, standing beside Shively and roaring down at them that he wouldn't be crowded off the road by anybody. LeeMaster, auction bound, had a leather curtain stripped back within the coach to shout that it was impossible to pass without an accident.

Elkins yelled back: "Plenty of room for everybody! Jes' don't try to crowd me, Shively!"

It was Brogan's first face to face meeting with Shaniko since the shooting; he thought how easy it would be to pull his Colt and quietly put a bullet through him. It was too close for even him to miss. The difficult part would come in court, and so he sat with his hands thrust into his coat pockets.

The road tipped down, affording a view of the crossing. The far bank was a fifty- or sixty-foot rimrock bluff up which a road had been chipped to the sagebrush flats. The near bank was more gradual, but still a drop, and the rocky bed of a spring branch had been appropriated for a descent to the creek. Water still trickled down the middle of the gravelly road and occasionally cut generous chunks out of it. To Wiley, it did not look wide enough for two Concords abreast, but Elkins seemed to think so and was lambasting everlasting hell out of the leather springs as he urged the horses on past, with one rear wheel off the road. Brogan had to grip the side rail, and only the broad leather driver's strap kept Horse Elkins in place. Suddenly he said: "Take the whip. He's going to try something."

They were booming down the ragged slot into the wide creek bottom. Elkins's leaders were abreast of Shively's swings. This was when Shively tapped his leaders over to the left, appropriating the whole road and the ford they were just entering. Wiley felt the coach lurch as the front wheels dropped into the muddy gutter; the tongue slammed the wheelers almost off their feet, and there was a bad moment of waiting to go over. Elkins shouted: "Let them have it!"

Wiley stood up and hurled the long buckskin cracker at the head of the off leader. The whip was as true as a rifle, fashioned of water-seasoned oak and braided rawhide, and it took a chunk out of the side of the horse's neck. It screamed angrily and hauled over. Shively stood up to fight his team, which was carrying him into the other gutter. The coach struck and lunged, went up on two wheels, and struck the ford that way. The horses for some mad reason started upstream. The Concord hung for about twenty feet, and then a wheel dropped into a mud hole and it slowly and wearily leaned over and lay on its side. Shaniko landed in six inches of muddy water with a splash like a bull moose starting across a stream. Shively landed among the wheelers' hoofs.

Horse Elkins cursed his team gently and affectionately all the way up the rise to the sage flat, and there, as they crossed it, he said: "If you'll just drop that whip back in the socket, Brogan, I think we'll make it on schedule, after all."

VIII

Wiley encountered Pete LeeMaster again in Garnet the next day, at the auction. LeeMaster had ridden up on a horse from a swing station. They bid against each other, but never locked glances. The feed barn went to LeeMaster, who could not be outbid after being whipped on the road.

Riding back with Horse Elkins on his down run, Wiley saw Jim Shaniko with a crew of four men at Sheep Creek ford making a road repair. Shaniko was on one knee at the edge of the little stream, panning gravel in a shovel. Elkins snorted.

"Some men can't pass a yard o' river sand without gettin' delusions of gold dust."

Brogan had moved to a room in a boarding house. Upon his return, he had a bath, changed to clean underwear, and sat on the bed staring out the window. A gray sky hung over the mountains. It was the color of his thoughts. They were about the foolishness of mankind in general and Wiley Brogan in particular. He had a pocketful of money and more coming to him every week. He had never in his life put out so little for so much. He had a new suit just like the old one but with sound cuffs. Around Cañon City, he had begun to rouse a sort of awe, as though he combined the derring-do of Wild Bill Hickok and the business sagacity of E. H. Harriman. If people knew he had once been a horse-breaker, they did not mention it. Only the other day, Foscoe, the banker, had said to him in the restaurant: "Well, what do you think? Is the Molly Maguire business going to raise freight rates?"

The two phenomena seemed totally unconnected, but Wiley said after some thoughtful probing of his food: "I've been trying to decide that myself."

He had been trying to decide too many things. Whether he was any happier now than he had been. If he were not, whether it was because he was shirt-tail cousin to a criminal or because he was in love with Dru. She was a sweet and attractive girl, but she was also a businesswoman. She was nice to him, but why not? They were partners. She was a lot sharper than he was, knew how to drive a bargain with a feed merchant or a horse trader, and maybe, if the opportunity presented itself someday, she would ease him out of the business so neatly he would think he was being promoted.

It all hung on the fact that he had come in to her with dirty feet. And that she had been willing to receive him. Their romance was as heart-warming as the mating of a dollar bill and a sawbuck. But he was certain now that he had done what the businessmen told him it was bad strategy to do in financial transactions. He had become emotionally involved with her.

He supposed old Elkins had apprised them of the race, but he went down nevertheless to make his report. Pennoyer was out somewhere, Mrs. Pennoyer was fussily posting letters in the cage, and Dru was at the roll-top desk. He sat on the edge of the desk.

She was involved in inventorying office supplies. For a moment, frowning over a total, she did not look up, and Wiley improved his time by admiring the clean grace of her body, the slender waist and long thigh lines, the small bosom making itself noticed despite a demure white shirtwaist. He sighed.

Then she turned quickly and put her hand over his, as casually as though she had been doing it for years. "Wiley, I knew, if you went out with Horse, something would happen. But this time I'm not going to scold you."

"I don't know what we proved. We got there first, but we lost the feed barn."

"At thirty-seven hundred, he can have it! You're even with Shaniko, too, aren't you?"

Brogan felt of his ear. "Not quite." Her hand was still over his; he turned it over and squeezed her palm. He carried her hand up to look at it. She wore a small ruby ring on a finger that did not matter. The tips of her fingers were slightly squared off. "Nice," he said. "Smaller than mine. But the fingers mean you could go ten rounds with me in a business deal and leave me punchy."

Her eyes disciplined him. "Wiley," she said, "you're as transparent as an ounce of ice. You've been thinking that we might come to resent you, haven't you? Do you think we could resent what you've done for the line, too?"

"What I did for the line was to get it a contract."

". . . And rebuild all the rolling stock, and train the horses so they were worth their feed, and . . . that's foolishness," she said.

Wiley knew all these things as well as she did; the line might never have amounted to a damn without him. Thoss Pennoyer knew as little about staging as an elk knew about trimming hats. It forced him to the realization that what was really on his mind was the left-handed position it gave him with her.

"Right," he said. "It's foolishness. But this isn't foolishness. I wish to the devil I were breaking horses again. There's one thing I didn't figure on."

"What was that?"

He jerked his thumb. "Can she hear?"

"When she's posting mail, you could fire a gun and she wouldn't hear."

Wiley bent forward and pressed his lips gently against

hers. She closed her eyes, but suddenly opened them and sat back. "For heaven's sake!"

"I didn't figure on you is what I was going to say. I'm what old Foscoe would call emotionally involved with you. And how can it go any further with . . . well. . . ."

"Because you made us take you in?" That cool, blue look of logic was in her eyes again, but mixed with it was a drop of unhappiness. "You're a simple-minded sort, Wiley. I guess all men are. What's really bothering you is that you don't think I'm good enough for you. Did you know that? You think you're depraved because you sold LeeMaster down the river, and you think I'm depraved because I let you. Why, anything you could do to Pete LeeMaster would be a kindness. But you're used to women who think they're ruined if they pass a pair of men's overalls hanging on the line. The funny part is . . . no matter how low a man may sink, he still can't get over the notion that almost any woman in the world would be lucky to land him."

Her face took on a surprised look, as though she had just seen the whole, wicked truth of this. She tipped her chin up and rose from the chair.

Wiley's pride was pinked. "That's a hell of . . . that's a tarnal thing to say to a man. Even a depraved man like me can't twist words the way a woman can." He stood. "Well, I'm glad we've got that cleared up. I'm a degenerate. But I'll stick around and run things in my depraved way until they're going smooth, and then I'll get out."

The side door opened and Thoss Pennoyer came in quickly and shut it. His pallid, mustached face was clammy. His bald dome was shiny with mist; evidently he had carried his hat from wherever he had been.

Dru gave Wiley a look that was a sort of bookmark to hold the place. She hurried to Thoss. "Dad, what is it?"

Pennoyer illogically put his hat on. "I don't know whether this concerns us or not," he said.

"From the way you look," Brogan declared, "I'd say it did."

"I was just down at the hotel. They had a Portland paper there. That fellow Skidmore has been arrested. He's being held by postal authorities for fraud."

IX

Wiley said: "Yep. That concerns us, all right." But no one else had the power of speech, except Mrs. Pennoyer, who asked plaintively: "What was that, Dad?"

"Nothing, Mother," Pennoyer said. He led the others into the parlor and shut the door. He sat down and dry-washed his face in his hands. He glanced up in sudden querulousness. "Brogan, you got us into . . . no, no, that isn't true. We all got into it together."

"That's better." Wiley was not panicky precisely. He felt more like a man in a forest who knows a cougar is stalking him, but cannot see it, and yet knows that, sooner or later, it will drop him. Something had been set in motion that must finally involve him. He knew that, but it was as far as his thinking went.

The organ began to pipe its feeble flutings into the room. Thoss Pennoyer sat swaying on the bench. "Rock of Ages" came forth to purify the atmosphere.

When the hymn had finished, Brogan sat quietly for a long while, peering out the window onto the alley. Distantly he heard the graveyard chatter of Dru and her father.

". . . but there really isn't a thing they can do to prove it! We hired him, but what's illegal about that? In fact, it wasn't!"

"That everlasting card," Pennoyer groaned.

"What does it prove? With nobody's name on it but Wiley's."

"I think I've got it," Wiley said, standing. "It's got only my name on it, and a forgery would be pretty obvious, in a different hand and pencil. Let's say you hired me after LeeMaster wouldn't, and I left the card there. Then this news broke. I didn't say a word. I just went up to the boarding house, packed my clothes, and got out."

In a solemn voice that indicated his religion was actually beginning to get a hold on him, Pennoyer declared: "Perhaps it would make it easier if we knew whether we really considered ourselves guilty. Do we?"

"That's beside the point. If somebody with a star on his vest thinks we are, he's pretty apt to convince us." Brogan put on his hat thoughtfully. "I've got a lot of thinking to do tonight. Unless some new evidence turns up, I'm leaving tomorrow afternoon."

Dru reached up to hold the lapels of his coat. "Wiley, I don't think you're a criminal. Do you think I am?"

"I think we're all opportunists. And there's a point where they begin arresting opportunists."

She pulled his head down and whispered into his ear. "Would you still love me if I were a criminal?"

"I'd bring hard candy to you every week. But I don't think I'll have access to a candy store."

He made it a point to observe his usual routine. When the stage came in toward evening, he saw that the horses got their roll and proper feed. He saw the last workman out before he locked the corral gate and went home. Only a few hours sleep came his way. But he was down at the station at six-thirty to open up. He got the stage off at ten o'clock, and still did not know whether he would be leaving on The Dalles stage at noon, leaving town for good.

At ten-thirty, he saw a heavy spring wagon loaded with Shaniko, four workmen, and their road tools ramble into town. It stopped at the assayer's narrow brick building and

Shaniko went inside. Then the superintendent, with a long and bilious look at the depot, drove on.

Something in the stare chilled Brogan. He went inside and cornered Dru and her father.

"Well, I'm getting out."

Smudges darkened the fine skin beneath Drusilla's eyes. "Whatever you want to do."

"All you've got to do is tell them you fired me for inefficiency. We don't know that they'll even ask."

"But if they do, you'll be safe in Idaho or Texas, and we'll be right here trying to keep from stammering."

"You don't think I'm walking out on you, do you? This is for all of us."

In the street a man ran urgently toward the corral. They stared at each other. Pennoyer went to the door. Horse Elkins was wrangling the big main gate shut. He was shouting. "He will, will he? By God, we'll see if he will!"

"Will what?" Brogan demanded, striding to the door.

"Shaniko! He's bringin' an army down the street, packing scantlin's and pick handles!"

Wiley reached above the door for the Henry repeater racked there. If they wanted fireworks—if Wiley Brogan had to leave town hanging to the tail of a skyrocket—it could be managed. He stepped into the yard and ran to help with the gate. Elkins was already locking it. Wiley said: "I'll handle them." He backed off about twenty feet from the gate and waited in the cold shadow hanging from the shake eaves of the depot.

Standing there, he saw Shaniko, unshaven and sunburned from his days on road repair, come to the gate and mount the stringers like a ladder. He swung a leg over as his crew swarmed after him. Brogan fired once, the gun's kick jarring his hat loose, and levered a fresh shell up. The men on the gate froze like chickens under the shadow of a goshawk. Shaniko's big face turned quickly.

"Shaniko!" Brogan called. "If you haven't had enough, I'll finish you off right here. But those shovel dancers of yours will watch from outside."

The swampers and hostlers from Mountain Stage were sliding back into the street. Shaniko dropped inside. Horse Elkins waited, holding his twenty-four-foot whip with the lash doubled back. Shaniko unbuckled his gun belt and let the Colt drop.

"I've seen dirty driving in my time," he said, "but that beat all! You wouldn't want to fight with scantlin's?"

Brogan said: "Take the gun, Horse."

Elkins caught the Henry, and Brogan walked to the woodpile. He matched a couple of sixteen-inch jack-pine limbs and threw one at Shaniko's feet. Men were streaming to the gate, shouting the word. Shaniko picked up the club. Wiley's stomach griped. Shaniko was a giant, a tousled giant in striped jersey, pants too short for him, and size fifteen boots. He was coming toward Wiley with his big shoulders sloping, the club resting along his neck, moving with a sidewise crab walk. Wiley was uncertain; he hoped he would be hurt early, and lose that fear so that he could go to work. He sidled around with a notion of maneuvering Shaniko against a wall.

Shaniko made a rush, feinting with his left hand to draw Wiley's club, then smashing down at his head. Wiley flung his own bludgeon up and parried it. He felt the vibrating jar of it to his elbow. Shaniko's feet were working like a boxer's, carrying him in and out. Wiley stabbed his club endwise into Shaniko's face, cutting him deeply on the cheek. Shaniko roared.

Somewhere a man was shouting: "Shaniko! Jim Shaniko!"

It got through to the superintendent; he frowned. Wiley, suspecting a trick, kept his eyes on Shaniko's face. He was aware of the man climbing the gate, waving a paper. "Shaniko! God's sake, man, what are you about?"

It was Ott, the assayer from across the street. Shaniko said: "Will you wait?"

Brogan stepped back and lowered the club. Ott came piling over the barrier, thrust the paper into Shaniko's hand, and began pounding him on the back. "For shame, fighting when you could hire men to do your fighting for you! You're rich, man! The dust you brought me was the real article!"

Shaniko looked at the paper, at Ott, at Brogan. He rubbed his cut cheek. Then he began to laugh, shouting, headlong laughter without any intelligence in it. He balled the paper and threw it at Brogan.

"Thanks, you little Mick! You work all your life for a dollar a day, and then a little hoss nurse like you throws you in a creek and you strike gold!" He tossed the club away and turned his back. "Go it, boys! I'm already staked out. Sheep Creek ford, and the devil take the hindmost!"

When Brogan went inside, Thoss Pennoyer was rushing about assembling tools, a change of clothing, and some blankets. "Brogan!" he yelled. "Saddle our horses!"

Brogan sat down. "I wouldn't ride fifty feet to stake a claim in any river he'd dirtied with his big feet. Come to your senses. Miners have been over every foot of this country up to ten thousand feet, and do you mean to say they wouldn't have panned along the road?"

"That's just where they might not! Right under their noses. He had the dust, didn't he?"

"Ott said so. I expect he ought to know."

"Well, I'm going up. Have my horse saddled."

Ten minutes later, a shawled and long-faced figure on his white mare, Pennoyer loped up the road with his pack horse skipping along after him.

X

Brogan witnessed the decampment of most of Cañon City. He rented every horse and wagon they could spare, and hung a sign on the gate: **No Horses. No Wagons.** Miners coming out of the hard-rock mines bought food, pick, and pan, rented a horse, and joined the parade. Merchants hawked flat tin gold pans in the street; the barrels of shovels before Ellison's Hardware sold like candy canes.

Brogan maintained his conviction that, if Shaniko were in it, something was as wrong as an aluminum nickel. Beyond this feeling, he was insulated from it all by his own worries. Something he had hardly thought of before, a new edge of the catastrophe touched him now. Poor Skidmore. He thought of the little man in the black stovepipe and short coat, who had been so eager to help a down-and-outer, so hound friendly that he evidently passed out a card of introduction to the wrong man at last. His formula had gone against him, his philosopher's stone had begun turning things to brass. Preachers would level bony fingers at him in their sermons, the honest and the uncaught would walk by the jail and try to decide which was his cell, but Harry Skidmore was worth six of any of them. He was a benevolent rascal. If all his philanthropy had been of the kind that had befriended Wiley, he had not make a dollar out of it.

It neared stage time. Wiley went into the depot. Dru was waiting for him. She held his hands. "Not today, Wiley . . . please. Not until Dad comes back, or we all move up to the claim."

"All right," Wiley said.

★ ★ ★ ★ ★

Horse Elkins took out a load of passengers and a sack of mail the next morning. By night, several men had come down with samples and small pouches of dust. They left these at Ott's and hustled on to the saloons. Later, Ott posted the news in his window.

Red Dog claim, J. Shaniko: Gold, 760 fine. Some osmium and cinnabar.

Mountain Queen, LeeMaster: Same.

Lucky Seven, Harkrider: Pyrites, chromite and cinnabar.

President Hayes, Hixon: Pyrites, chromite and cinnabar.

The list was long, but the amazing thing was that some men had found almost pure gold, while others were finding nothing but pyrites and mud. There were six men who had staked their allotted feet of placer in rich sand. Four of them were Mountain Stage men—Shaniko, LeeMaster, and two others. LeeMaster came back from the camp that night on his big bay mare, leaving his claim for Shaniko to handle.

With Pennoyer still up the hill, Brogan stayed over another night. An unshaven and raging Horse Elkins drove in at nine o'clock the next morning. He came lugging the mail sack inside. He stood in the middle of the room and announced:

"Well, sir, that takes the prize!"

Wiley said: "It does that. When'd you leave? You must have been on the road all night."

"I was. Believe me! *This* side of Sheep Creek! That's the same mail I took up. I dumped my passengers at the hotel on the way in. Those galvanized fools have tore up the ford and strung their rockers and riffles from hell to breakfast. I couldn't get across there with a jackass and a sulky!"

A scroll became legible. "Blocked, eh?" Wiley said.

"There's a hole as big as the Western Hotel where we used to cross. And that's the only fording place between here and Ironside Mountain. What are we going to do with this mail, and all the rest that comes in? Carry it in our pockets?"

Thoss Pennoyer came in shortly afterward. He had a little bottle of mineral flakes that he showed somewhat sheepishly to his wife and daughter. "It doesn't look high grade, but I do see some flakes in there. The black ones, see? When I turn it to the light."

Wiley took it out of his hand and threw it in the stove. "Let's go over and talk to Ott."

Pennoyer trailed him across the street, complaining in his old man's whine and getting no answer. Ott was in the rear of his shop, in the dusk of the furnace room. The iron door of his miniature furnace, cherry-red in a squat block of bricks, glowed in the dim light. The racket was almost tangible, the furnace shouting hoarsely, the compressor banging away, and overhead the hum and clatter of pulleys and belts. Ott, a fat, graying man, ruddy and sweat-beaded, was drawing a small cupel from the furnace with tongs. He saw them and with some flourish set the cupel down.

"There she is, boys!" he shouted. "There's the button! Let's see how much gold this fella's mining . . . and how much junk!"

There was a minute pinpoint of metal in the bottom of the clay dish. "Mister Ott!" Brogan shouted. "I want to ask you something! I've heard the balance of metals in any mine is as distinctive as a horse's shoe! Is that a fact?"

"That's right! The mint can tell you where any chunk of gold you sent them comes from! They got data on every mine in the country!"

"What about you? Have you got data on all the mines around here?"

"All the ones I work for! What is it, boys? I've got more

samples laying out there than I can assay in a month!"

"It'd be a favor to us if you'd kind of check and see if the dust these fellas are bringing in is like any other you've assayed!"

"You're right it'd be a favor!"

"A twenty-dollar favor!" Wiley shouted. He gave him a double eagle.

Ott said—"Hell, even for twenty dollars . . . !"—but he decided he couldn't work the button until it cooled, and, while he waited, he'd look about. They went back to the hall-like front office with its gaslight, safe, dark wallpaper, and assorted gold scales. Within the bank-like railing were a desk, ledgers, and cases of ore samples. Ott studied a while, made some notes, clattered his plates over it, and stared at them a while. Then he studied some more and sat back against the chair with his sheet of figuring.

"Well, if that ain't peculiar."

"What do you find?"

"These here samples are all *i-dentickle* with the gold from Ed Hosley's Wildcat Mine. They ain't on the same river, neither. They're forty mile apart. Now, boys, what does it mean?"

"Hosley's is out of Garnet, isn't it?"

"About ten mile. He gets his mail there, and his freight."

"And LeeMaster hauls some of his freight and I expect he brings things up for Hosley and Hosley pays him with dust. I was just trying to figure something out."

"What was that?"

"Why it would pay him to dump two or three hundred dollars' worth of dust into Sheep Creek and gamble he'd only get half of it back? If it ran Mister Pennoyer, here, out of business, I guess it would pay, eh? Mister Pennoyer has a pretty stiff forfeiture clause in the mail contract. Thanks, Ott. Tell the rest of the boys they might as well go home."

"I can't figure you out," Pennoyer complained. "I never know when you're joshing. Was all that straight?"

"Out of Scripture! LeeMaster figures he can stand a layoff for a month or so, but he knows we can't. We're getting too much mail and parcel post to carry by pack horse, and, if we tried, they'd never let the trains past the ford, anyway."

Pennoyer stopped in the street and stared toward LeeMaster's. "That's pretty damned bald, I'd say."

"Bald enough that I suppose eventually you could get an injunction. That would take about six months, figuring roughly, and you'd have to pay geologists and assayers from six states to stand up and say it was impossible for any two rivers to produce exactly the same stripe of gold. And then they'd begin contradicting each other, and maybe instead of you getting an injunction they'd decide to change the geology books."

Elkins was out back throwing chunks of bark from the woodpile at a horse, pretending to himself he was disciplining it for getting tangled in a trace. A headlong clatter of hoofs down the street signified the arrival of the stage from The Dalles. The varnished green sides glistened as it turned into the yard; it had evidently been through rain. They saw Pete LeeMaster stride across to the depot with one hand in his pocket, coattail flipped back and the wind riffling his black hair.

Pennoyer said tentatively: "I guess your stage leaves pretty soon, eh?"

Wiley chewed his lip. The time was now. But a man with two grains of conscience could not leave his friends in a muddle like this. "I'm going to see LeeMaster after a while," he told the old man. "I'll leave tomorrow. You're not doing anything . . . why not get Ott to put that in writing and take it up to the mines? The boys will be pulling out of there as soon as they see the assay sheets. I don't think most of them really believed it, anyway."

XI

He contrived an inventory of the things he would need. One dozen pick handles. Six quarts of whiskey. Five pounds of quarter-inch nuts. Powder and wadding for the shotgun. Understanding the psychology of stable hands, he reckoned the best way would be to declare a holiday when they came trickling back from the ford, commiserate with them, get them likkered up, and then begin feeding into them his own hatred of LeeMaster, of which he had a surplus. Pour enough whiskey down their throats and they'd go to battle over child labor in Massachusetts. With a real grievance, they would stumble blind drunk up the road to Sheep Creek, armed with pick handles, neck yokes, and anything else hard and heavy. When they began to sober, they would be ashamed to admit their foolishness, and keep going.

Yet, first, he aimed to talk to LeeMaster. The stage man was not reasonable, but he was intelligent, and it might be possible to show him that he had mixed cleverness and greed in the proportion indicated for tragedy. LeeMaster, wearing a heavy black coat, lava boots, and engineer's breeches was in a shed supervising the loading of a pack horse. At Brogan's approach, he turned. The long face with its look of hard, bony force did not react. He held a short length of rope in his hands, and cracked it once against a stanchion.

"I heard you'd left," he said.

"Not yet," Wiley said. "I want to get my hands on some of that gold first."

LeeMaster's eyes kept moving about his face. "That was quite a break for Jim and me. I'm going up now to get things set up right."

"It was a break, all right. Let's be sure it doesn't turn into a fracture. Got five minutes?"

LeeMaster tossed the rope on a bench. He went toward the station building with his long, pacing strides. There was a muscular vitality about him. He yanked the door open and went through ahead of Wiley, strode into his office, and shut the door forcibly. The early dusk of winter had already invaded the room. He took time to light a fizzing carbide light on an extension arm over his desk. He set a cigar smoking in the white heat, and his hand carried it quickly to his mouth.

Wiley looked him over with sour amusement. "You look like an honest-to-God gold miner, Pete. Do you always get togged out like that when you're going to throw some gold in a river and dig it out?"

LeeMaster accepted it as a rather bad joke. "With gold as hard come by as it is, I don't throw any in a river when I get hold of it."

"Not unless you stand to pan out more than you threw in. . . . So you've put the big britches on us now. We'll never get through till spring, and by that time it will be too late. Is that how it goes?"

LeeMaster pulled the band off the cigar. "I heard they hadn't done the road any good, at that. Well, roads can be rebuilt."

"This one's going to be. Tomorrow."

LeeMaster shook his head. "I wouldn't rush the boys. Any more than I'd rush a hound chewing a bone."

"But I'm going to tie a can to this hound's tail and get him out of my way. I'm going through, Pete. Like that." He smashed his fist solidly against his palm. "I'm going to have a jerry road through that hole they've dug by tomorrow night. And I don't think they'll do any more panning right there."

LeeMaster's pottery-brown eyes crinkled. He laughed

softly. "I admire your guts. You're talking as though you were still trying to decide whether to eat the world with tomato sauce or sugar. But you've known you were in trouble for quite a while, haven't you? And you're in it up to your ears now. Do you know a man named Kane?"

Wiley perceived all at once why he had failed to shake the stage man any more than he had. He said: "Postal inspector?"

"Have you seen him?"

"Not yet. But I figured there must have been some reason you went hightailing it over to the central Oregon station. And now you're wound up like an eight-day clock. So he's in town, is he?" He tried to carry it off complacently, but it lay in his belly, heavy and cold. "I've got a friend at one of the little P.O.s along the road. He tipped me off that he was coming."

LeeMaster's mouth eased into a smile, and he chuckled. "Wiley, I'm obliged to you. I did my best to get into this jackpot myself. What are you going to tell him?"

"Let's take it one step at a time," Wiley said. "What did *you* tell him?"

"Nothing. I just gave him the card. I told him I found it in the corral. Which I did."

"What did he say?"

"He didn't say a word. He looked at me a minute, and then put it in his pocket."

"He was probably thinking what a helluva friend you'd make, and wishing he had a dozen like you."

"You've still got a chance, Brogan. You could get out now. He doesn't know you by sight."

"You talk like I was on the dodge."

"Actually, I suppose you're not . . . yet."

"That's where I've got the bulge on you. You fitted yourself for the striped evening clothes when you salted the Sheep Creek mines."

LeeMaster's grip on his cocksureness lost traction. Salted was a bad word in a mining town.

"Ott discovered the dust you and the rest of your watered-down Buffalo Bills have been bringing in is from the Wildcat placers. There aren't any two dusts alike, you know. Or I guess you didn't. He says this amounts to salting a mine, which puts you right in the seat ahead of me."

"Ott is a two-bit four-flushing fool! If any Wildcat dust got spilled in there, it must have been from a Wells Fargo chest."

"There haven't been any Wells Fargo chests over that way yet. I doubt that they leave a trail of gold, anyhow."

Suddenly Wiley's panic had melted. In its place was a glossy surface of satisfaction, a sense of well-being. It was a feeling so suddenly acquired that he had to glance back to see what had brought it about. He donned his derby and gave it a tap. His rough Irish features were beginning to glow. LeeMaster saw it and pulled his brows in sternly, as though it were the essence of bad taste to smile over mutual hard luck.

"I'm beholden to you, too, Pete," Wiley said. "You put me back on my feet just now. For a while, I wasn't sure whether I was a train robber or what. It's that way, when you keep mulling a thing over and looking at yourself in the mirror until the mirror gets tired of looking at you. Come down to it, what did I do? I kept a pint of ninety-proof polecat juice from smelling up a whole county. I kept you from choking the Pennoyers and raising your passenger rates so high nobody but Jim Hill and E. H. Harriman could ride with you. The big thing is that I knew that when I did it! I wasn't dickering with you that day. I was sticking pins into you. I wouldn't have done business with you if you'd paid me in diamonds. I knew all about you after I smelled around town and met Shaniko and your competitors. What I'm getting at," he said, "is that if there'd been two Thoss Pennoyers shooting for that con-

tract, they'd have been on their own, as far as I was concerned. I wouldn't have lifted a finger to help either one of
them, or to get myself a job. But squeezing you out seems to
come more under the heading of bounty hunting. I've got an
idea I'll still be around tomorrow. If I am, don't get in my
way. I'm coming through like a brick smokehouse out of a
cannon."

LeeMaster stood there with the hard white light of the gas
fixture on his face and the cigar gone cold. "I hope you can
convince Kane of that," he said, then added several remarks
that would blister paint.

Wiley was not angered, but it gave him the logical opening
he had wanted. You couldn't go around punching people
without some kind of chalk line crossed. He took one step forward with his left foot, jarred LeeMaster in the chest as he fell
back, and brought his right hand in with all the gathered force
of his shoulder behind it. It feathered LeeMaster's cigar in his
mouth and snapped his head viciously. The stage man went
into the wall with a thud, reeled back a step, and reached
blindly with his hands. Wiley watched him fall against his
swivel chair and slump to the floor, not unconscious, but paralyzed, making deep snoring sounds in his throat and stirring
with slow, futile movements.

He went out, looked up and down the street like a man
surveying a piece of his own land, and walked up to meet the
man named Kane.

XII

No one had thought to build a fire in the stage depot. The thick walls of volcanic tuff held the dry, incisive cold. When Wiley entered the waiting room, Thoss Pennoyer was sitting on a bench with his coat collar turned up. Dru was fussing with things on the desk nervously. Mrs. Pennoyer was in the post-office cell.

There was no indication of trouble, no sign of the inspector, but Wiley played safe. Clapping his hands together briskly, he walked to the small iron stove.

"I guess there's no law against a fire, is there?" he said.

He squatted to whittle pitch-pine splinters, and stuff paper and splinters into the stove. He grubbed for a match. Then he saw the man inside the cage with Mrs. Pennoyer. Evidently he had been kneeling before the safe, out of sight below the half-height partition.

Brogan had brought only part of his optimism back with him. With the forceful gaze of the tall, loosely built, stern-eyed man on him, he had a jolt of cold shock. He tried to review in one flashing moment of prayer all the reasons why he was not guilty, all the sound country honesty behind his dishonest actions. He had an inspiration.

"Excuse me, mister," he said, "but nobody's allowed back there but the postmistress. Wasn't that the rule, Missus Pennoyer?"

The sweet, inconsequential little woman with the soft gray eyes and the skin like chamois stood at her wicket in the manner of a captain going down with his ship. "Yes, Wiley . . . but this man. . . ."

"My name's Kane." He said that as though it usually

86

brought forth skyrockets and a twenty-one gun salute.

"I don't care if it's Rutherford B. Hayes," Wiley said. "The rule is. . . ."

"I'm with the Post Office Department," said Kane.

"Oh!" Wiley threw the match into the stove. He went to shake hands with Kane. The inspector was big and broad, with a pallid face rutted and gouged with lines and tinged deeply under the eyes a brindle color. He turned immediately to resume his inspection of the safe.

"Better stay here," he said. "I may want to see you."

"You bet."

So they sat there trying to build a fire with three lumps of ice, he, Dru, and Thoss. They made pointless essays into the weather, business, the gold strike. But every spark fell into wet tinder. And every few moments one of them would glance over at Kane, running swift totals on a scratch pad, counting money in the cash drawer, asking Mrs. Pennoyer something about the posting and dispatch of mail. They observed that he had some difficulty moving about among the sacks of mail and packages. After a half hour more, he came out, shooing Mrs. Pennoyer ahead of him.

He stood by the stove, packing tobacco into a pipe. He lit a splinter of wood and started the pipe. He sat down, crossed his legs, and looked at them.

"Well, I might as well let you have it straight out," he said.

"Is something wrong?" Dru asked quickly. Her eyes were a little too wide, her inflection not entirely convincing.

"Wrong!" Kane bit out. "My dear woman, you're not running a warehouse here . . . you're running a United States post office! If you'd had one more sack of mail in there, I couldn't have got about at all. What are you going to do with the next sack of mail that comes in . . . throw it in the corner by the woodbox?"

They all laughed too loudly, too nervously at his pleasantry. Brogan recovered first. "It's the first trouble we've had, Mister Kane. The boys thought they'd struck gold up the line, and they tore the road to billy hell. We'll have it fixed up tomorrow and get back on schedule."

"How do you know you will?"

"We wouldn't have taken the contract if we hadn't been prepared to carry the mail."

"Did it occur to you that you could have sent the mail up by pack horse?"

"It takes a little time to get a pack string together. And I'm not sure we could have got horses through, even."

Points of light glinted in Kane's deep gray eyes. "Why not?"

"Some local opposition. It's straightened out now."

"Someone else who wanted to carry the mail?"

Dru came in lightly. "Oh, we've always fought with him. But we think we may have reached an agreement finally."

"I hope so. But I'd watch him. He's a sharp customer, if he's the man I think you mean. He bought me a lunch just to put this in my hands."

He balanced a small, white card on his knee, where they could all see it, the bold penciled scrawl staring blackly at them.

This will introduce Mr. Wiley Brogan.

Brogan grunted. "Where'd he get hold of that?"

"He told me you tried to use it to get job with him."

Wiley snorted. "The devil! I went down for a job, all right, but I got into a scrap with his superintendent and lost the card out of my hat. I suppose he picked it up. Say," he said, "you don't suppose he was trying to . . . ?"

Kane smiled and spun the card at the woodbox. "I suppose that's what he was trying to do. Everyone's heard about

Harry Skidmore getting in trouble, and I expect the assumption is that everything Harry did must have been crooked. Whereas he was a pretty good man, until he got to playing the horses. He needed money, and the quickest way seemed to be to take it out of the safe and cover it up in his books."

Mrs. Pennoyer said gently: "Why, wasn't that terrible?"

"It was terrible, Missus Pennoyer," Kane declared. "But it's no more terrible, in my eyes, than not getting the mail through. I'm going over to Baker, but I'll be back in a couple of weeks. I want every last postcard cleaned up! Otherwise, I'll simply have to see that your contract is cancelled. Do I make myself clear?"

They all agreed that he did, and they trailed him to the door and had his gruff good bye as he turned and walked off.

No one seemed to care to talk about it. Mrs. Pennoyer moved mail sacks around as though with evidence of good faith. Pennoyer went back and played a hymn. At last Drusilla closed her account book and turned to Wiley.

"Now I know you're a crook. You carried it off too well to be anything else."

He stared transfixedly through the window. "That's the funny part about it. I had a revelation a while ago. Just as I was about to hit Pete LeeMaster on the jaw, I saw a bright light, and a voice said . . . 'Hit him. *He's* the real criminal. Compared to him, you're God's right-hand-man.' So I did, and then I heard another voice. It said . . . 'A pox on your conscience, Brogan. Did you rob anyone? Did you cheat anyone? You put the heel to LeeMaster's neck, but that's an honest man's privilege. But what about the Pennoyers?' I asked . . . 'I held them up, didn't I?' "

She was listening raptly.

" 'Held them up, indeed!' the voice said. 'Was it that you accepted a bribe, or did you intend to really give service for value received?' 'Well, that,' I said. 'And you were in love with the girl and wanted an excuse to hang around, didn't you?' 'That, too,' I said. 'Well, then!' And right then," he said, "was when I knew I could look Kane in the eye and say . . . 'I'm Honest Wiley Brogan. As to the card, think nothing of it. It was all part of a favor I did myself, the Pennoyers, and the Post Office Department.' "

XIII

Brogan missed Pete LeeMaster's departure for the mines, but learned that Ott had been to see him and the stage man was missing. Then, about sundown, in a cold, sweeping dusk, men began trudging back into Cañon City. Ott's place was the first focus of activity; after that it was divided among the saloons. Press Malloy returned with a handful of Oregon Mail yard men.

When the men showed up for work in the morning, the downhill trickle had begun again. Wiley met the workmen with an armload of bottles and a handshake. "Boys, I think we'll all take a little holiday. That was a poor joke, and we need something to take the taste of it from our mouths."

He drew a cork and started the first bottle around, while he wound a corkscrew into the second. They congregated by the corral. Press Malloy stood at the gate, flinging his leg out recklessly and said that it was a hell of a doings when a man could salt a mine and get away with it. Brogan said he wasn't sure LeeMaster would get away with it, and Horse Elkins lowered the bottle quickly to ask what he meant.

"I'm going up and kick him to the devil out of our way."

Elkins said he'd like to see that. "You're bound to," said Wiley. "Before I can turn loose on him, I've got to show him a U.S. Mail coach, so you'll drive up first. When he turns you back, I'll step in."

Press Malloy laughed one short guffaw and said he'd like to see that, too; he might go along in the stage. "I don't know about that," said Brogan. "Anybody who goes up is apt to be pulled into it. I guess you'd better stay here."

"Pulled into it! You think I'd be hangin' back, suckin' my thumb?"

Brogan admitted he might need help. "He may back down, and he may not. He'll be fighting for his life up there. And we'll all be fighting for our jobs, because the inspector was through yesterday and read us the riot act."

He had planted the seed, and now he watered it generously with whiskey. But they were all still in bleary good humor, running more to affection for each other than for dislike of Pete LeeMaster, and Brogan suddenly got to his feet and said: "Well, boys, it's been a good party. But I've got to get up there. Hitch up a team for Horse. If you don't see us again, why, the best to all of you."

They moved into the horse barn. They fumbled a bit with the harness, had some trouble with the horses, but ended by getting the animals on the pole. Brogan began loading pick handles into the coach. Finley, the company blacksmith, a thick-necked man with the blackest fingernails in town, squinted.

"You ain't thinking you'll need them things?"

"I'm not going up to mend picks. It's a little matter of pride with me. When a man says I can't do a thing, I usually end up by making a stab at it. Press, you coming?"

Malloy hefted a pick handle and smote his palm with it. He drove a look of woozy truculence about the hangers-back. "Sure. I'm always ready to go out and fight for somebody's job that ain't got the guts to fight for his own!"

Finley drew in his chin. He was a ruddy fellow who wore collar-band shirts but no collar, and a mustache that was one-sided because he always chewed the left side when he was thinking. "That's a nice thing," he declared. "Nobody's asked us to go."

"I'm asking you now," Wiley stated.

Finley declared that he was always ready for a mill, and demanded whether the others weren't. They bragged and pounded each other on the back, and Wiley shoved them all into the stage before they could change their minds. He ran back to the office and acquired one sack of mail from Mrs. Pennoyer, to make the run official. He was loading the old shotgun of Pennoyer's with quarter-inch bolts when Dru came in.

"Wiley, what in heaven!"

"Just propaganda," he said. "We're taking up some mail. I think LeeMaster will quit, when he knows I'm still in circulation. If he doesn't, the boys and I know how to make him quit."

She gestured distastefully. "But . . . that horrid thing!"

"Shaniko's got a Colt that's just as horrid. Believe me, if there was any other way to rebuild that road than to go out and start building it, I'd take it."

"When do you think you'll be back?"

"Just as soon as we get the job done. If it's after dark, we'll be able to use some coffee and sandwiches." It would give her something to do besides walk up the walls, he reckoned. The men rushed to the bastions and the women manned the sandwich boards.

"You ought to take some sandwiches with you," she said, thinking one thing and saying the other, her eyes going over his face.

"Oh, we'll be all right. Well . . . take it easy." He grinned.

"You, too, Wiley." She stood in the doorway as he walked to the coach and climbed up with Horse Elkins. As the brake kicked off and the horses lunged into the collars, she waved and quickly turned and shut the door.

An hour of being jostled and thumped about, a cold wind

flapping in their faces, began to sober Brogan's army. They pawed over the pick helves and tried them for heft. Wiley could hear them making boastful talk to keep up their spirits. They all knew LeeMaster. They knew about the notch in Brogan's ear; they knew LeeMaster was fighting for existence, and they wondered how far he would go to make his brag stick.

They changed teams at Sawmill station and slung into the twisting climb that spilled over onto Two-Mile Grade. At the station, Brogan got inside with the others. From the top of the grade, he had his first view of what had happened at Sheep Creek.

Sluices, rickety flumes, rockers, and rock piles made a mile-long miners' battlefield of the wide gorge. Already most of them had deserted, but above and below the ford a few men still panned and shoveled. The greatest turmoil was at the ford itself. Lofty sandbars had been created by the digging of long trenches in the creekbed; the trenches had filled with muddy water, and a few men standing by them were unenthusiastically shoveling sand into a sluice.

As they rocked on down the grade, Brogan watched the brisk assembly of men at the near side of the ford, just where the road dipped. He sat there working a side hammer of his shotgun and trying to plan through what was bound to be a mighty planless affair, once it started.

Then the road pointed dead at the ford, and he could not see ahead without exposing himself. Wild cherry tangles rattled along the coach panels, and he knew they were almost to the creek. The brake shoes ground rustily. The sudden slowing of the stagecoach lifted him half off his seat. The coach stopped; they heard nothing for an instant but the blowing and stamping of the horses and the plopping of collected mud on the ground.

"You fellas ever saw a stagecoach before?" Elkins voice came.

Pete LeeMaster's voice had a nervous bite. "Turn it around, Horse. There's no way through here."

"I'm packing the mail . . . you know that, don't you? I'm willing to try 'er if you'll get out of the way. If you won't, it's a federal matter."

"So is this," Shaniko declared. "This is gover'ment mineral land."

Elkins said once more: "Get out of the road. I'm going through."

LeeMaster's voice was lower. "Turn it around, Jim."

Elkins snarled something, and Brogan exclaimed: "The dirty pigs are laying hands on the team!"

Finley and Malloy went out the left-hand door, and Wiley threw open the other. There were six of them in all, and they came out armed with white new hickory bludgeons.

"Roll 'er, Horse!" Brogan shouted. Elkins gave the leaders the buckskin but handed them in simultaneously, so that they reared above the dozen-odd men moving in to grab at head-stalls. They fell back. Horse let the team go, high-stepping into the midst of them as they plunged down the short tilt to the creek. Pete LeeMaster led the retreat, backing swiftly with his eyes on Brogan and his hand resting on the butt of his revolver. Wiley made a swift alteration in plan. He didn't like the cornered-badger look about LeeMaster. He did not trust the way he seemed to be trying to spur himself into something he was afraid of doing. He tossed his pick helve to the seat beside Horse and pulled the shotgun out the coach.

LeeMaster ran back through the sandbars into the wash. Brogan's men had made contact with the enemy. There were some good, solid cracks of hickory. They had the initial advantage, but some of the others had made it to tool stacks and were passing out sledges, shovels, and pry bars.

Up and down the wash, miners were running to watch the fight. Brogan, pacing past the now stalled stage, noticed that they kept out of it. There was a cleavage here as plain as a ruled line. LeeMaster's flunkies were the only ones standing up to them.

Wiley stopped on high ground to watch it. LeeMaster had pulled back to the top of a gravel bar, but Jim Shaniko, swearing and swinging, was in the midst of it with a shovel, standing off Malloy and Finley with great sweeps of the glistening blade. It seemed to Wiley that, torn up though the wash was, a way could be threaded through it without much shovel work. A good team could back and cut its way out of a bowling alley without upsetting a pin.

Brogan's men were already deeply into the wash, overturning sluices, hurling rockers aside. Round, washed boulders were beginning to fly as Horse Elkins moved in with his whip arm cocked. He let one go that caught Shaniko on the side and pulled away half his shirt. There was a long, bloody streak across his ribs. Shaniko dropped his shovel and clutched his side; recovering, he caught the shovel up again and surged into the stage driver. Finley, the blacksmith, was there to swing a roundhouse blow that took Shaniko in the belly. Shaniko went down.

LeeMaster was moving in, trying to tighten up his line by bawling at the men. There were five of them still fighting. Brogan shouted at Horse. "Roll her! Behind me!"

He jumped down into the wash and held the headstall of the near leader while Elkins climbed up and seized his lines. Wiley began to work through the gravel pits and piles, the shotgun laid across his left elbow with both hammers cocked. LeeMaster was screaming at his superintendent.

"Jim! Get back here!"

Shaniko pulled himself up once more, standing a moment with feet spread widely and blood running down his face. He saw what had happened to his men; he saw Brogan bringing the rocking Concord through the rubble. Wiley suddenly sensed that he had had enough. He was not afraid, but he was tired—tired of taking beatings and giving beatings. He saw Shaniko turn and say to LeeMaster: "I taken her this far, Pete. You take her from here."

LeeMaster said: "Get back here, Jim."

But Shaniko shook his head. "You're whipped, Pete. Ain't you got sense enough to see it?" And he stumbled aside through the washed cobbles.

LeeMaster drew his Colt. For an instant, Wiley thought he was going to kill the superintendent. But when he fired, it was a swift snap shot straight at Wiley, and the heart of him seemed to compress and then blow up. He heard a flat, meaty smack beside him. One of the horses screamed—that seldom-heard, shattering cry that is human, but worse than human.

He said: "Lay it down, Pete. Lay it down and git."

He heard the team threshing behind him, and Elkins's tongueless cries of rage. LeeMaster's thumb moved across the spur of the gun hammer and he brought the gun shoulder high. He said levelly: "You can cut that one out of the harness, but there'll be the same for the next one."

Wiley started toward him. "No, there won't. You're going back with me." It was someone else's voice he heard, or his own crowded through a tin horn, he thought. He was panicky and uncertain, but still walking forward.

LeeMaster pulled the gun down. He fired, and the bullet sheared down the stock of the shotgun and snagged wickedly through Wiley's bicep. In his panic, he pulled both triggers at once. The concussion and kick were magnificent. He went back two steps and fell flat on his back. He sat there with the gun lying at his feet, clutching his arm, and watched LeeMaster stumble around. LeeMaster's middle was a bloody cave. It was a sickening thing, and it was worse to hear him say: "By God, boys, I think I'm hurt! I'm shot, boys! By God!" He sounded as though it must be of the utmost concern to every man in Cañon City, that he, Pete LeeMaster, was injured. He was worse than that. He was dying, but incapable of realizing it.

A spring wagon carried Wiley back to Cañon City, with Horse Elkins going on up to Garnet. Malloy, Finley, and the rest stayed to push gravel around until a stagecoach could traverse the wash without dumping everything out of the rear boot.

Trying to recapture his dismal uncertainties of the last few weeks, Wiley discovered that, if anything were left of them, it had been burned out in those brief moments at Sheep Creek.

It was late when he reached Cañon City. He raised a doctor who cauterized the deep flesh wound in his arm and bandaged it. Then he turned his horse into a stall with a *morral* of grain, and went into the stage depot. A single lamp burned. At the desk, he saw Dru with her head on her arms, asleep. A big tray of sandwiches rested atop the desk; coffee bubbled slowly on the stove. Brogan came up behind her. Holding her shoulders gently, he kissed her on the cheek.

She awoke and caught a breath.

Wiley said: "This will introduce Mister Wiley Brogan. Always."

She pulled his head down against her cheek, drowsy and self-satisfied, as only a woman both sleepy and beloved can be. "Who needs no introduction," she said.

Texicans Die Hard

1

In Joel Harkrider's office it was cold and dusty. Some of the dust seemed to have rubbed off on Harkrider. He had the air of having missed sleep for years, of having consorted too long with law books and crusted ink wells. He was one of about a dozen Americans Charlie Drake and Cort Carraday had seen in Chihuahua City. He had an East Texas accent and a dispirited manner that made everything he said sound like an apology.

What he had to say to Charlie Drake, however, required no apology. Charlie looked at Cort Carraday, but Cort's gaze, as he stood at the window, was for a girl crossing the plaza.

Charlie said to the lawyer: "Well, I guess that's fine, but how about relatives? I never heard of a Mexican dying without leaving forty cousins."

Joel Harkrider smoothed the tender wrapping of gray hairs over his pallid scalp. "There's a brother," he said, "but he's well fixed, so there won't be any trouble from that quarter. But"—he shrugged—"this is Mexico."

Anything, his faded-blue eyes said, could happen in Mexico. A rich *hacendado* could die and leave everything he owned to a *gringo* who had saved his life. And the *gringo*, who happened to be Charlie Drake, could ride 300 miles and find out it wasn't a joke, after all. He remembered the portly, pleasant little Mexican who had made the mistake of flashing his bankroll in an El Paso saloon. It had been no business of Charlie Drake's that the man was followed when he left the saloon, but Charlie had made it his business—and had been in time to pull the attacker off Miguel Castillo's back in an alley. He had imagined Castillo had forgotten it long ago. But now he learned that Castillo had died of typhoid fever six months before, leaving a holographic will in Charlie's favor.

In the frigid little office they were waiting for him to say something. Charlie didn't know what it was going to be. They'd had great times, he and Cort. They'd punched cows, bucked the tiger, mined gold in New Mexico. Cort was tinder for the spark where a woman was concerned, and this had occasionally livened things. Already Charlie was looking at those days through a golden haze, as if they had happened a century ago. He had the wisdom to perceive that it wasn't being broke that separated men, but having money. And, while he sometimes got a little breathless trying to keep up with Cort, he wasn't going to see their fine times end.

He asked Cort: "What do you think?"

Cort turned from the window. He had dark, curly hair and strong features with a strain of wildness. His eyes were as blue as a desert horizon. "You asking me?" Cort grinned. He might have smiled that way if Charlie had asked whether he should let it ride again on red. He wasn't helping any.

Charlie scratched his head, while Harkrider arranged papers on his desk. From the campanile of the cathedral four strokes vibrated mellowly on the crisp fall air. "I reckon I could sell it," Charlie said.

"No doubt about it," said Joel Harkrider. "The brother I mentioned, José Castillo, is waiting outside right now. Speculate that's what's on his mind." He lined up three pencils, rolled his palm back and forth on them, and said mildly: "I didn't know ol' Miguel very well, personally. His own lawyer was a Mexican, but the man turned this business over to me because I speak English. But I do know Miguel was mighty fond of that *hacienda* of his. He babied it like an old husband babies a young wife. Reckon he had the only irrigation between here and the border. Best beef cattle, too."

For the first time, he had said something significant. He had said, in effect: *Castillo would whirl in his grave if his land went to his brother.*

Charlie asked pointedly: "Why didn't he leave it to his brother, then?"

"I guess he hated to see the land wrecked. You see, these people figure a range ain't overstocked until the cattle are standing in each other's hip pockets. But ol' Miguel spent some time in the States learning how they farmed and raised stock. It was a hobby and a crusade with him."

His eyes came up to Charlie Drake's face. Back of the bleached eyes was discernment. Harkrider knew a little bit about men, and he was taking a long look and a good look at this red-headed Texan who had come into a fortune and seemed worried about it. Charlie's was a pleasant face, lightly freckled, with brown eyes and a good jaw. But there was one thing wrong with it. It had no lines.

The lawyer frowned and looked away. Charlie saw that frown, and, because he could read men himself, he knew what it meant. This little transplanted Texas Blackstone had put him down as scatter-brained and irresponsible.

Harkrider muttered: "I reckon selling would be the easiest way out. Don't know but what it would be best. Down here a *Norteamericano* ain't exactly pampered."

Charlie said: "Let's talk to Castillo."

Castillo was an enormously stout, vastly untidy Mexican whose collar failed by a full inch to button and whose trousers looked tight enough to split. He was unshaven, and his large ears were choked in fat. Under his gray coat he wore a silver-mounted revolver. He carried a cane of inlaid woods, which he transferred to his left hand as Harkrider introduced them.

"What thing?" he exclaimed. "My brother . . . *que Dios le*

bendiga . . . is telling me of you. I have the summit of pleasure in welcoming you to Chihuahua."

Charlie did not smile at the butchered English, but replied in Spanish. "Thanks. To tell the truth, I thought it might be a joke when I got *Señor* Harkrider's letter."

Castillo's large head made a slow negative shake. "Hacienda Río Chula is no joke, *señor*. Three hundred thousand *hectáreas* are never a joke . . . a half million acres! My brother must have had an excellent concept of you."

"I hope so."

There was some talk without much point, and then *Don* José struck his palm with the head of the cane. "I merely desired to congratulate you, and to be the first to buy you a drink in Mexico. Eh?"

"That," said Cort Carraday, "is the first smart thing anybody's said. *¡Vamonos!*"

With his melancholy smile, Joel Harkrider opened the door. "Come back in the morning, Drake, when you decide what you want to do. Good luck."

On the street, in the clear amber sunlight of late afternoon, it was warm. Along the rutted length of Calle Libertad, carts lumbered through the dust and a few cowpunchers on lean-ribbed horses ambled past. All in all, it was a hungry-looking country—the burros were underfed, the peasants were bone and brown skin wrapped up in serapes, even the range, for the most part, was sorry-appearing. Before the cathedral, beggars and children thrust out dirty palms.

Cort dug down and found a handful of Mexican and American coins. He put some money in each hand and said: "Watch this!" He tossed the jingling silver on the walk. It was like a dogfight. Charlie looked away with a feeling of having witnessed something obscene.

Castillo escorted them to their own hotel, the Colonial. In

the lobby, a mustached old Mexican sat with a young, full-breasted girl in a dark skirt and one of those embroidered, low-necked native blouses that tease without quite promising. Cort made a low whistle that Charlie stifled with a glance. He anticipated enough trouble down here without hunting any. The girl was pretty, not yet twenty, he thought, with shining brown hair she wore inches below her shoulders. She met his glance coolly, and then looked at the old man.

They sat at a sticky table in the big, drafty restaurant. *Don* José washed his hands at a basin in the corner. He drank tequila, sucking on half a lime, and then drinking the liquor with short smacks. Then he threw the squeezed lime on the floor. He leaned back in his chair.

"First," he said, "I offer you the hospitality of my *hacienda* . . . El Molinillo. There is only one ranch in the state larger than mine . . . the ranch of Terrazas, and Terrazas is God."

"Where does mine figure?" Charlie asked.

Castillo smiled. "I would use it for a horse pasture. At one time, even Terrazas took off his hat to a Castillo. In the time of my father, before four brothers received their shares of the land, our cattle roamed a thousand hills."

Charlie saw clearly what was in his mind. He said: "*Vamos claros.* How much will you pay?"

Castillo shrugged. "I could use the land. I could not pay much. Already I am land poor. The taxes I carry would break the back of an ox. The *peónes* I feed would form an army. When they chop one stick of wood or grind one liter of corn, they consider they have been ill used. I could pay ten thousand *pesos.*"

A little fire lighted in Cort's eyes. Charlie shook his head. "Without seeing the land, I say no."

Don José spread his hands. "We will talk about it when you have seen the land, then. With me, it is a matter of sentiment.

If my brother had loved a worthless horse, I should buy it, for that reason. I offer no more than fifteen thousand, *amigo.*"

Cort's expression, almost wild, reflected the thought: *With fifteen thousand* pesos *we could bust the bank! The gals we could hug and the likker we could drink!*

Charlie was thinking of those things, too, but he knew José Castillo would jack a lot higher than this. "I might," he said, "take a hundred thousand."

Castillo laughed until he wheezed. He struggled out of his chair and offered his hand. "*¡Eso!* It is a pleasure to know you, *señores,* though you are totally insane. When you are near El Molinillo, do not forget me."

They shook hands again, and *Don* José departed, a vast, waddling figure in a wrinkled gray suit. Cort swore softly but savagely. "You had him in your hand, Charlie! He'd have paid twenty, if you'd worked it right." He could change quickly from blitheness to anger, and he was in a black mood now.

"He'll pay seventy-five thousand, too, and that's a bet. How do I know what I've got till I see it? Maybe I'll sell it to some syndicate for two hundred thousand."

"And maybe we shouldn't have come down here in the first place. They watch the women too close and the likker tastes like medicine." He looked like a big, worried kid who liked the fifth grade so well he distrusted the sixth.

"Tell you this much. I'm not figuring to stay. But when I go back, I'll be heeled."

When they went to the desk for their room key, the Mexican with the young girl arose from his chair. He was a man of less than middle height, his face brown, his eyes like jet, and the great black mustaches ragged. He wore tight *pantalones,* a leather vest, unpolished *tajas* to his knees. When he smiled, his face shattered into a thousand squint lines.

"I am Juan Bravo," he said. He looked surprised when this didn't register. "*Don* Miguel's foreman. He didn't mention *Don* Juan?"

Charlie shook his head. He lied agreeably. "I'd forgotten. Sure, he did. I thought we'd go out to the ranch in the morning. Would that suit you?"

"*A su servicio,*" *Don* Juan said. He beckoned the girl. Charlie thought she seemed truculent. "My daughter, *señores* . . . Tonía, this is *Don* Carlos Drake, of whom *Don* Miguel spoke."

The girl didn't offer her hand, but Charlie took it. The cocoa tone of her skin deepened. Her features were as fine as filigree. The dark eyes were shy, but the lift of her chin was proud. Charlie observed that nothing quite like her figure had ever come his way.

It was nearly dark outside. The odors of food came from the kitchen. Charlie herded them all into the restaurant. After dinner, the old Mexican began to talk of the *hacienda*. Presently he hesitated, and something pinched a frown into his brow.

"There are many Americans who own ranches in Chihuahua. Most of them live in the States and operate through a manager. Is that how you wish to run Río Chula?"

"I don't know. I may sell it. A man named Castillo wants to buy it."

Bravo did not cease to smile, but ghosts stirred in his eyes. He was hearing old, loved walls tumbling; his eyes were smarting from the smoke of dying hearth fires. "A fine man, *Don* José," he said.

Antonía made her first remark. She spoke clearly, looking at Charlie. "A great driver of slaves," she said.

The foreman brought his daughter under a compelling scowl. "My daughter means," he said softly, "that *Don* José has many workmen."

"I mean that he is a great sucker of blood, a slave driver. That where our people receive five liters of corn for each day they work, *Don* José's receive two. That where we raise hay for our animals, he cuts his on the prairies until there is no more to cut."

"Is that right?" Charlie said.

Under the slender, dark brows her eyes were hot. "*Sí*, that is right, and it is also right that the Americans my father speaks of ranch in the same way. You, *señor*, will also beat the land with a club until it is a desert. Tomorrow we will make smaller corn measures."

The café was cold, but *Don* Juan had achieved a glistening perspiration. He sought to interpret. "My daughter, she. . . ."

Charlie laughed. "Your daughter, she don't like *gringos*."

Tonía shook her head. "I like *gringos, Don* Carlos. I do *not* like *Americanos*."

Charlie extended his hand. "Shake hands with a *gringo*." In the border lingo, *gringos* were Americans who spoke the language and understood the ways of the Mexican. *Americanos* were the ones who kept a handkerchief over their mouths when they talked with one.

Tonía failed to see his hand. She drank her coffee, thought a frowning thought, looked out the door into the darkening street.

A stricken man, *Don* Juan arose. "We will be at the door with horses at whatever hour you say."

"Make it ten. We've got our own horses. Good night, *Don* Juan. Good night, *señorita*."

A volcanic mood descended on Cort Carraday. The ride from El Paso had required three weeks. During that time there has been no foofaraw and extremely little fluff. In their room, he commenced a caged pacing of the floor. Charlie lay down and regarded, on the ceiling, an interlacing of scrollwork in lavender, green, and gold. He was a quarter-horse, built for work or play. Cort was a thoroughbred, geared for speed.

"How much money we got?" Cort asked.

Charlie counted. "Fifty-eight dollars."

"That ought to buy us an evening. You can get some more from the lawyer in the morning. Let's find a game."

Charlie realized the pressure would go off gradually or in an explosion. He could have used some rest, but you had to take Cort the way he was. He got up.

They walked through the dark streets, finding nothing more exciting than a few *cantinas*. A dry, biting cold had invaded the desert city. Smoke of charcoal fires and the warm scent of spiced foods hung in the streets. About the city lay a ring of hills where fires winked in the night; beyond the hills burned the red glare of slag dumps. There was silver in the mountains of Chihuahua, and there were fortunes in cattle, but Charlie Drake and Cort were wondering where rich *Chihuahuenses* spent their wealth.

On Avenida Ogampo they heard a sound that arrested them both. Music—a tinkling echo of a *jarabe* to tickle their spines. Up the street they discovered the lights of a saloon. The old, familiar sight of batwing doors drew them like moths. They could hear the *click* of castanets and a dancing girl's cries.

Cort barged in first. He stood there in the smoke and light and clamor, arms hanging, the varnish of excitement on his eyes. "Ye Gods!" he said. "Ye Gods!"

It was in the tradition of an elaborate American saloon, a long bar measuring the left wall, gaming tables in the back, tables for patrons covering the rest of the floor, with a clearing for the dancers. The man was a slender Mexican as resplendent as a peacock. The girl was like a candle in the dusk of the room, her gown white, the skirt ringed with red, a silver comb like a crown in her hair. On the floor between the dancers lay a silver-trimmed sombrero.

Cort started through the crowd. Charlie caught him by the arm. "Anybody but her! Remember that night in Socorro?"

Cort brushed off his hand. For a moment he stood at the edge of the light, watching the girl in white bend like a willow as she went through the figures, hands on her hips. Charlie saw him reach up to unfasten his neckerchief. Then he was in the clearing and catching the girl's waist in the loop of the blue bandanna. She turned in surprise, and then smiled and called something to the musicians. The *jarabe* died. The music revived as a tango.

The crowd, resentful at first, began to shout: "*¡Ai-ee!*" Everyone seemed to think it was a great idea except the forgotten partner. He stood there for a moment, his mouth tight. Then he picked up the sombrero, turned his back on the dancers, and went to a table.

Charlie sighed. If Cort only had sense, just a little sense, being a saddle partner of his would have been less hectic.

He went back to the roulette table. For a while he watched the play. The table was crowded with well-to-do Mexicans and a few Americans—traders, ranchers, mining men. The game looked straight. He took the first chair he saw and backed the red for five. He won that and let it ride twice. Then he put five dollars on each of four numbers and on the second spin collected. Charlie Drake decided it was his night. He won enough that the other players began to watch him, and he ceased to watch Cort.

With a drink at his elbow, a stack of chips before him, and the good, stifling smells of a saloon in his head, he wondered how he could have thought of settling down to ranching. He'd go into dry rot trying to keep books. He was thinking these things when the sound of scuffling reached him. His head turned. There was no sign of Cort. No sign of the girl, either. An hour must have passed. Now he heard a crash of furniture and glanced at a door at the end of the bar. A large man was standing there, signaling the musicians. The music broke out in a riotous gust. The big smiling Mexican at the door crossed his arms and kept his back to the uproar from the room.

Charlie swept his chips into his hat and went around to cash them. His mind went like a clock. The ball was dancing once more. No one noticed him when he walked toward the guard. He made a roll of silver coins, which fitted his hand like the stock of a whip. The guard's face was brown and flabby, with a pocked nose and a cleft chin.

"The *excusado*," Charlie said. "Quick, *hombre!*"

"In the alley, out back."

"Which door?"

The guard uncrossed his arms to gesture. Charlie fired a punch at his chin. With the heavy roll of silver behind the blow, Charlie's fist drove the cleft chin into the man's neck. Across the saloon, someone yelled. Charlie slammed him on the side of the head and, as he went down, stepped across him to open the door. Without slowing, he got the whole picture of what was happening inside the room.

It was a cramped room containing a chair, a table, and a cot. The cot was overturned; the chair was smashed. The girl, looking frightened, stood against the wall at Charlie's right. Two men were holding Cort in a chair, while the *charro* dancer, thin and dandified, an exalted expression in his eyes, slashed at his face with a quirt.

Charlie closed the door and slipped the bolt. The girl screamed.

The dancer whirled like a cat. With all the strength of his

shoulder, Charlie hurled the coins in his face. A dozen cuts opened up. The Mexican went to his knees with his hands over his face, groaning. Charlie's gun flipped up. The men who held Cort straightened but did not molest their guns.

There were welts all over Cort's face. He stumbled from the chair. Charlie backed to a window and reached back to raise the sash. "*¡Vamonos!*"

Fists drummed on the door, but Cort Carraday paused to say: "Meet you outside. Cover me."

Charlie backed out. He saw Cort recover his gun from a corner and come back to stand before one of the men who had held him. He slashed this man across the face with the barrel of the Colt. He struck him again as he fell. The other man tried to run. Cort opened a four-inch cut on the back of his head. Then he took the *charro*'s quirt and slashed him in the face until he sobbed.

It was when Cort turned to confront the girl, the gun leveling, that Charlie yelled. He could see Cort's face; it was insanely twisted. "For God's sake, Cort!" he shouted. "Let her be!"

Cort fired. The silver comb on the girl's head was wrenched from the black hair. Her face was white as paper. Cort blew the smoke from his gun. "Thanks, *señorita*. Thanks for your good intentions."

As they ran down the alley, they heard the door crash inward. They made the corner just as the first shot pinked the night.

11

That night, Cort Carraday slept like a child. Charlie was disturbed. Cort had left his hat at the saloon; he thought there had been a letter in the lining. But no one molested them that night. In the morning they shaved and went out.

In Joel Harkrider's office, it was cold enough to grow a crop of icicles. The little Texan wore two sweaters under his box coat; his lips were blue and he kept his hand in his pockets. "Mexicans!" he complained. "Keep an office warm enough to support human life, and they start edging for the door. Castillo was in, by the way. He left a note for your partner." Surprised, Cort read the note, and let Charlie see it.

If Señor Carraday will call at my office on Calle Libertad, I shall be pleased to return his sombrero, which a member of the police discovered last night.

Cort grunted. "Why didn't he leave it here? Well, I'll meet you at the stable."

Charlie told the lawyer he had made up his mind to look over the land before he made any decision.

"The first thing, whatever you do, is to get squared away on your debts," Harkrider said. "I'd say ten thousand *pesos* would clear you. Load some of those Black Anguses into cars at El Sauz, dump them on a feeder in El Paso, and you're clear."

He offered Charlie his hand as he left, wistfully, as though they might not meet again.

They forded the Chuvisear River a little after ten, Juan

Bravo and his daughter leading up through the pass onto a sere, brown plain reaching north and east. Hills broke it at intervals. Across several of them marched low stone walls. Tonía turned to point at one of these.

"The great walls of Chihuahua," she said. "When *Don* José's workmen have nothing else to do, they pile stone upon stone." Her bitterness was irrepressible.

"What do they do on Río Chula?" Charlie asked her.

"They play with their children or tend their own gardens. That is . . . they used to." She gave him her back again, but it was a nice back and Charlie didn't mind.

Cort had said nothing since they left the city. Charlie asked how he had made out with Castillo.

Cort's shoulders lifted in a shrug. "Oh, tried to throw a scare into me about playing around with Mexican women. Said he got the hat from the police. They were going to lock me up. He advised me to head north, in case they changed their minds."

The old devil-may-care lights were not visible in his eyes. He looked bothered. Charlie laughed. "Don't let him throw you. He knows that if you go, I go. And if I go, I'll sell out quick and cheap."

Cort gave him a long, frowning stare. "Don't talk like a damned fool," he said. "We're pardners . . . but any fight I get into is on my own. We're not a corporation, Charlie."

"Funny . . . I always thought we were."

Cort's eyes watched Tonía's dark hair dance on her shoulders as she rode. "If I pull out, it will be on twelve hours' notice. I've got talkin' spurs. Don't you forget it. Just give me time to saddle and it'll be . . . *adiós,* Chihuahua!"

They came to a well-rutted road winding through a meager forest of piñons. "El Camino," murmured *Don* Juan, and Charlie's gaze traced the tawny roadway with respect.

Traders and travelers had been following that road since the days of Coronado; Indians had preyed upon it and self-appointed generals had led their peasant armies to death and glory.

Up ahead, Juan Bravo reined in his pony. He sniffed the air like a fox. Charlie pulled in beside him. "Smoke, *señor*," the foreman said. "Indians are good people . . . when one sees them first."

They proceeded cautiously. In single file, they came upon the still-smoking line of wagons.

They numbered four great-wheeled wagons whose oxen lay dead under the yokes. Fire had ravaged the train, leaving a black memory of charred oak and canvas. A barrel of flour was split open beside the road. Boots, hardware, and food stuffs mingled catastrophically between ruined wagon sides.

Death had taken some of the teamsters on the box, allowing others to sprint halfway to the pines or crawl beneath a wagon for protection. The body of a woman was sprawled beside one of the wheels.

A cold perspiration broke out on Charlie. Tonía's hands were over her face; her father slowly wagged his head. It was at this moment that Juan Bravo's pony plunged forward. Charlie saw it go to its knees and roll on its side, the foreman jumping clear, but even then he did not comprehend. The *crack* of the rifle struck through a moment later.

Cort Carraday was thrown ungracefully to the ground as his pony began to rear. Tonía sat with her face turned toward the cairn of rocks across the road, from which the shot had come. Charlie caught her about the waist as he dismounted, dragging her with him. Afterward, he did not know how he managed to pull his carbine out of the boot first.

There they lay in the dirt, the girl clinging to his arm while Charlie hunched around to get a shot at the rocks. He didn't know what the others were doing. He was too rattled to care. He saw the smoke of the second shot before he heard it. It stirred heavily through a slot near the top of the boulders. Charlie snapped off a quick shot that missed by six feet. He shook Tonía. "Behind the wagon!"

Terrified, she was slow to understand until her father seized her arm to draw her into the shelter of the mound of ashes.

In Charlie Drake's mind, road and trees and rocks were sketched like a battle plan. There were the road and an open space of fifty feet to cross, then the trees would give a furtive kind of security while he approached the rocks. He was convinced that there were only one or two men, left behind only the devil knew why. Otherwise, the attack would have been like a fist closed on them.

Someone was at his heels as he crossed the road. Cort. Charlie reached the trees and sheltered behind one. It was about the size of a Christmas tree, like the rest, hardly a hindrance to a good marksman. Cort spilled behind another. He fired as he landed. The bullet flattened itself on the blackened stone and soared over the trees with an expiring wail.

Charlie glanced at him. He was almost ashamed of his own nervousness. There was a fierce exultation in Cort's face, a savoring of the wine of danger. Cort loved a fight; he was totally without fear. He jacked a fresh cartridge into the chamber and spoke hurriedly. "I'm goin' to coyot' in behind them. Keep 'em busy."

Cort made a short run to the base of the rocks. He began to work around the pile. Charlie watched the sniper's nest a moment, and then he, too, sprinted forward. After he got a boulder between himself and the gunman, he felt better.

Now the moments crawled. There was no firing from the rocks. The breeze blew softly through the trees and the sun was warm on his back, making death seem a great improbability. At once a gun barked and a man yelled. Charlie reared up. High above him, a sniper lurched into view in a cleft in the rocks. The cool walnut of his gun was smooth under Charlie's cheek. It jolted, the butt of the gun setting him rudely back. The gunman jerked, fired his rifle into the sky, and took a step forward. He toppled face forward down among the rocks.

Lying on his back in the sun, the sniper did not look capable of frightening anyone. He wore the not-gray, not-white, pajama-like costume of the peasant. On his upper lip and chin were wispy black hairs. He appeared underfed and his skin was badly pocked. A stain widened perceptibly on his right shoulder, where Charlie's bullet had entered. A larger stain darkened his breast.

Don Juan tapped his nose. "This is not *bandido*," he said. "These hands have worked. A teamster, perhaps. . . ."

Then he looked up, and his eyes and Charlie's met. Charlie had a feeling like nothing he had experienced before. A sickness and a shame, a remorse that came up in his breast like a sob. He did not require Cort's puzzled exclamation. "Funny! He's been shot before. This blood on his chest is almost dry."

Don Juan had a depth of understanding. "*Sí, sí, sí*. We talk of that later, eh? Now, we bury this *pobrecito* and forget what has happened. We must hurry to beat the sun to Río Chula."

But Charlie could not hurry fast enough to lose the knowledge that he had shot a dying man, a wounded man out of his head with fever, who had fired at them in the belief that they had come back to finish him. For this man was the survivor of the massacre. He did not lose that dread, but he gained a hatred of the men who tricked him into murder.

★ ★ ★ ★ ★

At the railroad station of El Sauz, they broke westward into the hills. They passed a gate in one of Castillo's walls, and almost immediately a transformation in the range became evident.

There began to be a little graze on the ground. The cattle, an improved breed of longhorn, acquired a sleekness. Castillo's cows numbered thousands and were the poorest of Mexican culls. They entered a vast golden valley rimming out into blue uplands. He saw hundreds of hornless Angus cattle, fat as crib-fed steers.

Along a creek were acres of frost-bitten chili plants, festooned with red pods. He saw fields of alfalfa and corn. *Peónes* moved slowly along the rows.

It was now sundown. From the heart of this valley of sun-ripened grama and tobosa grass, he saw the scarlet flash of reflected sunlight at the rim of a long mesa. Indistinctly he made out the block-like shape of Hacienda Río Chula. A breeze rustled the dry grasses. It brought a prickling to Charlie's spine. It was like the whispering of a dead man, asking him to guard well these things he had loved, the land and the cattle he had cared for.

Charlie Drake wanted to. But he had an allegiance to the things he loved himself, which were freedom and good fellowship. And then he understood Cort's mood, for Cort was fearing the same thing he was—the end of the old, carefree days.

Before they had ascended the broken mesa to the *hacienda,* darkness filled the valley. Charlie's impression, as they approached, was of a small walled city with *torreónes* at the corners. Behind barred windows burned a few lamps. A great nail-studded gate opened to admit them. In a cobbled courtyard, hostlers took their horses. Tonía went off to the house

118

she and her father occupied within the walls. Juan Bravo escorted Charlie and Cort to the main section of the *hacienda*.

There was a kind of primitive grandeur to it all. The rooms were lofty, the outside windows tall and barred. Hides and native rugs covered the dirt floors, and the furniture was handmade of mountain juniper. There seemed to be six or eight bedrooms. It all added up to a crude frontier magnificence.

They ate in a spacious dining room. When they turned in, Charlie found himself in possession of a bed large enough for a horse. He went to sleep thinking of a little Mexican with ideas big enough for a king.

Very early, *Don* Juan awoke him by banging on the door. *"¡Patrón! ¡Patrón!"*

Charlie climbed out of bed and let him in. The foreman stood in the doorway, jabbering in Spanish and striking his breast with both fists.

"The fault is mine! I have not kept guards on them. I did not think the bulls could be moved without my hearing them."

Charlie began pulling on his trousers. "What bulls? What are you talking about?"

"The fine herd! Forty-five of our best bulls, too fine to be left on the range. The foundation of the herd. *¡Aii, santos!*"

Charlie got the rest as they hurried into the courtyard. The bulls had been quietly led from their stalls sometime during the night. The gate in the rear wall, through which they had passed, hung wide.

Charlie said: "Round up some riders, and wake up *Señor* Carraday. They can't be far."

While the cowpunchers collected, he looked over the ground. The earth of the big central court was a heavy clay mixed with straw and manure. Near the stalls it was wet, holding the impressions of many horse and cow tracks and of peasants' sandaled feet. Charlie kept looking until he found one pair of footprints common to each of the stalls. They had been made by small, high-heeled boots. A cowboy's—or a woman's.

He glanced around, his eyes moving down the line of workers' cottages against the *hacienda* wall. Children played there, and dogs lay in patches of sunlight; women knelt before *moledores*, grinding corn. In the doorway of her father's house, Tonía Bravo, a slender figure with a flash of red in her hair, leaned against the jamb to watch him.

Charlie walked across the yard, his spurs jingling. Tonía wore a short skirt that showed her slim tan legs. Her blouse was a pale green that enriched the warm tones of her skin; in the sunlight, her dark hair gleamed. Charlie stopped before her. She straightened with that casual grace of hers.

"Pase usted," she said softly.

Charlie went into the *jacal*. The floor was of packed earth covered with native rugs, bright squares of red and black and gray. The rawhide furniture was low and sturdy. In the air was a whisper of spices and the friendly incense of mesquite root coals, gray-red on the hearth.

"Such a pity about the bulls, *patrón!*" she remarked.

Charlie snapped: "Don't call me *patrón*. Call me Charlie, or Mister Drake, or anything but that. I've worked for a living too long to be called boss."

She gave him a glance that was demure but mocking, humble yet taunting. She repeated—"Charlie."—giving the "r" the faint Mexican trill that brushed the hayseeds out of its hair. "Yes, for an *Americano* that is better."

He started to retort sharply, remembering their conversation about *gringos*, but he turned, instead, to glance through a low doorway into a sleeping room. "Your room?"

She nodded. "But I don't think your bulls are in there."

His gaze slipped down her body to her feet; she wore sandals with flat heels. He went into the bedroom. One corner was curtained off as a closet. Charlie drew the curtain aside and looked down at several pairs of sandals and a single pair of low riding boots, of good kangaroo. He picked them up. He began to nod.

"It could have been you, at that," he said. "It wasn't a thing a man would have done."

Her chin went up. "So I am a thief, because I do not like *Americanos*."

Charlie dropped the boots and let the curtain swing back. "No, you're a fool, because you don't know when you're well off." In him was a sense of frustration and anger, because there was no way he could prove that her boots were the ones that had made the prints, and because, knowing it, she chose to banter.

When he went toward the door, she moved aside. "You will be ashamed," she said, "if the men who stole the bulls are caught with them."

"Surprised, too."

As he passed her, she said: "If you like, I'll apologize for having a pair of boots, *Don* Charlie."

It was the last tug at a frayed temper. He turned, the smile still on her lips, and caught her waist in the hard angle of his arm. She could outbanter him any day in the week, but he had his masculine superiority to fall back on, and the superiority of caste. He pulled her roughly against him. It was a saloon kiss. Her body was unresisting, but her lips, that he had thought the most beautiful he had ever seen, full and rich, the color of Burgundy wine in the sunlight, took the kiss impassively.

Charlie's arms dropped away. Her face colored; she

looked at the floor, her whole manner saying: *You have violated me, but it is the right of a proprietor to violate the women of his* hacienda.

It hit Charlie so he could only swallow. "I'm sorry, Tonía . . . ," he fumbled. "I . . . I only meant to. . . ."

She still would not look at him, and he turned at once and left the cottage. He was saddling his horse when he realized what she had done. Why, the damned little fox! She had played him to do what she expected him to.

He went back to his saddling. He thought: *I'll pay you back for that, Chata, and it won't be in liters of corn!* A moment later, he caught himself touching his mouth with his fingertips, trying to recapture the texture of her lips. *What would they be like if they cared to respond?* Charlie Drake decided to find out.

III

With a dozen riders, Juan Bravo waited for Charlie outside the *hacienda*. The nearest stream was Río Chula. They rode to the rim of the mesa to survey the valley, a tawny sea of whispering grasses. Below them were the irrigated acres along the river where it paralleled the mesa.

On the golden floor of the valley, the black shapes of Angus cattle were as plain as flies on a sun-shot wall. *Don* Juan led the men down the cliff trail. They dispersed across the valley to inspect the cattle.

Working with the foreman, Charlie rode for an hour down the valley before Bravo gave up. All of the animals were range animals. "It is what I feared," Bravo declared. "They have reached the hills."

They started back. West of the *hacienda,* the range crumpled into the first low barricades of Las Tunas Mountains. Here, the timber was scrub oak and cedar, and the ridges were not high but, beyond the mountains, ascended roughly to blue, timbered heights. Charlie was not worried about rustlers. The real danger was that the pampered herd bulls, fat and short-legged, would be injured on narrow mountain trails.

As they rode back, Charlie asked: "How long since the men have been paid?"

"Six months." Bravo rode with his wrinkled brown face turned straight ahead. "When do you hold the beef roundup?"

"This season. It is past time."

"Then we'll start it now and pick up the bulls as we go.

Send a man to El Sauz to arrange for cattle cars. And let the men know they'll be paid as soon as I get the cows across the river. This may have been a grudge trick."

Don Juan looked shocked. "It would not be possible!" But the small bright eyes began to ponder.

Down here, Charlie learned, they didn't pamper a cowpuncher the way they did in the States. A man was expected to exist on tortillas and beans, to wrap himself in his serape if he found the frosted ground too hard. He rode a wooden tree with a horn the size of a pie plate. He made his own rope, of rawhide, and, if he knew how to use it, he didn't have to splice it every night while the other men were sleeping.

Charlie's gang worked west. Cort went with him, grousing about the bad food and the hard work. He had always been more of a saloon cowboy than a ranch hand.

Within three days, half of the lost bulls had been found. But then they were in the mountains, with a thousand dead-end cañons in which cattle could hide. On the fourth day, Charlie found a bull lying on a steep mountainside with a broken leg. He shot it and left a *vaquero* to skin it for the hide.

Later that afternoon he discovered the torn body of another that had been killed by *lobos*. Before they were finished, Charlie figured his loss at four bulls. He sent the last of the uninjured animals back. That night he sat before the big campfire, feeling the good, scorching heat of it against his face. He was almost certain that Tonía Bravo had let the bulls out the gate. Yet it was harder for him to muster an outraged anger against her than it should have been. He tried to think of her as treacherous and crafty. He kept thinking, instead, of why she might have done it.

She had loved old Miguel Castillo for what he had done for her people. She hated Charlie for what some of his people had done to hers. He supposed that made them enemies. But when he turned in, what he was thinking of was the way her lashes veiled her dark eyes, of the warm, sweet pressure of her lips when he had kissed her. . . .

In the morning, José Castillo and his foreman rode up.

Castillo's fat body was borne by a Percheron of a horse. His saddle was of extra width, with skirts of *tigre* skin. Charlie remembered his appearance in Harkrider's office, and it came to him that the *hacendado* looked less cumbersome, less the dreamer after a dead dream than he had seemed in Chihuahua City. There was a sureness about him that was not quite arrogance; in his ability to look at a cowpuncher without seeing him, there was a cavalier disdain. But with Charlie and Cort, he was affable.

"*¿Qué cosa?*" He dismounted by the branding pen, a vast ambling figure with a gray-and-red poncho over his shoulders.

Charlie shook hands with him. Castillo introduced his companion. "Vasquez, my foreman."

Vasquez was a large, dark Mexican with somber features and melancholy Indian eyes. His costume was a leather jacket, straw sombrero, and bull-hide chaps. He had a heavy, loose chin, heavy shoulders, and lean hips. Vasquez said— "*Su servidor.*"—but the flat Yaqui eyes denied that he would ever be the servant of anyone.

"The daughter of *Don* Juan," said Castillo, "told me you had started the roundup. I found you by your branding fire. A little late for the *rodeo*, eh? The price is not now so good."

He could say the gloomiest things with the pleasantest manner, Charlie thought. "Better late than never." He shrugged.

Castillo lit a brown cigarette and watched a calf take the brand with a prolonged bawl and a puff of smoke from cooked hide. "Good calves," he said. "Fine calves."

Vasquez regarded them with a smile at the corners of his lips, the way a raiser of bulldogs might regard a poodle.

"On the way up," Castillo went on, "I saw some calves which did not look so good as these."

Cort Carraday had a stiff, unsmiling stare for the Mexican. "What do you expect from longhorn cows?" he countered. "Black Angus heifers?"

Castillo shook his head. "I mean . . . sick calves."

Charlie looked at him sharply. "The herd's been vaccinated," he said. "There shouldn't be any sickness."

Vasquez shrugged.

"Perhaps they were mavericks. But these calves did not look good."

"Where are they?"

"Not far from here. Six kilometers."

"Let's have a look at them," Charlie said.

Castillo tugged at a large ear. "A pity to take you from your work," he said. "But it seemed that you should know. *Vamonos.*"

Charlie turned the tallying over to a cowpuncher. He glanced at *Don* José's face as they started. Castillo retained that complacent smile. Charlie began to be angry. If there was herd-sickness, he wanted to know about it. But he got the impression that Castillo was moving pieces on a checker board.

Once, as they rode, Castillo maneuvered in beside Cort and spoke to him. Cort rapped out a reply that silenced him, but it did not quiet a barbed tendril of curiosity that began to turn in Charlie's mind. He remembered the day Cort had called alone at Castillo's town office. And now he recalled Cort's preoccupation when they left town after his visit with Castillo. . . .

They passed through a gap onto the apron of the plain.

They were in the longhorn country, where the grass was closer-cropped and the water less plentiful. Vasquez jogged toward a motte of leafless trees around a water hole. A handful of yearling bulls began to shy from them. The Mexican put his pony to a lope and threw one of the animals. Cort was there to make the tie.

In the weak autumn sunlight they gathered about the bull while Castillo's thick fingers explored one of the forelegs. A muffled crackling came from a heavy swelling under the red hide as he pressed it. Castillo looked up. Slowly he withdrew his hand.

For one instant none of the men spoke. Charlie's thoughts were less of the bull than of himself. He tried to recapture the spirit, for a moment, of the old, untroubled days of having nothing more serious to perplex him than how to make two pairs beat a full house, the days when he had let somebody else worry about whether or not a calf was sick. What was in every man's mind was blackleg—the killer of herds.

Vasquez groaned. "The devil! That it should be so close to your own land, *Don* José!"

Castillo arose and rubbed his hands together. He wagged his head. "Naturally these animals will be destroyed and buried on the spot. I would recommend a fire of brush on the ground over which they have been grazing. It is possible that the sickness may be arrested."

Charlie was too sandbagged to think clearly. When you said blackleg, you said catastrophe. The treatment for an infected herd was to destroy it.

"In Mexico," Castillo said thoughtfully, "it is customary to destroy the entire herd in which the disease breaks out. The authorities insist on it. It has been found least expensive to the vicinity as a whole. Of course, that is ruthless and unnecessary."

Charlie continued to stare at him.

Castillo sadly shook his head. "It is time, *Don* Carlos, to decide for yourself whether or not an American is able to run cattle in Chihuahua. Our authorities distrust you. They will make it hard. And, of course, I cannot let you cross my land to the railroad with such animals."

There was a rustle of movement. Cort's gun was suddenly in his hand. Before they knew what he was doing, he had put a bullet into the head of the downed animal. On the broad plain, the shot rang flatly. Vasquez stepped back, alarmed. Castillo's fat-choked eyes stared.

Cort flipped out a pocket knife. The animal was still moving, but he squatted to make a long cut the length of the cannon. There was little blood, but an oily liquid bubbled from the wound. The foreman, Vasquez, laid a hand on his shoulder, the fingers biting.

"*Hombre,* to release such matter into the air is murder!"

Cort wiped a finger in the stuff oozing from the cut. He sniffed it, showing the finger to Charlie. But Charlie already understood. He faced Vasquez angrily.

"Sweet oil! A vet's needle and a pint of sweet oil, and you've got Mexican blackleg. You work best at night, don't you, *compadre?*"

Vasquez's face began to redden. He turned on Castillo as much resentment as a workman dared show *el patrón.* "Did I not say . . . 'of a pig, expect only ordure?' "

Charlie bent to wipe his hand in the blood, oil, and dirt on the ground. He wiped it across Vasquez's mouth. Vasquez struck at him, and Charlie slammed him on the side of the jaw. Vasquez stumbled back into Castillo. He shook his head. The black eyes, fuming in his dark face, hardened. It was when he reached for his gun that Charlie lost his temper.

Vasquez was just a stride away. Charlie started the punch

as he moved toward him. His knuckles smashed into Vasquez's mouth and the blood came. Vasquez's gun was out but the man was too stunned to bring it up. With his fist, Charlie knocked it to the ground. He threw a high one that opened a cut in the Mexican's brow. Fumblingly Vasquez reached for Charlie's throat with his hands. Charlie grinned and let him close. Vasquez's eyes lighted up with a savagery, but just then Charlie brought his fist up under the man's chin with a force that lifted him to his toes.

Vasquez made a windy noise. He went down. He lay between Charlie and Castillo as accusatively as a pointed finger.

A good general, Castillo refused to be panicked. He made a convincing show of bewilderment. "*Don* Carlos, I say to you that it was not I, nor any of my men, who did this! Vasquez is a stupid man with a bad temper. We rode by the calves. You can see for yourself that one must notice. . . . Apparently you have enemies."

Cort laughed. "Now tell him about the day I ransomed my hat."

Sturdily Castillo returned his gaze. "What I said to you was for *Don* Carlos's good. I said . . . 'Persuade him that he cannot succeed.' "

"You also said there would be five thousand *pesos* waiting for me at El Paso if I did."

Castillo colored but said unashamedly: "*Pues,* this is Mexico. I am a businessman. Here we transact business by the shortest line."

Charlie was confused and angry and hurt. It was in his mind that, if Cort had not hoped to collect the money, he would have told him immediately about Castillo's offer. Not that he would have been a party to treachery. But if Charlie had gone broke, perhaps Cort would have been willing to accept the money as a windfall.

He walked to his pony, found the stirrup, and mounted. "*Don* José," he said, "you may be right. Maybe an American can't run cattle in Mexico. But this is the wrong way to convince him. All you've done is to show me that my line riders should go armed. Starting today, they will. Anybody we find riding through the herd without an engraved invitation from me had better be armed, too."

IV

With the idea of getting a line on the calf count in the longhorn pasture, Charlie headed west into the foothills, taking a round-about way back to the branding camp. Cort said once: "That bastard would kill his grandmother for the gold in her teeth. Blackleg! They don't stand around cropping grass that way when they've got blackleg." Then he appeared to forget the whole incident. As they rode, he whistled, and after a while taunted: "Didn't I see you coming out of Tonía's *jacal?* Not looking for a Mexican wife to go with your ranch, are you?"

Charlie had not shaken the distemper his suspicion of Cort had put him in. He told the truth about Tonía. "I'd bet double eagles to *pesos* she turned those brutes out the gate. But I can't prove it by high heels, when I wear them myself."

Cort chuckled. He started to roll a smoke, and Charlie had a small pang of jealousy, watching him. He was the same easy-going cowpoke who had crossed the border a few weeks ago, irresponsible, carefree, with no more ballast than a canoe. Charlie was already dragging the leg iron of responsibility. He knew he would have to get this thing off his chest, sooner or later.

"Why didn't you tell me Castillo tried to bribe you?"

Cort popped a match with his thumbnail. He didn't answer until he had the cigarette going and had snapped the match in two. "Why worry you? Everybody had been trying to throw the fear into you. I told him to go to hell, and that was the end of it."

"Castillo didn't seem to think it was. He was still counting on you helping him."

Cort gave him a pained look. "Charlie, for Pete's sake! If you'd inherited a horse, I suppose I'd be riding off on it the first time you turned your back."

Charlie stared at him a moment. Then he grinned and the tenseness went out of him. "Cort," he said, "you should have shot me for asking that. I forgot you're going to make your fortune backing the double zero."

"Don't forget it again," Cort said. The wind took the smoke he exhaled; the same wind took the last of Charlie's suspicions with it.

The plain broke into hogbacks and eroded barrancas. A strong east wind combed the grass and buffeted the piñons and cedars. The range tilted up, rising steeply to a chain of mountains faced with pipe-organ formations of stone. The cañons deepened; the timber grew heavier. Along a thread of silver water they discovered cow tracks. The stream led them up a twisting cañon that opened into a little park sentried with pines. On the still air hung an odor that set Charlie's mouth to watering. It was a moment before the illogicality of a civilized odor like that of beef stew in a remote spot such as this struck him.

He looked at Cort. Cort was staring at him. Before either of them could speak, the sand between their ponies' hoofs was disturbed by something that struck a long, shallow furrow and went whining past them. The rifle shot slammed down from a ledge a split second later. A high yell followed it. "Get out of here, you buzzards! Get out fast!"

It was a girl's voice with a vixen edge that raised the hair on the back of Charlie's neck. Right now there was nothing to do but keep both hands in sight and turn his horse back. He said: "Yes, ma'am."

The bank went up steeply from the trail. The ledge was formed where a cleavage occurred in the sloping pile of rotted

132

stone. Brush grew in the crevices, and among the thorned wands of an *ocotillo* burned a blue spark of metal. The girl lay at the base of the plant, almost hidden.

Cort rode ahead of Charlie, back down the stream. "Ma'am," he called, "you talk good English for a native!"

There was no answer from the ledge. Charlie's rein hand touched his rope, lying coiled over the saddle horn. He wondered what kind of gun the girl had used, that it required no re-cocking. There had been no *clink* of metal since the shot. Somebody, he figured, was rattled.

As he passed beneath her, nearly hidden from her view, he lifted the rope and tossed the loop onto the ledge. There was a gasp, and then a scrambling as he spurred downcañon, taking a dally about the horn. He looked back and saw a girl with braided yellow hair, clad in overall pants and a pony-skin jacket, come sliding down the rough face of the stone. The gun clattered along ahead of her.

She lay still for a moment after she landed, so that they were at her side before she came up, swearing and fighting. Her face was scratched, her hands bled, her shirt was torn so that the white skin of her breast was exposed, in sharp contrast to her deeply tanned face. Cort caught her arms. She tried to bite him. He laughed and held her tighter. But Charlie saw desperation in her face and a genuine terror.

"All right, we'll get out!" she said. "Drive a sick man and a girl out, and laugh about it!"

"Who's *we?*" Charlie asked. "We didn't know anybody was here."

She scanned him closely. He observed her body relax. Cort released her then. "And I didn't know you were Americans," she said. "I thought you were some of those dirty bastards sent down here to run us out. I mean, me and Pop. We're traders, but Pop's too sick to move. Yes, and I killed one of their steers!" she said defiantly. "It was that or starve."

"One of *my* steers," Charlie corrected. "This is my range, lady. If your dad's sick, why didn't you come out for help?"

The blonde hair tossed. It was long and braided, with a sheen of pure gold. The eyes were gray, giving a kind of animal sharpness and beauty to her face. Even in shirt and Levi's, she couldn't have fooled anybody. The curves under the shirt were soft and full; the Levi's were snug across the hips.

"I wouldn't ask a Mexican for help if I was starving," she said bitterly. "They raided us this side of Chihuahua. We had five wagons of trade goods. They killed all of our men and put a slug in Pop. He came down with a fever before I could get him out of their damned country." The cleft chin went up. "Why don't you turn us over to the *rurales?* I killed one of your steers, didn't I?"

Charlie stared at her. So this was the last remnant of the massacred wagon train! He felt an immense pity for the old man and the girl. But even at this moment, Cort could find something to joke about. He held her by the chin and with his handkerchief dabbed at a deep scratch on her cheek. "For a kiss," he said, "I'd square that with my pardner. Is my credit good, Charlie?"

"It's good with me." Charlie grinned.

The girl gave Charlie a close look, and then stared at Cort. And right then, Charlie knew there was going to be a meeting of the wild strains in each of them. Soberly she peered into his eyes. Then she smiled. "I've never kissed a man without I knew his name," she said.

"Cort. Cort Carraday."

Her slim brown arms went around his neck. She kissed him on the lips, long and clingingly. When she stood back,

Cort looked more like a man who has been hit on the chin than kissed. For the first time in his life, a kiss had reached him.

"Do I need a receipt, Cort?" the girl asked.

Cort's face burned. He took a long breath. "What name would I put on it if you did?"

"Amy Sheridan." She turned and walked up the stream, limping a little after her fall.

The camp was hidden behind a shoulder of rock, consisting merely of a high-sided freight wagon with a canvas top and some crates piled around a fire on which a Dutch oven bubbled. On a clothesline was an odd assortment of man's clothing, a girl's, and long strips of sun-dried beef. She went to the back of the wagon.

"Pop! There's a couple of men here."

It was not a man's voice that replied. It was a hoarse, windy whisper that death sometimes uses.

"Lord, girl, why didn't you . . . ?"

"They're all right, Pop," Amy interrupted. "Americans, and one of them owns the land we're on. They're going to help us."

She beckoned them. Charlie looked in at a skeleton under a blanket. There was the ugly, sweetish smell that dying men have when they have suffered long in unwashed blankets. Charlie did not see the mouth move, but he heard the man whisper.

"Got any whiskey, mister?"

"Plenty, where we're going. Can you stand a ride?"

"If it kills me, it'll be a blessing."

Charlie and Cort rode up to where the mules were staked. They harnessed them to the wagon. Cort offered to help Amy drive. They tied his pony on behind and started down the cañon.

★ ★ ★ ★ ★

They wore out that night on the prairie, five miles from Hacienda Río Chula. At noon they hauled through the gate into the courtyard. Amy stood in the middle of the yard, staring at the slotted towers and the great block of masonry forming the front buildings.

Tonía appeared from her cottage. Charlie smiled at her meeting with Amy Sheridan. Tonía stared at the golden, braided pigtails; she frowned at the roughness of the girl's clothing. Then she smiled and murmured—" *'Uenos días.* "—but Amy, with her suspicion of anything Mexican, did not acknowledge the welcome. She looked at Tonía critically and turned to Cort.

"She's pretty." It was an accusation.

Cort began: "Oh, she's just. . . ." He glanced at Charlie. "She's the *mayordomo*'s daughter."

Charlie had an instant's resentment. *She's just one of the natives,* Cort had been about to say. Just a Mex. But Mexes had pride and intelligence, and sometimes they had beauty. Sometimes they had all three. In Tonía's face he saw that she had interpreted Amy Sheridan's manner, if she could not understand the words. He tried to make his orders sound more like a suggestion than a command.

"Find them some dry, clean rooms, will you? And see that there's a fire, and some broth and whiskey for the old man. He's pretty sick."

Tonía nodded. It appeared that she comprehended a little English. She instructed Charlie in Spanish: "Thank the *señorita* for me. She is pretty, too. Blondes are always prettier than brunettes, no?"

"All depends on how they act," Charlie told her.

In some unused rooms off the chapel, Tonía had furniture installed, fires laid, and clean blankets spread. While the rooms were warming, Charlie had *Padre* Alonso, the *hacienda* priest and physician, examine the old man. Dick Sheridan, the trader, saw his brown skin and cursed him. The *cura* said nothing, taking his pulse silently, examining his eyes, and finally left the wagon.

"He will die in a week," he said softly. "It would not be a kindness to bring a doctor from Chihuahua. It would simply be an unkindness to the doctor."

For a while Charlie thought about it. As they were carrying Dick Sheridan into the bedroom, he decided to tell Amy. She took it the way wild things always take catastrophe, wordlessly, with calm fatalism.

She looked across the walls toward the timbered mountains. She said: "I'll pay them back, Charlie. I'll pay them back!"

They went back to the cow camp that afternoon.

It was nearly three weeks before the branding was finished. With the cattle drifting toward the pass, Charlie took the bulk of the crew back to Río Chula to get the Anguses started. He was selling only 100 *corrientes*, good beef cattle but not the stuff to build a herd with.

As the tired, unshaven gang of cowpunchers trailed into the *hacienda*, *Don* Juan spoke to Charlie. "What shall I say to the men about the *fiesta, Don* Carlos?"

"What *fiesta?*"

"The *fiesta* of the roundup!" The old man looked surprised. "It was the custom of *Don* Miguel before the cattle drive to do so. . . ."

Charlie smiled. "Start the fires," he said. "And tell the cook I don't like too much garlic."

He went over to the rooms behind the chapel, where Dick Sheridan and his girl were staying. He had heard nothing of them in two weeks. He had a small fear that Dick Sheridan would be dead, and perhaps a fear that he would not. It seemed useless for a man to suffer hopelessly. But Sheridan, clinging like a dying puma to a rotten shred of life, lay in a half coma in his bed. The stench in his room was sickening. Charlie got out.

In his room, Charlie found a letter from Joel Harkrider, with a postmark two weeks old. In their easy-going way, the servants had figured it could wait on the roundup. As it happened, it couldn't.

Charlie read it, while his mind began desperately to figure ways and means.

Friend Drake: Hope you are doing well. Have to tell you, however, that a suit has been brought against you for collection of some notes I didn't know existed. Castillo acquired them from a bank. The principal was only 4,000 a year ago, but the way they figure interest down here, it amounts to 6,000 now.

You've got until the 17th to pay up. After that, the ranch may go on the block. Better sell those cattle and get the money down here.

It killed the *fiesta* atmosphere like a bullet. The 17th! That gave him one week to make the trip to El Paso and get back! He could do it, but only if his cattle cars were on time and he found an immediate buyer.

He spent that day checking and re-checking dates and figures.

All that afternoon, smoke from the barbecue pits hung over the ranch. In the kitchen, the slapping of women's hands shaping tortillas was incessant. The tang of cooking chiles invaded every room.

Off Charlie's bedroom was a large patio, the heart of the *hacienda*. The entrance to it was through an arched passageway. At dusk, lanterns were hung from the rafter ends and food began to be carried in and arranged on upended barrels. The workers commenced streaming in. Cowboys wore their finest outfits and sombreros. The girls who did the meanest chores about the ranch were mysterious, dark-eyed creatures in full skirts and embroidered blouses.

Someone strummed a guitar. Suddenly there was focus to the excitement. They were pairing off for the dance. Charlie had been anxious to stay out of it, but Juan Bravo dragged him over to Tonía. "She is one to speak too quickly," he said. "But there is not a better dancer on Río Chula."

The music was in full swing, but no one danced yet; they were waiting for the *patrón* to start it. Charlie was desperate. All he knew about dancing was the Varsoviana. He looked into Tonía's face and saw there a laughing enjoyment of his plight. With a sort of desperation, he recalled the quick, rhythmic stamping of the dancers in the Chihuahua saloon. He took Tonía's hand and gave her a spin. His spurs set up a musical rattling as he went out to meet her, hands on his hips.

He kept up the bluff, somehow, until the rest were dancing. Tonía looked surprised. She still smiled, but it was a smile without a sting. Charlie almost wished she had kept the other smile. He was afraid of her when she looked that way, afraid of forgetting his resolve to keep his distance from her and let her know her place. Under his hand her waist was like a reed. He could have enjoyed it, except that he was beginning to step on her toes. He was lost.

Over on a bench, Cort Carraday sat with Amy. She wore a long gown Tonía had lent her. Her blonde hair was braided and arranged in a kind of corona over her head. Charlie hated to break them up, but he had to get out of this. He got Cort's eye and signaled him.

Cort said something to Amy and came to relieve him. Charlie said to Tonía: "Excuse me. I've got to see about the wine."

He sat beside Amy. It was not over thirty seconds before he knew he had made a desperate error. Army's eyes, as she watched Cort and the Mexican girl go through the figures, had a strange, wicked shine. Suddenly she turned to Charlie.

"Don't you want to dance?"

"I wish I could."

Amy laughed. "Sure, so you could dance with your little *amiga!*"

The odd part was, Charlie felt a species of jealousy, too. Cort, who had the light heart for it, danced like a Mexican. Once Charlie saw him kiss Tonía's cheek. She turned her head away, and through the moving pattern of dancers their eyes met; she was laughing. Charlie felt Amy tense, her fingers clenching the edge of the bench. *Cort, you damned fool!* he thought. *She's not the kind to use jealousy on. She'll cut your heart out.*

Charlie began to hum a little louder than his mood called for. He decided maybe he was hungry. "How about some chuck?" he asked Amy.

She took his arm, giving it a squeeze. As they passed through the arch, she tossed a backward glance at the others.

At the smoking barbecue pits, Charlie filled their plates and got pottery cups of coffee. They went back. As he started to eat, Charlie glanced about for Tonía and Cort. Amy was looking for them, too.

They were gone.

V

Charlie started to rise and nearly tipped his plate over. His heart was hitting his chest with little jolts. Was Cort crazy? Not only to try to make Amy jealous, but to fool around with a decent Mexican girl as though she were a saloon entertainer.

Amy was suddenly on her feet. She tried to pass him. He caught her wrist. "What's the matter?"

"Nothing! I'm going to my room." In the lamplight, tears sparkled in her eyes.

Charlie tried to pull her back down on the bench. "They've probably gone out for food."

Amy tore loose from him. "They've gone, all right, but not for food."

She ran down the walk and through the arch.

Something had happened to Charlie's food. It was sawdust. Something was wrong with the wine. He realized that something would remain wrong with them until Tonía came back. He thought: *What happens is up to her. A woman can end a party any time she likes. It's none of my business what she is.*

But that sick breathlessness stayed with him like the jolt of a saddle horn. Charlie Drake was not one to deceive himself. He came to a decision. He would send her and *Don* Juan out to the last line camp on the ranch. He would bury them where he'd never see her again. It was one thing to dislike a woman, and another to be in love with her at the same time. It was going to happen to him. He was not going to be made a fool of by a girl who despised him both for what he was and for what he was not.

Someone stopped beside him, and he looked up to see

Cort. Cort sat down. His left cheek was red, but he was grinning.

"She's a keep-your-distance girl, Charlie. Don't you forget it."

"What happened?"

Cort chuckled. "The usual. Just as I thought I was making time, she slapped me."

"I didn't see her come back."

"She said she was going over to her shack for a while." Cort glanced about. "Where's Amy?"

Charlie drank his coffee. "Where do you think? Cort, if you don't end up by hanging, you'll finish with a woman's fingernails cutting your jugular vein."

Cort looked pleased, his dark, good-looking face flushed. "She wasn't jealous?"

"If you don't think so, just hike over there and try to explain."

Cort scratched his head. "It might be a good idea, at that."

Gradually it came to Charlie that Tonía's few minutes were extending beyond a half hour. In his mind a red flag of suspicion fluttered. He had almost forgotten about the lost Angus bulls, but now he was recalling that only a couple of cowpunchers were on guard around the big corrals outside the *hacienda* where the holding herd was penned.

He walked to the courtyard. It was in full darkness, but he could hear the sounds made by the animals in their stalls. He turned to search the *jacales*. There was a light in Juan Bravo's quarters. Charlie knocked.

"Tonía!"

Getting no answer, he opened the door. The place was empty. Charlie strode across the ground to the gate. The heavy bolts had been slipped and it stood open a foot. He silenced his spur rowels with match-sticks and passed through.

In the night the sounds of the herd were restless. Far out on the mesa, at the most distant edge of the great cedar-pole corrals, a *vaquero* sang to the cattle. Charlie approached the main corral.

Suddenly he saw them—a single file of steers, ambling unhurriedly from the corral. At the same time, he saw the figure at the left of the gate.

She did not see him at once. She must have changed her clothes, for the white gown would have blazed like a torch in the darkness. Only her face showed, a pale oval against the darkly massed herd. Charlie began to walk toward her.

The cattle sensed him first. A big Angus steer just poking its head through the gate swerved. Charlie moved in fast. He slammed the gate and swung to catch the girl, darting toward the *hacienda*. On high heels, she was not difficult to overtake.

He held her from the back, feeling the softness of her hair against his face. Over the white dress she wore an old poncho of her father's, a plain dark serape with a hole in the center for the wearer's head.

Charlie said: "You Mexicans have a saying for this. *¡Huele, y no perfume!*"

After a long time, Tonía spoke, tightly. "I am not sorry I tried it . . . only that I was caught."

"I believe it," Charlie said. "And I believe you could give lessons to a sidewinder for treachery. I knew it was you who let the bulls out. And I knew you'd try to let the cattle out tonight. Why?"

Tonía wouldn't answer. She was still breathing hard; a thin rind of moon brushed shadows into her face, emphasizing the thin cheeks, the pulsating hollow of her throat.

"So now," Charlie said, "I've got to fire your father, to get rid of you. And I need him."

"Then don't fire him. Punish me, but let him stay."

Charlie's lips smiled. "I wonder how you would go about punishing a thief in skirts, with a red comb in her hair?"

She shrugged. "Castillo would know. He has had men whipped to death. I don't think it would matter to him what kind of clothes a thief wore." For an instant she was silent, her eyes going over his face. "I like *Señor* Cort," she said. "I like him because he doesn't pretend to be what he isn't."

"So you still think I've got a blacksnake in my suitcase."

"If a rich American left his ranch to a Mexican, wouldn't you wonder why? *Don* Miguel met you only once. Yet he left his ranch to you when he died. And the lawyer who held the will was an American, too. I've kept hoping someone would find the real will before you take all the cattle north."

Charlie laughed. "So you didn't know the will was held by a Mexican, who turned it over to Harkrider because he spoke English!"

The impact of it was in her eyes. She had fabricated a legend around him, a dramatic lie in which he was a conniving American cattle thief. And now that he had dissolved it, she was groping. It gave him a little better understanding into her mind, too, into the love she had for the ranch *el patrón viejo* had built.

"You're lying." She said it positively, yet she was still searching his eyes.

"You can ask Harkrider. Not that it matters. I suppose I should fire your father and you both, just to be safe. But *Don* Juan is a good man, and he doesn't hate *gringos*. So I'm sending you where you can't do any damage. They need a cook at Noche Buena camp. That's twenty miles across the hills."

Although her chin went up, Charlie knew he had touched her. "If you do, my father will quit," she declared.

"I've got a notion that, if I tell him who killed his favorite bulls, he'll run you out there himself."

He was suddenly enjoying it. For the first time, he had her on the defensive. She knew she had been wrong, and wanted to apologize, but she was going to be very sure before she humbled herself. "*Don* Charlie," she said thoughtfully, "you could tell him. Then he will watch me himself."

Charlie shook his head. "You're too dangerous. You're *muy peligrosa.*"

She was quick to sense that he was half bantering. A light from the *hacienda* was reflected softly in her eyes. "Then watch me yourself," she suggested.

"I don't want to watch you."

"Are you afraid of me? I don't carry a knife."

The breathlessness that had overcome him while she was with Cort came over him again. He had a desire to possess her the way he had that first morning, but he remembered how that had gone. He said gruffly: "All right. You can stay. But, if it happens again, it will be one for the police."

As he started away, she caught his hand. "Charlie! I'm sorry. I was wrong to suspect you, and I was wrong to let the bulls out. But I didn't know. . . ."

At the gate, Charlie turned roughly. "I was wrong, too. I had a nice, easy life and now I've lost it. I hate being a *patrón,* and I hate being in love. But I'm both."

He held her arms tightly, but she did not pull away. In the darkness, it was hard to tell whether she smiled. She said meekly: "They say being in love is nice."

"No. Only this part," Charlie said, "is nice." He held her closely by the arms, bending to kiss her. He knew how it would be, and he was crazy enough not to care. The amazing part was that it didn't go the way it had before. Her arms, slim and strong, moved up and around him, holding him. Her lips were firm and warm, half parted. . . .

The gate stirred rustily on its forged iron hinges. They both started. The voice of *Don* Juan blurted: "Excuse me . . . I did not know." Then: "Tonía! Why are you not . . . ?" At once his glance recognized Charlie. He looked startled and unhappy. "*Patrón,* I am sorry. But I had a message, and, when I did not find you inside, I thought to look out here."

In Charlie's face and neck, the blood surged violently. "What was it?"

"That ten men are riding up the cliff trail. The guard in the west tower saw them. It would be well to bar the gates. A precaution. It is possible they are *rurales,* what you would call Rangers."

VI

They stood in one of the *torreónes,* a squat adobe tower with tall rifle slots that guarded the approach to the *hacienda.* A penetrating chill filled the small angular room. Cort had come up with Charlie and Juan Bravo. Only a few men had been sent to the roof to take up guard. Down below, the rest still drank wine and ate barbecued beef and danced.

Hoof sounds rattled on the dark night air and a moment later a file of horsemen came over the rim of the mesa. Bravo studied them. "*¡Rurales!* But why?"

Charlie and Cort linked glances. Charlie was thinking of the saloon fight in Chihuahua. The horses hauled up before the gate, restless under harsh Mexican bits. A lean rider in a tall sombrero struck the gate with the barrel of his rifle.

"*¡Abra!*"

"For whom?" Charlie shouted down.

"Captain Villalobos. Of the Rural Police."

Don Juan breathed: "*Sí.* It is Villalobos. I know him."

"What's the trouble?" Charlie demanded.

"*¡Fugitivos!* Must we shout here in the cold, when there is the smell of a *fiesta* inside?" The *rurales* laughed. Captain Villalobos added: "We look for two Americans, an old man and a girl. Have you seen them?"

A look of panic struck into Cort Carraday's face. Charlie knew what had to be done. "We haven't seen them," he said. "But come in and warm yourselves."

He faced Juan Bravo, not knowing how to ask it. There was no reason why the *segundo* should perjure himself for a couple of Americans. Nor was there any reason why Charlie

Drake should, except that he thought the Sheridans had suffered enough down here, and that the trader would die if he were moved.

With a short brown forefinger, Bravo tapped his nose rapidly. "In the grain shed. No . . . they may feed their horses. ¡Aii! In the bell tower, above the chapel. Meet your guests, *Don* Carlos. I will see that it is done."

Charlie gripped his shoulder for a moment. "For this kind of work, there's a bonus."

As they went down, Cort said: "Thanks, kid. You're taking a big risk for an old man and somebody else's girl."

Charlie shrugged. "I don't know what the charge is, but I know they'd lock them up till they rotted."

Villalobos led his men into the *hacienda*, shadowed, tall-hatted men with serapes muffling the lower halves of their faces. The captain dismounted and studied closely as he shook his hand. The eyes of Villalobos were bloodshot from the wind; his face was spare and hard and his hand had the texture of dried rawhide.

"Where is Juan Bravo?" he inquired.

"He's with a herd, out back. I've sent for him."

Through cold, silent lanes between the buildings, they moved toward the warmth of the barbecue fires.

"Border jumpers?" Charlie asked.

"Murderers. They ambushed a party of traders on the Chihuahua road. Vasquez, Castillo's foreman, informs me he saw a wagon proceeding this way a few days after the murders."

He glanced at Charlie, and Charlie did not permit himself to look at Cort. Cort was the one it must have hit hardest. He was the one who, if Villalobos told it correctly, was in love with a pretty murderess.

The *rurales* ate like hungry dogs. Some of them had drifted into the patio by the time *Don* Juan hurried up, rubbing his hands together. He and Villalobos embraced in the Mexican fashion, pounding each other on the back and lying about how they had missed one another. Bravo affected shock when he heard of the crime.

"But of course they are not here! Still," he said, "it would be well to search. It is possible they were smuggled in on a load of hay."

Captain Villalobos grunted as he tore a strip of beef from the chunk he held in his fingers. "We will search."

They moved into the patio, where Villalobos drifted among the workers. He recognized Tonía and paid exaggerated compliments, over which she laughed. Her father hastily told her what had happened. "Naturally," he said pointedly, "they cannot be in the *hacienda.*"

Her eyes widened a little. She looked at Charlie, and then at Villalobos. "Impossible," she said. "The walls are much too high."

"But the gates are wide," said the captain, smiling.

He showed no haste to begin the search. It was a cold night and his attention was first for food and drink. Thus Juan Bravo was able to get Charlie aside.

"The old one is out of his head. When I tried to move him, he threatened to kill me!"

Out of the corner of his eye, Charlie was conscious of Villalobos's attention. He said casually: "I hadn't noticed, *Don* Juan. We'll bring another keg up right now." He disengaged his key ring from his belt and called to the *rural.* "Will you excuse us, Captain? The wine's running low."

"A catastrophe." Villalobos smiled.

Charlie and *Don* Juan went into the main building. Immediately Charlie strode through the rooms toward the *zaguán,* the arched passageway off which opened the chapel. The

Mexican scurried at his heels, a dark shadow with clanking spurs.

"But if we go in, *patrón*, he will kill us!"

"I'll go in first. He doesn't trust a Mexican."

He stood a moment in the dark passage, his eyes and ears alive. Quickly, then, he crossed to the chapel. He rapped lightly and Amy's voice came from the darkened room. "Charlie?"

"Open up! Villalobos will be here any minute!"

The door was unbarred, and, in the ruddy surge of the hearth, Charlie saw Amy standing with an enormous cap-and-ball pistol in her hand and behind her, a lean right-angle on the cot, her father crouched with a rifle in his hands.

"He's crazy as a loon," Amy whispered tensely. "I can't get that thing away from him."

Charlie stepped inside. At once Dick Sheridan raised the gun. "Get outta here!"

Charlie went toward him. "It's me, old-timer. Charlie Drake. The law dogs are howling outside. We've got to move you."

"Git back. I don't keer if you're Daniel Boone. I'm watching out for my ownself!" The long gun trembled.

"Pop! It's Charlie. They'll kill us if they find us here, stand us up against a wall and shoot us without a trial. You know these Mexicans!"

"Shore do. And I'm about to kill one. Pass that chair, *hombre*, and. . . ."

Reaching the chair, Charlie hesitated. If there were more time! The rifle was heavy; he saw it begin to sag in Dick Sheridan's hands. Now he rested his hands on the back of the chair. "Amy's right, Dick. You don't stand a chance with them."

While he talked, the chair lifted and soared gently toward

Sheridan. At the last instant, the trader perceived what had happened. He tried to squirm aside, but the chair was descending on him. The long barrel was struck down. Charlie ran toward him.

There was a magnificent roar, an end-of-the-world explosion that filled every corner of the room with redness for one shattered second, and then expired. A lead ball caromed savagely about the plastered walls for an endless interval.

Bravo sprang into the doorway. *"¡Patrón!"*

Down the corridor, the *rurales* were running.

"I'm all right," Charlie snapped. "Head them off. Amy and I will move him."

He stepped in close and brought his fist solidly to the point of the trader's chin. Dick Sheridan went limp. Amy had closed the door and replaced the bar. Charlie could just discern her, a slender taper against the dark panel.

Several men ran up. Questions were fired like birdshot, and in this moment Charlie knew that unless *Don* Juan were superhuman, it was all up with the Sheridans, and probably with him.

Don Juan was saying coolly: "It could have been an owl, *compadres. ¿Quién sabe?* I heard a noise and came out to see. I saw it on the wall and fired. It disappeared. Owl or man, it should be on the ground beyond the wall."

Footfalls rushed away.

Charlie lit a candle and placed it in Amy's hand. "The stairs behind the altar. Bring your blankets."

Silently they traversed the dark chapel. Amy held the door open and Charlie groped inside. The steps were perilous even if a man did not have 150 pounds of dead weight to carry. They mounted in tight spirals to the belfry on steps a foot wide. Charlie was breathless and dizzy when they came out into the clear black night of the belfry. They spread the blankets and made Dick Sheridan as comfortable as possible.

Charlie told Amy to tie him and put a gag in his mouth. "If he starts yelling, you're cooked. And if they look at *Don* Juan's gun and find it hasn't been fired, you're cooked anyway."

When he went down, he dumped water on the hearth coals. He obliterated all signs of occupancy and left the door unlocked when he departed.

He looped back through the house, secured a keg of wine from the cellar, and returned to the patio. It was deserted of all the men. He joined them outside the walls. There was no trace of an owl or a man. Villalobos's manner was that of a whip coiled to crack. He led his men back into the *hacienda*.

With patient thoroughness, he brought his attention to every square foot of the ranch house and outbuildings. He did not miss the tanning shed or the harness room. He spent a moment or two in the chapel. He glanced in the room the Sheridans had occupied. Here he hesitated a moment, while Charlie's heart stopped. Had he noticed that the air was too warm for a deserted store room? But he strode on out.

When the search was finished, Captain Villalobos made a decision. "It was a false alarm. The old ones are too quick to fire. Nevertheless, it is too late to ride farther tonight, *Don* Carlos. With your permission, we will pass the night in the courtyard."

Charlie had hay spread on the ground for the men, and then turned in. But he lay sleeplessly, thinking of an old man dying in the freezing night air of the belfry, with a girl and a mute corroded bell for comfort. Then with tingling warmth he recalled the last moment with Tonía. *Being in love is nice,* she had said. Did she know it could be inconvenient, as well? In his mind still lay, like a half-completed chart, a plan. The things he and Cort were going to do when they left here, the places they would see. Roulette in Buenos Aires and Río; a girl for each arm in Tehuantepec. But even Charlie Drake knew that you could enjoy none of these good things if you kept looking back over your shoulder.

In the morning, with the night's frost still on the red, tiled roofs, the *rurales* rode out. Charlie dressed and hurried to the chapel. Juan Bravo had already brought the Sheridans down. Amy was shivering, pinched with cold. Her father was delirious. He rambled through mad conversations punctuated with shouts. Amy regarded him wearily.

"I had to keep him gagged all night. He was yelling like a fool." Then the sage-green eyes flicked to Charlie. "What did they say about us?"

Charlie lit a cigarette. "It was a little different from the way you told it. Villalobos has it that you murdered a party of Mexicans."

Cort was putting mesquite roots on the growing fire; he did not look up.

"Villalobos," Amy snapped, "is a damned liar. Well . . . maybe I didn't tell the whole story. I didn't talk about the mercury, did I?"

Charlie drew on the cigarette and watched her, and wondered how much you could believe of what Amy Sheridan said.

"You can't make a living hauling shoes and chiles back and forth across the line. So once in a while Pop bought a few flasks of mercury at the Puerco mines and smuggled them into the States. I guess we got the reputation of carrying bar gold around with us, though. Before we left Chihuahua this time, we found where somebody'd been poking around in the wagon. First night out, they raided us. We got away with only one wagon and our skins."

She came up to Charlie and took the cigarette from his

lips. She drew on it and gave him a defiant smile. "You see, I'm really a pretty tough character, Charlie. Sometimes I smoke. And I kill Mexicans. And I don't give a damn whether you believe me or not."

"You'd better. If I don't, I'll lock you up and send for Villalobos."

From the corner fireplace, Cort interrupted: "Don't be clowning. You know what happened. The old man must have punctured a couple of them. They went back and told how they were attacked, and down came the *rurales*."

Beyond the door, heatless sunlight burned on a patch of ground. Charlie squinted at it. "That's good enough for me," he said. "You'd better stay until things are quiet, Amy, after your father . . . after he's all right."

He walked to the corral. Juan Bravo had fifteen riders ready for the beef drive to El Sauz, where the cattle would be loaded into cars.

"Best that we both go with the cattle train," he informed Charlie. "I am acquainted with the tax collector. Sometimes the pinch can be made less painful."

A week ago, Charlie would have been afraid to suggest to Cort that he stay behind. Today he took it calmly. "How long will you be gone anyways?" he asked Charlie.

"Four or five days." Charlie grinned. "Got it bad, haven't you?"

Unsmiling, Cort seemed to look beyond him. "I don't know. Maybe next week I can't see her for trail dust."

"I hope so. We've got some riding to do after I come back. I may sell out. I've got Castillo in a corner now. He knows he's going to have to pay."

Cort shook his head. "Don't ever think you've got a Mex in a corner. That may be when he's just fixing to pull something out of his hat. Don't forget it."

All the ranch women and the numberless children were standing outside the wall as the herd moved out. Juan Bravo wore his pride like a silver-trimmed jacket. He had raised these cattle; they were, his manner said, just a little better than any cattle in Mexico. His men, too, were overly casual about it all. The women smiled and nodded, while the children ran along beside the cattle.

At the wall's corner, against the whitewashed roughness of the bricks, stood Tonía. Her slim legs, the waist that was like a reed, were sketched against the light wall. She waved, and over the muted shuffling of the hoofs he heard her cry: *"¡Que te vaya bien!"*

Te—the pronoun as intimate as the brush of a girl's lashes on your cheek. Charlie smiled and waved back and felt like a damned fool; at the same time he warmed with the pride women have always kindled in men by persuading them they are doing something spectacular or brave.

She waved again, and, when he turned, it was to be confronted by *Don* Juan's thoughtful, frowning gaze. *Don* Juan shifted his glance to the herd. Sometime later, he said: "If you have daughters, *señor*, have ugly ones. That one is an anxiety. Last summer it was Felipe. Last spring, for two months, she was in love with Ysidoro, the tanner. And now again she acts like one in a fever, singing and laughing when she is not dreaming at the window. In a day's time, she can fall in love or decide she hates the man."

There began in Charlie an oblique jealousy for a series of lovers he had never met. . . . "I guess," he said, "they're all thataway."

"No. Not this way. Tonía is the worst who ever lived." *Don* Juan shook his head and spurred ahead to whoop a steer back in line.

Charlie felt less exhilarated as they rode on.

VII

A miracle had occurred at El Sauz. On the rusty siding between the mountains and the dunes stood a dozen cattle cars. Charlie had waited for cars as long as two weeks. Two days' delay, this time, would have finished him. In a windy red dusk, they loaded the cattle.

The stationkeeper brought a yellow flimsy to Charlie at the camp beside the tracks. "A train will pick your cars up at midnight, *señor*."

When the train arrived, *Don* Juan picked two men to ride the cattle cars, watching for downed animals. He and Charlie shared the caboose with a couple of taciturn trainmen.

They rattled northward along the base of the mountains. Every now and then someone would throw a chunk of coal in the stove. Against the windows flushed the first gray touch of dawn. Worn with the trail, Charlie nodded, moving through a purgatory of half-finished thoughts that he picked up, examined, and lost before reaching any conclusion.

He thought he had not slept, but suddenly a crash of couplings jarred him awake. The lantern bobbled in the half light. Under them, the wheels ground to a halt.

Charlie looked at the brakeman. "Is there a stop here?"

The brakeman, fat, unshaven, and grease-stained, lumbered to the ladder. "Not here. We are in the *médanos.*"

He poked his head out of the cupola and immediately pulled it back in. Up the tracks they could hear a man shouting, and then the rattle of a door. The brakeman descended. He sat down and held his hands to the fire.

"What is it?" Charlie demanded.

"A hold-up, *señor*. It is no business of mine. They will not disturb us if we leave them alone."

Don Juan secured his carbine from a corner and on the way to the ladder stopped before the trainman. "No business of yours! Make this your business, he-goat!" With the butt of his gun, he shoved the man over backward in his chair.

Charlie seized his gun and strode to the ladder behind him. The brakeman sat up He appeared more disturbed than angry. "You will be murdered," he declared. "And for what? For twelve cars of cattle."

Bravo stepped onto the catwalk. When Charlie reached the roof of the caboose, he found him crouched there, appraising the scene ahead of them. All around were the sand dunes, with a rickety fence of slate on the west side of the tracks to hold back the drifting sand. A pearly shore of daylight lay on the horizon, but night had not fully yielded the desert.

Eastward, about 100 yards, Charlie picked out the forms of eight or ten horses tended by a horse holder. An *ocotillo*, half buried in sand, failed to hide this group. Charlie nudged Juan Bravo. Bravo acknowledged it by a lift of the chin. He pointed ahead along the flat crescent of cars halfway through a curve.

"*¡Mire!*"

The engineer and fireman stood beside the pompous little Mexican locomotive with its fuming diamond stack, in charge of a man with a carbine. Nearer, three men were standing beside a cattle car while others, inside the car, endeavored to chouse the animals out. There was no ramp, and the steers were resisting.

Another man was running down the tracks toward the caboose, a chunky figure in baggy trousers and loose coat, a shell belt sagging on his hips.

The battle formation, to Charlie, appeared full of loopholes. He spoke rapidly to Juan Bravo. "Down the ladder and under the cars. I'll scatter their horses. You scatter the men up the line."

Bravo scuttled down the irons. Charlie descended until just his head and shoulders were above the roof line. Out there in the sand, the horse holder was having difficulty. Charlie laid the barrel of his gun across the catwalk. At this instant a force lifted one of the wooden strips so that his gun was jolted out of line. There was the unresonant impact of the bullet and almost simultaneously the report of a rifle.

He twisted and saw the gunman. It was the man who had been approaching the caboose. He had gone to one knee to squeeze off the shot. In a sprawl, he went against a car and out of Charlie's view. But not out of Juan Bravo's. Charlie heard the compressed *thud* of his shot. He watched the rustler falter back into view and crash to his knees, losing his gun, and then slump heavily forward.

In Charlie's ears was the pounding of his pulse. His hands were not quite steady; he was glad to have a rest for the gun. He leveled into the brown mass of the horses and let the hammer fall. A pony reared above the others. The tender tried to yank it back into line, but it had pulled free. It took a couple of tortured lunges and went down. Another horse reared and the horse holder lost this one. He shouted at the men by the cattle car. One of them ran to help him.

Charlie fired again. With a target the size of a feed barn, he couldn't miss. A horse dropped, rolled, and began to kick. Charlie winced. He thought: *It can't hurt worse than chewing a Spanish bit every day.*

Now the horse herd was all over the landscape. They were running, buck-jumping, kicking at saddle girths. The outlaw running from the tracks grabbed the reins of one and was yanked off his feet and dragged.

Charlie scrambled down the ladder. Juan Bravo was already two cars ahead. When Charlie reached him, he was spraddled behind a truck, his gun thrust from between the wheels. Charlie took a spot near him. Above them, cattle were moving restlessly in the car.

Bravo's old smooth-bore crashed. One of the men at the gate of the cattle car went back, his arms doubled over his belly. He sagged to the sand, while his partner snapped his carbine to his shoulder and fired at the flash of Bravo's weapon. The bullet ricocheted off an iron wheel. From the interior of the car sprang two men who sprinted toward the horses. The sand, heavy and deep, dragged at their ankles. Charlie pulled a bead, and then hesitated. It was like popping tin cans off a mud fence. He had an idea they were out of this fight.

A prolonged wail of the locomotive's whistle caused him to stare up the tracks. The outlaw who had held the engineer and fireman was dodging through the brush. Down the line of cars reverberated a series of crashes, as the couplings jolted. Black smoke went up from the stack; the drivers skidded and took hold.

Charlie crawled out. Bravo followed a second later. They let the cars rattle past until the caboose approached. Charlie caught the grab irons and went up. As he reached the top, he heard the popping of rifle fire from far off. A few bullets tore the panels of the old Mexican Central cars, and then the wheels were hammering exultantly and the powdery dust of their passing drifted in behind.

They entered the warm caboose. The brakeman had pulled from his shirt a medallion on a silver chain that he held in his fingers. *Don* Juan paused before him, an aged, bandy-legged rooster of a man. "No business of yours," he said scornfully. "No, it was business for men." He spat at his feet, and sat on a bench near the fire, scowling at the chinks in the stove.

Charlie began replacing spent shells. Juan Bravo shook his head. "It was not like Castillo. He was not formerly so crude. Of course, he did not want the cattle. He merely wanted to frighten you. But it is shameful."

No, Charlie thought, *it was not like Castillo. It was like somebody else, who was more direct.*

At Juárez, the dusty pueblo across the shallow Río Grande from El Paso, Charlie sold the longhorns. He received enough money to make his peace with the tax collectors and drive his Aberdeen-Angus cattle across the river. *Don* Juan and the other men, having no immigration papers, remained at the stockyards until Charlie returned from the bank that afternoon, just before train time.

Bravo was puzzled by the new bag of cheap leather that Charlie carried. "The take." Charlie grinned. "Nine thousand dollars gold, American. How'll you have yours?"

The engine whistled and they waded through the horde of peddlers selling reeking leather goods and poisonous-appearing food. Bravo frowned. "This is Mexico, *patrón.* A draft would have been better. From Chihuahua, our men would have brought silver *pesos,* which are heavy. One man cannot carry enough to make robbery profitable."

Charlie shrugged. They took seats in the chilly, littered coach. "What makes this heavy," he said, "are these." He indicated their guns.

"*¡Eso!*" *Don* Juan agreed. But he was a man in whom worry flourished, and he carried his misgivings in his eyes.

It was midnight when they reached Río Chula. Charlie slept with the bag beside his bed. He had not seen Tonía in four days, and he found himself anxious for her. Phrases of *Don* Juan's hovered around him like mosquitoes, keeping him awake.

Last summer it was Felipe, and before that it was Ysidoro, the tanner. She is the worst who ever lived! A father's duplicity to keep an only daughter? Or a warning dropped to keep a man from making a fool of himself? The warning was a little late, if it were that.

Charlie did not show up for breakfast until ten o'clock. The dining room doors were open onto the patio, so that the high-ceilinged room glowed with the light of the sun blazing on whitewashed walls. The stone walks had been scrubbed and shone wetly among the dead winter plants. As Charlie sat there drinking the odd stuff Mexicans called coffee, Cort and Amy came in through the patio.

With the light behind her, Amy's hair shimmered with fine golden lights. She was wearing a short skirt and drawstring blouse that Charlie suspected were Tonía's, but the way she wore them made them hers. She had the slender legs for a short skirt, the tanned arms for a sleeveless blouse. He found a change in her. The worry had gone out of her face. Her eyes had a brightness and her whole manner an intensity that made her noticed.

Seeing Charlie, they looked startled, and then Cort reddened and some inkling of what had happened came to Charlie. He decided to let them bring it up. They sat across the table from him.

"How's your father?" he asked Amy.

Amy paused in the act of mixing hot milk and coffee elixir. Charlie saw her bite her lip. Cort glanced up.

"The night you left," he said. "He's in the graveyard up on the hill."

"But he won't stay there," Amy said softly. "Someday I'll

have him moved back to Texas."

There was a pause, while a girl entered on bare feet to bring *pan dulce*. Cort's mood changed. He caught Charlie's glance. "You can congratulate me any time you want."

Somehow Charlie felt sunk. He couldn't believe that it would wear, for either of them. But he mustered the heartiest air that was in him, reaching over to shake Cort's hand. "I thought so! When did it happen?"

Amy reached for Cort's hand. She gave Charlie an almost defiant look. "Yesterday. We knew it was going to happen, so it might as well be quick! We thought we'd stay until things cool off a little."

"As long as you like," Charlie told them. "I'll be going into Chihuahua tomorrow to see Harkrider. I've got just twenty-four hours to square those notes of Castillo's. Otherwise, I'm on my way home, broker than I was."

He had brought the money sack with him. Cort frowned at it as Charlie rose and started out. "What's that?"

"Double eagles. And I'm living with them till I leave."

It was an odd thing, Charlie thought, that the caressing look Amy gave the bag as he walked out was almost the look she had given Cort when she took his hand.

VIII

Charlie left the bag in the office. He went out and smoked a cigarette on the wall of the horse corral. He had baited a trap, and now he was in a kind of terror of hearing the snap of its ruthless jaws. Too many small, furtive tracks had come to his attention recently. Hacienda Río Chula was like a coin purse left on a saloon table. A lot of hands itched for it, leaving it alone only because the owner might be observing. With the lights out, the same hands might become bolder.

Charlie pondered it until his mind seemed to go out of focus. As he sat there, it was suddenly as if he were in a strange place. He looked around at the tall, whitewashed walls, with their guard towers, at the rough mountains to the west. The smells were of charcoal fires and the hot animal stench of the tannery; the sounds were quick rattles of Spanish and the rolling of corn grinders outside the kitchen. Foreign sounds and smells, things he had nothing to do with.

What was there to hold him if he wanted to leave? An obligation to a dead man was no obligation at all. He thought of the rude camaraderie of roundups in the Red River country; his heart expanded until it seemed to choke him.

He dropped from the wall. *Texas, here I come! Dealer, let's have three aces! And set 'em up for the house, bartender.* Cort was tied up, but he could still break away. Charlie Drake was going home.

Juan Bravo was at lunch. He left his place at the table, making sweeping motions with his arms to welcome him. *"¡Pase! ¡Pase usted!"* Then he stood rifle-straight and smiling, awaiting his orders. Tonía appeared in the kitchen door.

163

Charlie wished these people wouldn't be so damned polite. They made you feel obligated. He accepted coffee. He was aware of Tonía's presence in the room, and once he caught her eyes and the look he received was gentle and yet reproving. He could have asked her to sit down, but *Don* Juan, he knew, would be horrified. In Mexico, women knew their place.

Now that it was time to say it, he could not. What about Tonía? What about these people who had been spoiled by good treatment? Castillo would know how to take care of them. He fashioned a cigarette, got the warm smoke in his lungs, and said: "I'm going to Chihuahua tomorrow, *Don* Juan. I'm going to sell the ranch."

Something in the bottom of the Mexican's coffee cup kept his eyes. "As you wish," he said.

"I guess an American is better off in America. Look how it's gone! I lose four of my best bulls, tell lies to the *rurales,* and Lord knows how that'll come out! They hold up my cattle cars. The Indian sign's on me, that's all."

"Perhaps Mexico is not to blame for all those things."

Charlie gave him a close look and wondered how much he, too, had noticed. "Whoever's to blame, these things didn't use to happen to me."

Bravo sighed. He smiled wistfully. *"Éstes bien. Ésta bien. "* He sipped his coffee.

Charlie's glance narrowed on him. He was beginning to understand that this little wrinkled cowpuncher's craft was a deep and subtle thing.

In a moment, Juan Bravo arose. "At the time *Don* Miguel died," he said, "he left in my care a box for you. It was to be yours whenever you decided to leave." He went into the bedroom.

Tonía came quickly to Charlie's side. "So you are not

afraid of José Castillo, but you are afraid of a woman!"

"What woman? Amy?"

Tonía tossed her dark braided hair. "Of me! You thought what happened the night of the *fiesta* was like a . . . a troth. And you didn't know how to break it except by leaving! Did you think it meant so much to me?" She said that with tears standing in her eyes and her underlip trembling.

She had Charlie off balance with the aggressiveness of her attack. "I knew how much it meant to you," he said. "Your father told me about Felipe and Ysidoro and the rest."

"Felipe?" Tonía's head turned quizzically. "He is my cousin! And Ysidoro is seventy years old." She put a cool forefinger under his chin and tipped his face up to hers. There was the beginning of understanding in her eyes, something indignant mellowed with something tremulous. "What did my father say about Felipe and Ysidoro?"

Charlie stood up. "Weren't you going to marry Felipe last summer?"

A woman had never laughed like this before, he thought. Clear water laughed this way when it tumbled over marbled rocks, with a thousand glints. "I have never been about to marry anyone," she said. "The morning after the *fiesta,* my father said . . . 'Little birds who fly too high fall far.' He was hoping to discourage me. Did I fly too high, *Don* Charlie?"

Charlie had her hands in his. "You could fly a lot higher than Charlie Drake," he told her. "Would you like Texas, Tonía?"

She could keep the frown from her face, but not out of her voice. "I could try to like it."

At that moment, Juan Bravo returned with a wooden box in his hands. He saw at once what was occurring. With his oblique diplomacy, he preferred not to notice. He placed the box on the table. "We will want hot milk for the coffee," he told Tonía.

The box was stout, with the imprint of an ammunition firm on the lid. Bravo pried the lid up with a knife. He pushed it over to Charlie.

Inside, there was an envelope sealed with red wax. There were dried red chiles, pottery cups containing corn, oats, and *frijole* beans. And there was a dull silver coin. Charlie saw that the envelope was inscribed with his name. He opened it.

My excellent American friend. What I now make to you is a request for the burial of my land, which you are about to kill.

In this box you will find the first corn harvested on Hacienda Río Chula, the first chiles, the first oats and *frijoles*. The *peso* was the first money received from the sale of a purebred steer from the State of Chihuahua. These mementoes you will burn.

I hope that Juan Bravo and his people did their best to please you. I am sorry that the ranch did not. You understand that in selling Río Chula, the land will be permitted to die as the rest of Chihuahua is dying.

For this reason, my last wish is that you spend one hundred *pesos* for a wreath that will be hung above the main gate. *¡Adiós!*

Miguel Castillo N.

Charlie closed the letter thoughtfully, creased the parchment fold with his thumbnail several times, slipped it into his pocket. Juan Bravo had gone to stand by the window, watching an ox-cart lumber in with a load of hay. With his finger, Charlie stirred the fat yellow corn in the brown cup. He sniffed the chiles. His thumb rubbed the tarnished *peso*. *Damn a man who wills you a set of hobbles!*

He looked again at the coin. His eyes lightened. *Heads I*

stay . . . tails I go. The coin flashed, came down in his palm; he slapped it onto the back of his other hand. Tails. Charlie hesitated. *Two out of three,* he thought. The second was heads. On the third toss, tails again showed. Charlie thought a moment, grunted, and threw the coin back in the box. Hell! What could you tell by a coin? You had to go by your conscience, even if you had only discovered it recently.

He took the box under his arm. "In the morning," he said, "I'll go to Chihuahua. The debts ought to be paid off. I won't sell just yet."

He placed the box in the office, beside the money bag on his desk.

He wore the day out in drinking wine in the patio, smoking, and feeling like a cattle baron. By dark, he was sure he wouldn't like playing the cattle baron often. He could feel the wine, and his mouth, from the tobacco, tasted like a saddle horn. Cort and Amy showed up for dinner. Cort was flushed. He had been drinking, too, and not wine. The smell of brandy was on him, although Amy was quiet and sober.

They ate and departed. Charlie got the impression that marriage was beginning to work up saddle sores on Cort Carraday's hide.

He went to his room and remained there until all the lights were out. Then he walked on unspurred boots to the office. He took a rawhide chair in a corner, where the moonlight did not reach.

Around midnight, shadows drifted silently through the patio. He heard a side door *creak.* Presently footfalls approached the office. Someone stumbled and a soft curse reached Charlie's ears. The knob turned.

A whisper scraped dryly through the silence. From the door, a tall shadow and a short one advanced to the desk.

167

Charlie heard the *chink* of metal as the leather bag was lifted.

He struck a match.

There was Cort Carraday's startled grunt and a whirl of Amy's skirts as she turned, but Charlie did not look at them until he had the lamp burning on the table beside him. Cort's long body faltered back against the desk. He gave Charlie a loose grin and with mock delicacy replaced the bag on the desk.

"We were just making sure those double eagles were being taken care of right," he said.

Amy's small white teeth flashed. "Shut up!" She turned on Charlie a vixenish stare. "Sitting back in a corner like a spider waiting to catch a fly! So you thought we were after your dirty cattle money!"

"Well, it isn't exactly money," said Charlie. "It's just iron washers. I sent the money to Chihuahua by draft."

Cort was drunk, foolishly, thickly drunk. He put an arm around Amy's shoulders. "Sweetheart, you get the best ideas."

She thrust him away so that he fell into a chair. A decanter of wine stood on a cabinet near him. He reached it, pulled the stopper, and drank from the bottle.

Charlie rolled a cigarette. "I'm glad of one thing, Cort. You had to be drunk before she could talk you into it."

"Talk him into it!" Amy spat. "He has some ideas of his own."

Charlie shook his head. "It's my fault as much as anybody's. I've bungled this whole thing. We've been partners in everything else, but I've hung onto this cow spread like it was my last dollar. I'm going into town tomorrow, Cort. I'm going to have Harkrider cut you in for your half, legal."

"The hell with that," Cort said. He drank again from the decanter; a spill of red wine trickled down his chin and onto his shirt.

Amy lifted her chin defiantly. "We don't want any part of your damn' ranch! The sooner we get out of here, the better. That's the only reason we . . . came in tonight. You've got to have money to buy your way out of this country."

"You'll have enough. But you can't take the train. Not with what they're waiting to hang on you at the border. There's got to be another way. Got any ideas, Cort?"

Cort was nodding over the bottle. Amy stepped to his side and knocked it to the floor. Wine and shards of pottery went all over the tiles.

Charlie sighed, as much for the death of things past as for what had occurred.

"Better get him to bed. I'll take him to town with me tomorrow. The lawyer ought to have some contacts."

IX

During that short but dusty train ride into Chihuahua, Cort was silent. They had left their horses with the stationkeeper at El Sauz. Cort was a little uncertain as to the details of last night, but enough lingered with him to sour his mood. He masked his shame with a waspish temper.

In Joel Harkrider's law office, it was as cold as ever. A thin-cheeked girl labored over a copy book in the outer office, a shawl over her shoulders. When they entered, the first thing Charlie was aware of was José Castillo's brown bulk in a chair beside the desk. Vasquez, his *segundo*, stood at the window. He turned to regard them without expression, heavy-boned and somnolent, with insolent Latin eyes. Castillo, the gentlemen schemer, offered his hand and had it refused. He exhibited no resentment.

"An unfortunate thing, that of the money," he said. "My brother was always one to borrow of the wrong people."

"Were you always one to buy the notes up behind his back?"

Harkrider, the withered little Texan behind the big desk, cleared his throat. "To get down to business, Mister Drake...."

Charlie said: "I deposited the money to his account in the bank this morning."

Harkrider glanced at Castillo, and then stared gloomily at his desk. He began marking the blotter with a rusty pen. "That brings us to the next matter," he said.

"Uhn-huh," Charlie said.

"This," sighed Harkrider, "is one of those matters which is generally costly to the defendant whether he wins it or not.

170

And I may as well advise you that *Señor* Castillo has a good chance of winning his case."

"He's trying to break the will," Charlie remarked. "Is that what you're working up to?"

Harkrider made a deep mark on the blotter. "That," he said, "is right. While I am sure the will is perfectly proper, there is the point that the lawful heirs have certain rights. . . . And it may strain a court's credulity to believe that Miguel Castillo would have left his ranch to a man he had met only once."

"Castillo," Charlie interrupted, with a glance at the *hacendado*, "you're a very stout man."

Don José smiled, trying to think ahead of the American. "*Sí*, I am *muy gordo*. I enjoy my food."

"In fact, I don't know how you ever got up the stairs to this office. But I know how you're going down them!"

He seized the back of Castillo's chair and hauled forward on it, so that the rancher was levered onto his feet. Then he slapped a palm against the seat of his pants and caught the back of his collar with the other hand. Cort had the door open by the time they struggled up to it. Vasquez, the foreman, lunged in to grapple Charlie. Cort laughed his old, exultant laugh and slammed his jaw with a larruping right.

Charlie marched the vast, shouting form to the top of the stairs. A shove, and *Don* José was taking gigantic leaps in a fight to recover his balance. Halfway down, he missed a step. He went to his knees like a bull. He rolled the rest of the way. He lay there a moment and then, coming onto all fours, shook his head.

Charlie went back.

Cort was dragging Vasquez from the office by one leg. He hauled him to the top of the stairs and rolled him down. They went back in and Charlie closed the door.

"I wonder if that was legal?" he asked the lawyer.

Harkrider had not moved from his chair. He looked pained. "Legal or not, it was a mistake. He's a Mexican citizen. You're. . . ."

". . . a *gringo,* and sick of knives tickling my back. Mister," Charlie said, "we want some advice, and we want it quick. My pardner's in a scrape. He's got himself married to a girl the *rurales* are looking for. A nice girl, but. . . ."

"Amy Sheridan? Bet they're looking for her!" Harkrider gave Cort a close look. "You don't look like a man to get tied up with a bunch like. . . ." He caught himself. "Well, it's just hearsay. But the story is, Amy and Dick Sheridan are only two of a gang of about twenty bad 'uns that have been making a good thing out of the freight trails."

Cort's face darkened. "You've been listening to too many *rurales.* Why didn't the rest of the gang jump us when we found them?"

Harkrider made a careless gesture. "They had to split up for a while. Like as not, wherever you found the old man was the rendezvous."

Charlie hurried in. "It doesn't matter what they say. Amy is Cort's wife. They've got to get out, and the train's not going to be any help. I was thinking maybe they could make it across the hills to Sonora."

Harkrider rolled a pencil between his palms. Then he proceeded to the door and glanced into the reception room. His secretary had vanished. He closed the door carefully and returned to his seat. As he spoke, he began to write.

"There's a man named Armendariz, in Guerrero. I've done him some favors. If you can get that far, he'll see that you get horses and grub for the trip to Cananea. Have you got any money?"

"Enough," Charlie said.

Harkrider handed Cort the note. "Sew that into the lining

of your boot. And, for the Lord's sake, don't let the *rurales* get hold of it!"

They had a drink at the *cantina*. There was now nothing to hold them in town, but there was no train until morning. They had taken a room again at the Colonial. Yet neither of them seemed anxious to go back to it. A cold wind flapped through the streets, blowing trash before it. They emerged into a ruddy dusk and began to walk.

Suddenly Cort gripped Charlie's arm.

Charlie followed his gaze. At the corner, a pair of policemen conferred while staring up a side street. They turned to look the other way, and in the next moment they were gazing at the Americans.

"Those guys," Cort said, "look too busy to be killing time. I'm getting the hell out of here."

Charlie pulled Durham and papers from his shirt pocket. He said: "You're jumpy. If they're looking for us, it's about Castillo. We'll pay the fines and walk out of the station."

Cort's thumb nervously rubbed at the cartridges in his belt. "It's not about Castillo. It's about Amy. That damned priest! He must have reported the marriage. Charlie, I'm getting out."

He turned and started away.

Charlie caught up with him. "Not this way. You're *asking* them to follow us."

Cort's face was all hard planes and angles. "I can't take a chance. If they jug me, Amy will give herself up. That's the kind she is."

"Is she?" Charlie said.

Behind them, the policemen were running. Charlie seized Cort's arm and hauled him through an open door. They entered a saddle shop, full of shadows and the stench of poorly cured leather, cluttered with sawhorses supporting saddles, and containing just two men. A simple-looking *vaquero* was seated astride a roping saddle, testing it. The proprietor, bespectacled and stooped, stood beside him.

Charlie flung three saddles into the doorway, piled a sawhorse on top of them, and walked straight through to the rear of the shop.

The saddle maker found his voice. "*¡Santisima!* Are you insane?"

Charlie opened the rear door and pushed Cort through. "Absolutely!" he said. He slammed the door and they began to run. It was three blocks to the hotel.

Charlie snapped at the clerk: "*¡Doscincuenta!*" He snatched the key and they strode up the stairway to the second floor. The Colonial was a spacious, drafty old building of two stories, built around a disheveled plaza where a fountain played drearily and withered vines climbed to the gallery of the second floor. As he unlocked the door, they could hear excited voices in the lobby.

Charlie locked the door and slid the enormous carved chest in front of it. In the darkening room, objects were just visible. He confronted Cort. "Now, what?"

Through the tall window, Cort stared down upon a dusty side street veiled in shadows. It was an avenue of small grocery stores, shops, and leafless trees. Before the inevitable corner *pulque* shop stood a horse under a wooden roping saddle. Cort opened the window.

"Somebody down there is about to donate me a horse. Can't talk you into coming with me, can I?"

"I wish you could. But it wouldn't be any good, this time. And it won't be any good for you. I'm telling you the odds are ten to one that this is over the ruckus with Castillo."

"I can't gamble it."

They were running up the gallery now. A fist struck the door three times. *"¡Abran!"*

Cort walked to the window. For a last moment he faced Charlie. "I've learned something, son. Never slow down. If you do, they'll hang a mortgage on you. Keep moving, and you're your own man."

"They've already hung one on me."

"Then pay it off. Sell that outfit for ten *pesos* or ten thousand . . . but sell it. Charlie, this country is poison. It's poisoned me, and it's going to poison you. I've married into a gang of night riders, and you're being pulled into a family of *paisanos*. And I don't know but what I've got the best of it, at that." He turned and let his long legs through the window.

"What about Amy?" Charlie asked.

"Tell her . . . tell her I'll meet her at the spot where we found her and her old man. So long, Charlie. Name your first kid after me."

In the street, there was the heavy *thump* of his falling. A moment after, Charlie heard him running.

X

They kept Charlie at the police station most of the night. At four o'clock, the last of the searchers after Cort Carraday reported back. The night and the desert had devoured him. Shortly after, they let Charlie send for Harkrider.

The Texan passed a half hour in a back room with the *jefe*. Both were looking pleased when they emerged. Harkrider brought Charlie his hat and gun and merely said: "This will go on your account."

Outside, he told him: "It's none of my business, Drake, but if you want to hold onto your cow ranch, you'd better be more careful of your friends. You ain't Carraday's type. He'll bring you nothing but grief."

"I'll argue about that," Charlie said. "He won't bring me any more grief, because he's gone. And we're pretty much peas out of a pod, come down to it."

The lawyer shook his head. "You've no more polish than a mesquite root, but you're steady and tough. In a month you've sobered up, got a few lines in your face, and taken hold like a man." He shrugged. "None of my business anyway. But . . . be careful about Amy. Good luck."

The morning train put Charlie on the ground at El Sauz at noon. From there it was a ride of several hours to the *hacienda*. In late afternoon, he turned his horse into the corral. Amy had been waiting for him. She hurried from the back of the chapel as he walked across the courtyard.

She looked white and sick. "Where's Cort?"

Charlie took her arm. "Take it easy, kid. He had to run for it."

176

They entered through the patio, Charlie telling her. He closed the door of the office and from his wallet extracted a thick fold of fifty-*peso* notes. "Take this," he said, "and start packing. You'll be traveling light. Cort will meet you at the spot where he found you. I brought his horse back from the station."

Amy tucked the money inside her dress. She no longer looked frightened. In her face was a keen attention. "I'll need a horse for Cort," she said. "He'll have ridden the heart out of that plug he got away on."

"I'll bring them out right after sundown. Don't leave until it's completely dark. Can you manage it?"

Amy smiled, with masculine frankness. "Charlie, I was managing it when you were wrangling horses. Living with Pop was pretty brisk sometimes."

At sundown, Charlie saddled the horses and left them near the gate. He tolled *Don* Juan over to the office on the pretext of making arrangements for distribution of wages the next day. He kept him there until eight-thirty.

The big, easy living room, with its natural wood furniture and woolen and hide rugs, seemed to echo its emptiness. Charlie went to his bedroom and tried, lying on the bed, to read a Mexican newspaper three months old. But in his breast a very large ache would not be eased. The past was being buried tonight. It was the unjoyous end of joy.

Don Juan awoke him by tapping on the door. His mission in life seemed to be to upset Charlie's sleep. Charlie lit a candle and prowled to the door. Juan Bravo, small and stiff-necked, acted strangely. It was 3:00 a.m., but he was still fully dressed. His face looked frozen. He kept his gaze somewhere over Charlie's head.

"*Don* Carlos," he said, "I have tried to close my eyes. But this is too much."

"I don't doubt it. What's too much?"

Bravo said pompously: "If you will inform my daughter that her father has been aware for three hours that she was not in her bed, I shall be grateful. This comes of trying to raise a motherless daughter by oneself. It is a man's own business what he does, but in Antonía I am hurt."

"How much brandy," Charlie asked, "do you have to drink to tie on one like this?"

Juan Bravo's eyes at last met Charlie's. A curious expression came to them. "Are you saying that . . . Tonía is not with you?"

Charlie jumped. "With *me?* Why should she be? *Don* Juan!"

Bravo looked frightened. "If I have been wrong, *patrón,* cut my heart out! But I knew the girl loved you, and that night I saw you kiss her, outside the wall . . . I thought . . . when I could not find her in her bed nor anywhere else. . . . *Don* Carlos," he whispered, "where can she be?"

It hit Charlie Drake so that he had to sit down. He massaged the back of his neck with stiff fingers. The sluggish treadmill of his mind would not move.

Juan Bravo toured up and down. "She has never done it before! She is a good girl, never one to worry me. I lied about Felipe and Ysidoro. She has loved no one before. But I feared for her to love one so far above her."

"Above her." Charlie walked to the dresser for his tobacco. "The sooner you understand I'm a forty-a-month cowpoke, the sooner you'll understand me. Maybe she went for a ride."

"She seldom rides." *Don* Juan snapped his fingers. "There were two horses, saddled, near the gate when I came to your office. Perhaps she. . . ."

It sank coldly down through Charlie from the back of his

neck to his heels. "I'll need a horse for Cort," Amy had said. For Cort? For Tonía! For her hostage! Amy Sheridan had not got away with his gold, but she had taken something she knew to be more precious. . . .

In the empty room Amy had occupied they found a letter for Charlie.

Don't worry about your little Mex, partner. You can have her, or the ranch, but you can't have both. You've got the deed to this place in your office. I've seen it. Endorse it over to José Castillo and bring along the payroll money. He's paying for the deed. You're paying for the girl. Is she worth it? Come to the cañon where you and Cort found us. Come alone. You'll be guided from there.

After he had translated it for Juan Bravo, the foreman regarded him with an expression of confused emotions. Charlie stood frowning at the paper. At last, *Don* Juan asked bluntly: "*¿Lo vale ella?*"

Charlie passed a hand over his eyes. "It's not a question of whether she's worth it. It's a question of whether or not they'll stick to the bargain. Because Amy hates her."

The silver was too heavy for Charlie's horse to pack any distance. Charlie led an extra horse loaded with Tonía's saddle and the bulging rawhide saddlebags. Sunup caught him searching for the entrance to the cañon.

He had drawn *Don* Juan a map. Bravo knew the spot and sketched in some ridges and side cañons surrounding it. He put his finger on one point. "They would be here. There is a cave."

The shortest way was, of course, straight down the valley

and due west. That was out of the question because anyone following Charlie would be observed. Other than this, there were precipitous trails that would take many hours to follow. And he might have picked the wrong spot. He was still undecided about what strategy to follow when Charlie left.

Amy had said nothing about coming unarmed, and Charlie Drake was packing all the hardware he could carry. His Frontier Colt was at his hip. An old double-barreled pistol of Miguel Castillo's was strapped beneath his armpit. A nasty-looking knife was tucked into his boot. Of course, they would take the Colt; they might not find the others.

Crossing the first rank of hills, Charlie rode up the main cañon into which the other emptied. As yet, the sun had not thawed the frost patches under the trees. When he saw the familiar sandy wash, something awoke in him. His heart commenced to slug.

All these hours he had tried to think of it only as a dangerous job he had to perform, as something physical, not emotional. Now he could tie his attention neither to Amy, nor Cort, or Castillo. It was all Tonía, a refusal to believe that they would touch her, a horror that they might. Memories drifted before him like smoke: Tonía teasing and Tonía angry; Tonía's tongue making his name sound almost romantic; the way she had looked that last morning when he told her he was going away.

He came to the spot where Amy had fired at him and Cort; an instinct caused him to rein in. From the ledge, a man called in bad Spanish: "Alone, *gringo?*"

"Unless you count my horses."

The outlaw stood up, a small and solid-looking man in white linen pants and shirt, his red serape wound about his upper body. He carried an old-style rifle as long as he was. "*Momentito,*" he said.

He came into sight presently on a scarred jughead of a horse. He gestured that Charlie was to follow him. They crossed the cañon floor and began to ascend a shelving ridge. There was no question of his being in danger of a shot from the back. He had a hostage.

Charlie sniffed. By the smells, he judged they were approaching the camp. Five minutes later the Yaqui shouted something and they passed a kink in the cañon to enter the camp.

At first Charlie saw only the scattered piñon trees, the boulders, and an icy trickle of water winding down the middle of the slot. Then, among the trees, he discovered the camp. It was as filthy as only a bunch of Mexican renegades could make one. Entrails of slaughtered beeves lay stinking on the ground fifty feet from the cook fires. The horses were tethered too close to the beef hung on a rawhide line. Flies abounded.

Men were coming into view, but Charlie's eyes were entirely for Tonía. He counted a half dozen Mexicans and Yaquis; he saw Amy standing beside the bare flicker of a tiny campfire, with Cort seated near her. He found the lanky form of Castillo's man, Vasquez, standing with crossed arms, sullenly, near a rope horse corral. And no sign of Tonía.

Amy approached. Cort continued looking down at the smokeless fire with brooding eyes. Amy was wearing her own clothes again, Levi's and shirt and a brush-popper jacket. They suited her, making a frame for the vixen grace of her.

"You're a trusting one, Charlie." She smiled. "We've got you, the deed, and the money, and you haven't even seen the girl."

"Have you?" Charlie countered. Someone took his saddle gun and plucked the .45 from its holster, but it did not alter his cocksure grin.

Amy's glance narrowed. "We'd better have. But relax, cowboy. She's in the cave, yonder, being a good girl. Coffee?"

"Don't mind," Charlie said.

Amy sat Charlie across the fire from her and Cort Carraday. Vasquez drifted over. A cup sat beside Cort. By the color of its contents, Charlie deduced that he was drinking either tea or whiskey, and the cup was not steaming. "I see you made it out of town," he said. Cort grunted.

Vasquez tossed his cigarette into the fire. "This place," he said, "does not smell well, and I have business elsewhere. If he has the paper, I will give you the money and say *adiós*."

Amy's sage-green eyes stirred. "Your move, Charlie."

Charlie patted his shirt. The hard feel of his hide-out gun was pleasant. "Right next to my heart. Let's all bring our hole cards out first, though. The way I figure this, you must have cut Vasquez in on it when Cort and I went to Chihuahua. When I had the money to retire the notes, Castillo was ready for the next move. You're acting as a real-estate agent in this deal, in other words, except that we're both paying you commission."

Amy stirred her coffee. "You're both winning, aren't you? He gets a ranch, you get a girl. No accounting for the taste of either of you, but. . . ."

Charlie sipped the strong coffee. "He gets my ranch, and I get my own girl back. But . . . I'll dicker with you. You show me the girl, I show Vasquez the deed, and Vasquez shows you the money."

Amy had a macabre sense of humor. "You aren't going to pay for a dead horse, are you? Cort," she said, "bring her down."

Cort did not move. "Bring her down yourself. I'm out of this since you dragged her into it."

Amy's lips tightened. She snapped at one of the Mexicans. "Bring the girl."

Vasquez pulled a fat chamois sack from his jacket. He struck his palm with it; coins clinked softly. "I am not concerned with whether or not this *yanqui* gets his woman. Is there any reason I must spend my life in this place of offscourings?"

"Sure," said Charlie. "I haven't got my woman, yet. So Amy hasn't got her deed."

Cort looked at him with a frown. That was the danger—that Cort would get wise. Cort knew it was not in him to stall over a business deal. And he was stalling desperately. Somewhere, *Don* Juan and a gang of cowpunchers were groping over the hills, hunting for a certain side cañon.

The outlaw brought Tonía to the fire. She was tousled; there was dirt on her face, and she rubbed at the marks of ropes on her wrists. She saw Charlie, then, and what happened to her eyes brought a lump to his throat.

"This is a funny time to propose," Charlie said seriously, "but I want to get something straight. If I buy you from these people, I'll be a poor man. With that understood, do you still want to marry me?"

Tonía glanced archly at Amy. It came to Charlie that she had achieved some kind of obscure feminine victory over Amy, which he wouldn't understand. "Carlito," she said, "you must teach me English, so that I shall not be ashamed before your people."

Cort's head came up. The strange thing was, he was looking off across the cañon beyond the horses, not at Charlie. His eyes widened, and something happened to his coloring. Something happened to Charlie's heart, too. Juan Bravo was back there, and Cort had just spotted him. It was the only thing Charlie could think of that would hit him that hard.

Cort turned casually to Amy. "Sweetheart," he said, "you're a nice kid, but you've picked up some wrong ideas somewhere. This kidnapping business . . . it seems like I won't be able to swallow it, after all. I'll tell you what. Let's take Vasquez's money away from him, let Charlie have his girl and his ranch, and get the hell back to the States!"

Amy's eyes were as cold as cave ice. "Drunk again," she said.

"Cold sober," said Cort. He stood up, and Amy stood up, and Vasquez's manner sharpened. With his eyes still on Amy, Cort snapped: "Take her, Charlie, and get out. What happens between me and Amy and this Mexican pig, here, is no worry of yours."

Charlie took one step toward Tonía, and Amy snapped up the light carbine she had been handling as carelessly as a quirt. "Stay back! Cort, you'd better give me your gun until you're sober."

Vasquez, perceiving that trouble was building fast, stepped forward. "The paper, *gringo*." Vasquez extended his hand.

Charlie unbuttoned his shirt. He reached inside and got the warm, rounded butt of the gun in his hand. Vasquez edged forward to seize the paper. When the gun roared, smoke and wadding rolled against his body. He gave a convulsive lurch and one hand clutched his shirt.

Charlie closed with him, dropped the empty Derringer, and groped for his Colt. Amy snapped the carbine to her shoulder. As a shield, Charlie realized Vasquez's body would be as effective as a blanket. He waited for the impact of the shot, while trying to support the Mexican and at the same time to find his gun.

Suddenly the cañon was filled with the tumbling echoes of gunfire. *Don* Juan's men, wherever they were, were pouring their fire fully upon the trapped outlaws. Tonía, partially hidden from Amy's view, ran at her, clutching for the gun. Amy shifted like a cat. In an instant, it was not Charlie Drake under her sights, but Tonía. That would have been all right with Amy Carraday.

What she had not counted on was Cort. Cort had drawn his gun. "Drop it!" he yelled. "Drop it, or I'll . . . !"

Amy did not drop it. She turned, the carbine jolting in her hands. Cort fell back. He had been hit, high in the left shoulder, but still he faced her, and again he said, in a voice drained of all its force: "Drop it."

Amy's hand worked the lever. A sickness was in Charlie. He had Vasquez's gun, now, and he let the man fall. Yet he did not fire at Amy. He would not need to. Cort was chivalrous, but he was not crazy.

Charlie heard the heavy blast of the .44. He did not look at Amy. He heard her gun *thump* on the ground. He heard a wondering whisper. "Cort! You've. . . . shot me. . . ."

There in the cañon, Charlie Drake buried what was left of his past. Cort Carraday lived an hour, long enough to clear his conscience.

"It was that damned Castillo, Charlie. I never thought money meant anything to me until the day in Chihuahua when I went after my hat. He put a stack of gold pieces on his desk and told me a guy like me needed something like that for security, or I'd wind up cadging drinks. He told me to sink it in a ranch some place, let somebody else operate it for me, and take the profits. He knew me better than you did, Charlie. Better than I did myself. He told me to think about it. And the hell of it was, I did. But until . . . Amy, I decided to drop it all. Then. . . ."

Charlie knew the rest. He felt no ill will to his old saddle partner, just a vast pity. Cort was a poor lonesome cowboy, and he knowed he'd done wrong.

As they left the somber shadows of the gorge, it grew lighter, until by the time they reached the plain the warm sunlight made the whole thing seem a dream. Charlie Drake was willing to leave it that way. It was a dream somebody else had had. And now he and Tonía were going to make some dreams of their own.

High Iron

I

High in the Sierra Nevadas, where the magnificent shoulders of the Donner Pass hold up the sky, there is a tie siding with the cryptic name of Barbara Bly. There is nothing pretentious about this siding—a few ranks of ties, a gravel pile, and some blackened planks torn off a snowshed. Hardly the kind of thing a girl would want to give her name to, unless she happened to be a very unusual girl. Barbara Bly was.

You could have asked John Duff about this, and the way he would have evaded the question, while his color gave him away, would have told you considerable. He would have remarked that any girl who had spent all her life in railroad camps was bound to be unusual. She could talk railroading like a hogger. She could walk through a gang of rough Irish track laborers, and not a man of them would have dared smile, unless she smiled first—which, however, she generally did.

At the time the railroad marker bearing her name was installed, she was nineteen years old, had chestnut hair, gray eyes, and a figure as trim as that of any of the little woodburners on the Central Pacific Railroad, which her father was helping to build. Her real name, as a matter of fact, was Barbara Carney. Barbara Bly was the name she gave herself when she deserted the railroad for the stage.

Yes, deserted. The daughter of an Irish railroad engineer deserting the iron! It caused something of a scandal in the trade. And what it caused in the heart of Johnny Duff was a sad thing indeed. But maybe it was his own fault. Maybe, if he had handled her differently the day the accident happened at

Bloomer Cut, she would have given a shake of the head to the stage, instead of a nod. But there was no doubt that it would have meant a compromise with the railroad, and Johnny's love of the iron was something just short of worship.

Those were the days when men all over the country were just beginning to realize there was something pretty grand about the business of railroading. Grown men wiped locomotives for ten cents an hour, and thought it worthwhile just for the chance to get into the cab now and again. Firemen decked themselves out between runs like Louisville steamboat mates. Engineers—well, it seemed as if nobody could do quite enough for them. Johnny Duff was in the construction end of the trade. On the Central Pacific books he was down as **Assistant Superintendent, Charge of Construction**— and don't ask how a young buck in his twenties landed a job like *that!* Only Johnny and a few others knew just how it had come about. The point was, he had it. And he wasn't going to let it slide even for Babbie. Maybe that sounds stubborn. Yet it isn't fair to make snap judgments. They had their reasons, both of them. In a way, her leaving the road was the only thing she could have done. This, if you are interested, is the story of Babbie Carney and Johnny Duff.

Johnny Duff swung from the mess car into the damp chill of the right of way. He stood in the darkness a moment, smelling the weather. Clouds had been gathering for days, and now, in the cold pre-dawn, the air was wet with mist. Down the tracks the morning supply train shouted her arrival; there was rain in the sound of the whistle.

He walked down to the chief engineer's car, fastening the frogs of his coat. Over the stir of workers and wagon teams, he now could hear the locomotive pulling through Sailor's Ravine: puff-and-clank, puff-and-clank-and-wheeze. Her great yellow eye bobbled into view, raked the hillside with light, and bore suddenly upon the camp at Newcastle Trestle.

In the murky wash of the headlight, gang foremen moved about on horseback, assembling sleepy crews. Wagons and teams jostled each other along the right of way. Inside the telegraph car, the key was already awake; through the window Johnny saw the operator, his head propped on one hand, taking down a message. There were lights in the other cars, too, the boarding cars where late risers were tumbling out of bunks, in the engineers' car and the offices. Over there in the grayness, 1,500 Chinese were trotting from their ramshackle tent city.

Johnny put his foot on the iron ladder of Chief Engineer Carney's rolling home and swung up. Ed Carney was finishing his coffee, and Babbie, at the stove, had her back to him. She wore a dish-towel apron, and her chestnut hair was pinned high in a pre-breakfast coiffure.

Johnny said: "Let's pick her up, Ed!"

Babbie glanced at him over her shoulder. "He hasn't finished his breakfast yet," she said. "Sit down and have some coffee." She had on her pre-breakfast voice, too—crisp as bacon.

Johnny got a cup, and Babbie poured coffee with one hand while with the other she kept the skillet tilted so that the egg bubbled in deep fat. The lamp, on a shelf over the stove, brushed her cheek with warm magic. Her face was almost thin, the lines of it well defined. Her nose was short, with a tilt, and the eyes Johnny looked down on were gray, although now he could see nothing of them but the long dark lashes.

Those eyes didn't bother with Johnny Duff much, anyway, Johnny being railroad to the core, and Babbie Carney being a rebel from the good life of dust and iron. All she could do, her old man being in the trade, was to run it down, but at that she fought a pretty good war from the shanty car.

Johnny stood by the door to drink his coffee. Once the morning supply train had shunted in, he was on springs; he could never sit down until dark. Payroll Section listed him as **Duff, John J., Assistant Superintendent, Charge of Construction.** He was field marshal, battering ram, and crying shoulder for the Central Pacific Railroad; therefore his office was wherever powder blasted, sledges sang, and locating crews dragged their chains. It was as good a way as any of growing old—only, the gray came a little faster.

"How many rail cars came up?" Ed asked him.

"Couldn't tell. If they don't start sending up some powder, you won't need rails, anyway. We'll be chipping at Bloomer Hill with pocket knives in another week. The cut hadn't moved three feet when I left yesterday."

With a fork, Ed attacked the egg Babbie placed before him. "And what are you going to do about Kearns and McKewen?" he demanded. "They haven't been cold sober in a month. Every night they take off for Hedenburg's store as soon as it's dark. They get back about time for work. But Kearns is the best rail setter you've got, and you don't find telegraphers like McKewen twice in a year."

"I'll keep them until I have to can them," Johnny said. "Sometimes I think we'd be smart to put in a sutler's store and sell beer. It might keep them out of hog ranches like Hedenburg's. If it was only the two of them, I wouldn't worry. But Hedenburg's is getting to be a habit."

"Beer won't hold those boys," Ed declared. "If there's whiskey within ten miles, they'll have it."

Babbie walked to the table with a cup of coffee. She sat down and cupped her hands about it. "To hear you two talk, you'd think trouble was new to this business. I don't remember a job yet where Pop didn't fall off a trestle, have a

strike, or lose his eyebrows fourteen times in explosions."
Babbie could tell you all about railroad life; she had lived
nineteen of her twenty years in boxcars. Suddenly she sprang
up. "Heavens, your toast!"

Ed's chair scraped. "Put it in a bread pudding for me.
We've got to unload those flats." Ed was in his fifties, big and
ruddy in the Irish way. There were two deep ruts between his
eyes. His hair was getting thin, except for a reddish brush in
the center, and his skin, soft as a baby's, never stopped
peeling.

Babbie turned back from the stove. She shook back a
strand of hair that had fallen across her forehead. "That's
three days in a row," she told her father. "You promised when
you took this job, you wouldn't go back to eating like a tie
bucker."

Ed kissed her on the cheek. "I'll make up for it tonight.
That supply train's been early every day this week."

They jumped down. Babbie, hands on hips, stood in the
doorway and watched Ed button his jacket. She said, so
coolly you might have missed the irony in those gray eyes:
"They tell me there's a place, over the hill, where the day
doesn't start when a whistle blows, and you can hang out a
wash and it isn't gray with train smoke by noon. You can even
plant potatoes, and know you'll still be there to dig them. Of
course, any railroad woman would say you had to die to find a
place like that. But one of these days I'm going to start
walking, and see if I can find it!"

The door banged. Ed laughed. "The kid's about got herself convinced she don't like railroading. Someday I'll park
her in a hotel when I go out on a job. She'll find out how
much she don't like it."

Johnny did not comment. He knew how real was this dis-
taste of Babbie's for railroading. He only wished he could

have known earlier how she felt. But all he could see, at first, when Ed came to the job after two other engineers had bungled it, was the way she fitted into the life. She had taken over the slatternly boxcar and created a little cosmos of civilization in the dirt and clamor of the camp. She was an efficient, novel, and amazingly pretty element in his life. Johnny never had a chance. Before she knew him well enough to open up on railroading, his eyes were following her around, and he underwent an acute high blood pressure whenever he watched her walk up the grade toward him, bare-legged, high-breasted, with the beauty and clean grace of a doe. And her voice—when she sang, all the nervous energy that was forever churning around in him was quiet, and for a little while it lay still and purred.

Gradually he found out that the only part of her life she wanted to remember or talk about were the winters in a Boston school, where she'd studied subjects like French and algebra and singing. He learned these things in time to keep from making a fool of himself, but not in time to do his heart any good. Johnny Duff, who was used to trouble, added one more headache to his list.

In the cold mist, Johnny and Ed hurried down to the supply string, where sparks swirled upward from the big diamond stack. Foremen were already checking in their supplies and turning them over to muleskinners. Johnny got a wagon and walked down to the powder car. About half the black powder he requisitioned was coming through. At Bloomer Cut, work was almost stalled. The men known as the Big Four, backers of the road, cried because the C.P. hadn't tapped the rich traffic of the gold fields; yet they cut supplies and wages every month.

Johnny ran the door open, respectfully. That door was faced with sheet iron and edged with India rubber. He knew at a glance that he had been shorted again. He checked the kegs out, and found only sixty. Sixty kegs to feed into holes that cried for a hundred!

He sent the powder wagon on up the grade; it was three miles to the camp at Bloomer Cut. He shouldered back up the tracks, through the tangle of horses, wagons, and workmen. Johnny Duff was tall—too tall for his weight, so that his arms and legs had a long, loose-coupled action. Around his eyes were the fine lines that come early to men who work in the open. His forehead, where his hat shaded it, was fair, but below that every inch of his exposed skin had the hue of the red-brown California earth.

Chinese were carrying rails and fittings from flatcars to wagons, to be carried around the camp train, which blocked the tracks to the grade up ahead. A couple of engineers stood with Ed. One had a roll of blueprints under his arm.

Johnny showed Ed the tally. "I'm going up and have a talk with Huling," he said. "It's about time I got his figures on just how much he needs to finish the cut. Then I'm going down and fight for it."

Ed grunted. "For all the good it will do you. All those boys down in Sacramento really want is to scatter ties and iron along a right of way and collect the subsidies."

Johnny saddled his horse, and in the growing daylight rode down the ravine, under the trestle that was so new the timber ends were still varnished with pitch. He ascended again to the right of way and rode along the trackless red path grooved into the hillside, passing through pear orchards and oak groves and the first scattered pines.

The Big Four, he thought grudgingly, were not quite so black as Ed and the rest of California painted them. They were scroungers; they were pirates of finance. But they had courage. He remembered how they had scrimped two years ago to find $50,000 to back Theodore Judah, a railroad engineer from the East with a wild dream of building a railroad across the Sierras to meet the Union Pacific somewhere on the plains. They were just four Sacramento merchants then— Collis P. Huntington, Mark Hopkins, Charles Crocker, and Leland Stanford, purveyors, variously, of hardware, dry goods, and groceries. And more than once, Johnny Duff knew, their assets as railroad czars had fallen far short of what they had owned as merchants.

Johnny himself came in for criticism frequently. What was a man of his age doing as assistant superintendent of a railroad construction crew? This was a point the Big Four never discussed. They kept him because they had to. They kept him because nobody but Johnny Duff knew how the Central Pacific was going to get across the snag-toothed Sierra Nevadas. Nobody!

These were the kind of mountains, like clods dumped out of a sack, over which you didn't just start building in a general direction, as a good engineer could almost do in the East. Johnny had been in Theodore Judah's surveying crew when he was searching for some route a railroad could conceivably follow in crossing the mountains. The nation was just becoming interested in a Pacific railroad. In the two years Judah surveyed, trying this pass and that, dragging rod and chain from sea level to 9,000 feet before he found the only possible route, Johnny was the only man who stuck with him. When Judah talked railroad, Johnny forgot all about salary. But Judah died, with the railroad barely started, and on his death the amazing discovery was made that he hadn't left any maps. He had either destroyed them or never made any. He simply knew where the road was going. So did Johnny. It gave him a club he was not slow to use. Judah's fear had been that the Huntington crowd would cut costs until they had a jerrybuilt road that nothing but a handcar could ever run on. Johnny made them coax him, chiefly with a written agreement to build according to Judah's specifications. In the end, Johnny Duff agreed to swing the sledge if they would hold the spike steady.

11

The ceiling of gray mist was slow to break up. Through the pressed-down atmosphere rolled the heavy throb of a black-powder blast. Digory Huling, Johnny's boss powder monkey, had his men out early. Digory was a Cornishman, the best powder man Johnny had ever known, who he had stolen from the hard-rock mines a few months ago. From the sound of it this morning, he was trying to tear the top off Bloomer Hill with one shot. But it was not until Johnny Duff saw the workman running down the grade toward him that he knew he had just heard the heavy tread of disaster.

The workman ran up close to the horse so that it began to rear. Johnny controlled it, while the Chinese gestured up the hill, screaming: "Clave-im! Clave-im!" A cut on the man's cheek mixed blood and dust. There was powdery earth in his hair and clothing.

Johnny had to raise his hand to stop the rush of chopped Cantonese. He wrote on a pad from his hip pocket: **Accident at Bloomer Cut. Send shovels and doctor.** He sent the Oriental on down the line with the message.

He found the camp of forty Chinese wildly astir. For shelter, tents had been pitched within the narrow slot their drills, doublejacks, and black powder had blasted into the tough meat of Bloomer Hill. The walls of the cut, rising eighty feet above grade level, showed why every foot of the advance at this section had been shot. Under a thick hide of shale, the hill was solid rock and conglomerate. Half the tents appeared to have been buried beneath the slide. Twenty or thirty Chinese were moving boulders, shoveling, clawing at loose earth with their bare hands.

Johnny found Colbeck, the clerk, the only white man in camp besides Digory, attempting to move a stone with a bar. Johnny got on the bar with him.

"He's caught it for sure, Mister Duff!" Colbeck panted. "Him and about ten others! I don't know what the hell happened. A spark must have fallen in a powder keg while we were eating."

Three men had already been dragged out and now sat against the cut wall near the breakfast fire. They held handleless tea bowls in their hands, stunned but not badly hurt. It might be another story with those under the deeper angle of the talus. Johnny grabbed a shovel and went to work as soon as the stone was moved.

A few minutes later a hand was uncovered. It began to clutch wildly as other hands scooped the rubble away. A Chinese, half suffocated, was unearthed. Johnny's heart tightened. In a few more minutes they could hope to find nothing but bodies under the slide.

It was his own shovel that struck the mining brogan. With that two-and-a-half-inch sole, whose foot but Digory's could be inside it? He shouted, and other men came to help him. But the Cornishman lay, loose-limbed, on the ground when he was pulled out. They carried him to the fire.

Johnny washed the dirt out of his mouth and nose. He looked small, like an injured child, for he was not a large man, except in breadth of shoulder. He cut his own hair, running the clippers straight up the back and sides, a vigorous little man whose pride was the golden belt buckle he had won in some wrestling bout in the old country.

Faintly, when he bent over him, Johnny could hear a light breath. He started rubbing his wrists. One of the Chinese knelt to pinch Digory's nostrils and breathe into his mouth, forcing the air into his body with the bellows of his own lungs. Digory coughed, opened wild eyes, and began to fight.

Johnny was giddy with relief. He took his first deep breath in twenty minutes. A workman brought a bowl of China tea. Digory drank, spat, and began to curse, the rich profanity of the Cornish tin miner. Ed Carney and a dozen other men rode in. Shovels and bare hands attacked the slide, but it was an hour before the last workman was taken out.

It did not go so well with some of them as it had with Digory. There were broken bones and cuts. Two of the Chinese were dead when they were taken out. After the casualties were on their way down the grade, Johnny began to ask questions.

"Hit come," Digory stated, "just as we were eatin'. I've been leavin' four or five kegs atawp the cut for splittin' breast 'oles. Domned if a spark didn't set off the works!"

They started up the hill. The switchbacking trail lifted them to where a small area had been hacked clear of brush. Here the powder had been stored. The clearing was now a pit that funneled into the cut; when the shot went off, a slide of dirt and rocks had been started that poured down the rock wall like ore from a loading bin.

Standing there at the edge of the slot, Johnny looked down on the camp. The tents were being put up again. The fire had been re-started. Imperturbable workmen, used to accidents and tragedy, returned to their parsimonious breakfast of dried cuttlefish, rice, and tea. It occurred to Johnny that eighty feet was a long way for a live spark to ride; there wasn't a sign of a spark now. He asked if the kegs had been covered.

"With rain threaten'," said the Cornishman indignantly, "would I be leavin' them out to soak?" Then he saw what was in Johnny's mind. He took his gaze frowningly back to the hole left by the blast. " 'Tis a long way up, at that! And coom to think of it, why didn't the shot go straight up? There was nothing to send it down . . . no tampin'."

A tiny scrap of red paper caught Johnny's eye. He picked it up, and they all looked at it, Digory and Ed and Colbeck, the clerk. All of them had worked with powder enough to recognize the scrap of paper torn from a dynamite cap. They all knew, too, that caps were used with dynamite or nitroglycerine, but the Central Pacific was using black powder.

Digory was remembering out loud, while his calloused palm slowly rubbed the golden belt buckle. "A couple of fellows been goin' by here near every morning, drunk to the heyes. This morning they stopped and wanted coffee. I'll say they needed it, Mester Duff! I gave them a pot, and they drunk it, and went on down the grade. It wasn't long after that the rocks begun to fall."

Ed said: "Kearns and McKewen!"

Johnny's mind went slowly and carefully. "Maybe," he said. "Maybe not. Put your men to work cleaning up, Digory. Don't say anything about this. We don't want any excitement until we're sure."

He and Ed were the only ones with horses, the other horsemen having gone back with the injured. While the men returned to work, they began to look for sign. But the freight trail passing near the cut bore the impression of hundreds of horse and mule tracks. They split up, to check the road in both directions.

Johnny rode west, toward the main work camp. The freight road twisted in and out of tall manzanita jungles, passed through a sparse grove of second-growth pines, and traversed a pear orchard on a hillside. Kearns and McKewen had only a corner of his thoughts. He was thinking about Ben Hedenburg, who ran the store and saloon on the Auburn and Nevada stage road, where Kearns and McKewen and too many other workmen spent their evenings. Liquor was cheap and plentiful at Hedenburg's; the big sutler would always carry a man till pay day. But liquor was not all he sold. You could buy mining supplies there, too—pans and rockers, dynamite and caps. Johnny was wondering if Ben Hedenburg had realized what the men intended to do with their powder when he sold it.

From the medley of tracks in the deep road dust, a file of boot prints struck off into the orchard. Johnny sat straight on the saddle, his feet thrusting against the stirrups, searching through the columns of black trunks and bare branches now frosted with white pear blossoms. Petals were scattered on the ground. Where the boots of this man had pressed, the petals were crushed into the earth.

He left the road and saw, 100 yards away, the flash of a plaid shirt. He spurred the horse. "Hold up!" he shouted. Then he recognized the broad back and thick neck, overgrown with red hair, of Tim McKewen, the chief day telegrapher.

McKewen floundered on over the irrigation ruts. Johnny came alongside and sprang down with both feet in the middle of McKewen's back. There was no fight in the man when he came up. He was soddenly drunk; his underlip was moist, and his jaws were frowsed with a four-day beard. His tongue fumbled out the cheap lie with which he had armed himself.

"We only set down to rest up there, Mister Duff! Kearns, he knocked out his pipe on a keg. I said . . . 'Kearns, sure that was a damn' fool thing to be doin'!' We hadn't gone on a hunerd feet when. . . ." He covered his face with one clawing, wretched hand. He was sobbing. "I'm a church-goin' man, Mister Duff! I wouldn't willingly take the life of a fly. But we ran. We didn't know . . . we was scared."

"Where's Kearns?" Looking into the little bloodshot-eyes,

advertising their guilt, Johnny was sick.

"We split up. Mister Duff, as sure as the Lord looks down on us. . . ."

"Empty your pockets," Johnny said.

McKewen's mind chewed on this for a moment before his hands went into the pockets of his sagging denim trousers. He pulled them out, his fists full, and just then the import of it reached his face. He moistened his lips.

Johnny said sharply: "Well, open them up!"

McKewen's arms fell to his sides. He kept his eyes on Johnny. His fingers opened, and a small clutch of objects dropped to the earth. On the ground by his right foot lay a copper five-cent piece, two silver dollars, a horn pocket knife—and a dynamite cap.

III

At eleven-fifteen, Johnny marched his prisoner into camp. McKewen seemed stunned and had not spoken all the way down. Johnny ordered him into a boarding car. He went inside the dark, dusty interior and searched the Irishman's hammock and gear for weapons. Then he turned on him sharply.

"Did Hedenburg know you were going to do it?"

McKewen sat on the hammock with his hands hanging between his legs. "I reckon so, Mister Duff. But it was one of them damned things a mick'll do when he's drunk. You can take it or leave it, but . . . we done it for a joke! We got to laughin' over how it would be to see them chinks come a-pourin' out of the cut!"

"Who suggested it?"

McKewen hesitated. "It was all pretty gay up there last night. Faith, I don't know whose idea it was! But me an' Kearns took it up, and, when we'd done with drinkin', we bought the dynamite and started back." A light of recollection touched his face. He said: "I remember how it was! 'I'll sell you the powder, boys,' Ben says, 'but I want no part of the joke. But if you're determined to do it, be damned careful of your teeth when you crimp the cap.' So you see, Mister Duff, there's nobody to blame but me and Kearns."

Johnny frowned. Somehow this sudden nobility of McKewen's regarding Hedenburg was out of character. Hedenburg was as guilty as the railroad men for selling dynamite to drunks, and McKewen must know it. The suspicion was strong in him that the sutler had ribbed them up to the whole thing. But a suspicion like that called for a motive, and

204

who but a homicidal maniac would propound such a ghastly joke? Hedenburg was too shrewd to be considered a maniac of any kind.

Johnny posted a guard at the door and left.

The noon whistle sounded. All the discordant noises of the railroad ceased. Sledges were thrown aside; the rattle of earth from the embankment into the fill ended; iron peddlers parked their jangling carts. From the trestle and from the grade beyond it, Chinese came on the trot to their group messes, while the outnumbered white laborers tramped to their immutable fare of beef, beans, bread, and potatoes.

Ed rode in just before the whistle sent the men back to work. He was empty-handed. Johnny met him at the horse corral. "It looked as if he was heading for the stage road," Ed announced. "I thought I'd be sticking my nose into something if I tried to take him at Hedenburg's, without a gun."

"I caught McKewen," Johnny said. "We'll have to turn him over to the sheriff at Auburn tonight and go after Kearns. My guess is that Hedenburg jockeyed them into it."

Ed hoisted his saddle to his shoulder and faced Johnny. "How long are you going to let him get away with it?" he demanded. "I don't know what he's got against the road, but you can bet that the grief he's made hasn't all been accidental. And he'll keep right on making it until he's stopped."

Johnny frowned. "The law won't close him up, but maybe we could hang a padlock on him ourselves. What about tonight, when we go after Kearns?"

Ed deposited the saddle among those of the riding bosses. "Why not? Even if he gives Kearns up, we can take him with the most possible trouble. Come around after dinner."

Darkness came early, the sun sinking gloomily into banks of cloud and fog over the valley. Johnny spoke to six of the gang bosses at dinner. They were men he could count on, hard men, railroad men who knew no profession but the iron. Afterward, he secured his Navy Colt from his quarters and strolled on, through the darkness, to Carney's car. A night mist was cool on his face. He knocked at the door and called: "OK, Ed!"

A chair moved, and someone crossed the floor. Then Babbie's voice said: "Pop! Where are you going with *that* thing?"

Ed stood in the doorway, buttoning his coat over the revolver he had not succeeded in hiding. "We're taking a prisoner up to Auburn," he growled. "Johnny found out Kearns and McKewen set off that blast this morning. We've got McKewen."

Ed came down the steps. Babbie was right behind him. She stood in the light from the door, hugging herself with cold. She saw the horses under saddle near a pile of ties.

"A gang like that to take one man to town?" she declared. "I didn't come to the railroad yesterday, Pop. You're going to close up Hedenburg."

"The Irish," said Johnny, "don't need crystal balls, as long as they've got their women."

"Is it funny?" Babbie asked.

Ed said: "No, honey . . . it's not. Only . . . it's got to be done. He set himself up there to make trouble. He's got to be taken care of before something else happens like this morning." He started for the horses.

Johnny hesitated, wanting to say something to make Babbie understand it wasn't as chancy as she thought—no worse than cleaning out a den of rattlesnakes. But he could think of nothing more reassuring than to smile and say: "Don't worry. I'll make him stay outside with the horses."

Her silence, the long, grave look she gave him, stole his smile. She said: "You're young, Johnny. I wish I were half so

206

young. Then I might be able to take this life. Every week some man forgets to take his foot away when the rail comes down, or a blast goes off prematurely, or somebody falls off a trestle. And every time I see the doctor saddle his horse, I think . . . what if it's Pop or Johnny?"

"You take risks in any business." Johnny shrugged.

Babbie gave him a tired smile. "I know. Only . . . maybe not so many. I suppose I'm talking like a mother sending her little boy off to school. But if you two come back with holes in you, I'll wrap up this darned railroad and send it back to Sacramento for keeps. No, go on . . . they're waiting for you." She gave him a push. Johnny went, with the perverse satisfaction of the warrior going to battle, who knows he leaves someone behind to worry over him. . . .

There were other saloons strung along the streets that climbed steeply to the business center, but Hedenburg's caught elements that settled to the bottom of the hill—teamsters, hauling in from Sacramento, miners with a little dust to spend and a big thirst to kill.

They decided that it would be best for Johnny to go in first, Ed following. The rest would enter in pairs, distributing themselves about the room. Johnny's lanky stride carried him across the porch. He walked into a low-ceilinged hall where all a man could take in, at first, were the noise and the heat. A big iron stove, squatting in a tub of sand, started a process that the bodies of overheated men continued. They stood at the bar, ringed the gaming tables, and shot pool in an alcove at the rear. A music box was beating out: "She May Have Seen Better Days".

Noise went with each of these operations, shuffling and arguing and loose-jawed laughter. Johnny stood at the end of the bar for a time before he was noticed. He had time to map out the place. His gaze searched for the man Kearns, but he did not see his baldhead and rounded shoulders in the room, nor had he expected to. Then Ben Hedenburg, presiding behind the bar, approached him.

He slapped both hands down on the pine and waited, smiling. He was a robust man with dark skin and pale eyes; the hair that should have been on his baldhead grew from his lip and jowls in an unkempt black mustache, and a fringe of beard around his wide jaws. He wore a buckskin shirt with dark rings margining the armpits; close up, he smelled rankly of perspiration and sour, chewed cigars.

Johnny ordered beer. Hedenburg drew a foaming schooner from a barrel. When he set it down, Johnny asked quietly: "Where's Kearns?"

Hedenburg's smile dwindled; two lines appeared between the gray eyes. "Who's asking?" he said.

"Duff and some others."

Hedenburg rubbed his nose. "Kearns and McKewen left about five o'clock this morning. They haven't been back. Why don't you put those boys in a corral, Duff? They're good customers, but, my God, can they raise trouble!"

"Let's skip the sparring," Johnny suggested. "I've got McKewen in jail for manslaughter, and I'm going to put Kearns in the same place. Let's take a look in your back rooms."

In the backbar mirror, Johnny saw Ed's face reflected. Then Hedenburg did the unexpected. "It's what you get for trying to help a worthless down-and-outer!" he deplored. He selected an iron key from a bunch that hung on his belt. "He's in Number Six. Damn the Irish fool! What happened down there? He said he'd got in a fight and somebody was gunning for him. Wanted me to hide him."

"Is that what he said?" Johnny asked, smiling. He went through the door at the end of the counter into a narrow, unlighted hall. A little light came from the door; at intervals along the hall yellow blots of light paved the floor.

Number Six was dark. Johnny put the key in the lock and turned. He threw the door open. Within, a bed suddenly creaked, and a man's weight made the floor planks whisper. A voice clogged with fear rasped: "Ben?"

IV

The round, cold eye of Johnny's Colt looked into the room. He moved inside. "It's Duff," he said. "Don't be a fool, Kearns. You may get off with manslaughter, if you don't make trouble now. But if you do. . . ." In that small space, the blast of exploding powder was staggering. For one instant the room seemed to blow up with light. The flash showed the form beside the bed; it gave Johnny a target. Kearns's bullet had gone into the wall. Shaken, Johnny squeezed off his shot; the recoil lifted his forearm. Again he fired. In the orange burst, he saw the rail setter stumbling forward with his hands blindly reaching.

He heard him fall. The ropy gasping of the man's lungs held him there, aghast; stronger than any feeling of relief was the realization that he had shot a man, had probably killed him—that the bullet that had been in his gun an instant before was now in Kearns's body.

Shouts from the saloon turned him back to the hall. He was sweating, but it was a cold, unhealthy sweat. He had never even pointed a gun at a man before. It had come instinctively. Someone banged into the hall; he backed into the room. It was Ed's voice that called out.

Johnny walked toward him. "I had to shoot him," he said. "He fired at me."

Ed's grasp on his arm, hurrying him back to the saloon, was reassuringly solid. "Forget Kearns!" he said. "Hedenburg's started things! He ducked when the shooting started . . . came up at the other end of the bar with a shillelagh. I don't know how many men he's got, but the rest are heading for the door."

In the smoky twilight of the saloon, half the lamps having been extinguished, panic shook up the reins. Hedenburg was moving fast down the wall to the rear alcove, where startled pool players were dropping their cues to run. He began to break cues over his knee, tossing the tapered butts to employees who were beginning to rally.

"Ten dollars and a quart of whiskey for every head you break!" he shouted.

From the confusion of pounding boots, overturning chairs, and grunting, swearing men, two forces began to work out. Most of the crowd wanted no part of this affair but to get out. The dozen employees who flocked to the big sutler quickly deployed into a rough skirmish line, with Hedenburg as a bearded general in the center. Johnny's gang bosses, armed with pick halves, moved in on the saloon men.

Johnny scooped a stein off the bar and hurled it at Hedenburg. It hit the saloonkeeper in the shoulder. Hedenburg wheeled, roaring his fury, and charged. It was poor generalship. Without a leader, the skirmish line broke up. Railroad men now picked their adversaries and went to work. They were outnumbered but not outmanned. Theirs was a hard trade, in which fighting was considered a rare, off-hours treat. A shillelagh was their tennis racket.

The saloon was emptying fast, so that the fighters had all the room they needed in which to maneuver. There was a smell of smoking wicks; Hedenburg had managed to darken half the lamps. Johnny had only a confused idea of just what went on. He had his gaze on Hedenburg. The sutler, a black ebony shillelagh cocked, strap about his wrist, was a sight to break up a riot. He came at Johnny, kicking chairs out of his way. Johnny broke a chair over a table and took one of the legs as a club.

He hoped Hedenburg would rush him, but the

saloonkeeper was craftier than this. He stopped short of Johnny and made a couple of feints, moving around lightly on his feet. He kept his left shoulder up, those narrow gray eyes studying Johnny across the greasy buckskin parapet. The blunt end of Johnny's weapon went into Hedenburg's face like a sword. Hedenburg grunted; his nose began to bleed.

He came in, then, the shillelagh flashing. Johnny flung up his club; he felt the impact to his teeth as the chair leg splintered. The shillelagh found his ear, glancingly, but it set off a red explosion in his brain. He threw the splinters of the chair leg away and went after Hedenburg with bare hands. The saloonkeeper's throat came into his grip as he lurched after him; he was choking and cursing and forcing him back to the wall, with the sutler threshing savagely. A rack of colored balls boomed stutteringly upon the floor. Johnny began to hammer at the rough features. Hedenburg, taken by surprise, was suddenly in trouble.

In the semi-gloom another man came up silently. Johnny did not sense him until he had sprung onto his back. Hedenburg tore loose, spitting blood. Something flashed into Johnny's vision as the man on his back held his neck in an arm lock and reached around with his free hand. A knife—that was his first thought. Then he saw that it was the saw-toothed ring of a broken bottle.

One arm was still free, he reached for the other's wrist as the bottle slashed. He caught it, but an edged tooth of the brown glass ripped his ear. Blood spurted against the wall. They stood like that for a moment, muscles locked against muscles. Hedenburg came in again, but suddenly he staggered and his hand groped up to his head, and just then a yellow pool ball dropped to the floor. He went down, heavy and loose, like a shot steer.

It slowed Johnny's adversary for a moment. While his attention was on Hedenburg, Johnny hauled the man over his shoulder, slamming him on the floor. He grabbed a billiard cue and put him out of action with two blows.

For the first time Johnny had a chance to look around. There was one skirmish still going on—an Auburn man in a corner standing off three railroaders. The music box finished its five-cents' worth with a run. The battle ended while Johnny watched. The big room seemed quiet. Railroad men stood among the shamble of tables and chairs.

Ed came up with a bruise like a turkey egg under one eye. He turned Johnny's ear to the light. "My God!" he exclaimed. "If you aren't a sight! Your ear's torn half from your head." He sent two men for Kearns, and the rest of them began to drag fallen gladiators out the back. When it was all done, lamps were smashed on the floor. The building was blazing well when they departed. . . .

It was necessary to take Kearns's body to the sheriff's office and make a report. The sleepy deputy who was on duty knew about McKewen and Kearns and the trouble at Bloomer Cut; he was not inclined to become interested in the case, other than to ask a few questions and take down their story laboriously in cramped handwriting.

End of track, when they returned, was silent. On the hillside, coals from evening cook fires made rosy puddles. A turned-down lamp burned in the telegrapher's quarters; as they passed the string of boarding cars, they could hear the lusty snoring of tired workmen. The gang bosses turned in here, except one man who had a head cut to be stitched. He and Johnny walked to the infirmary car. Ed had hurried on to reassure Babbie.

The doctor pulled on trousers and boots while his patients waited on straight-backed chairs. One end of the car was partitioned off as a rude operating room. Grumpily, hungry for sleep after being up until late with victims of the cave-in, the doctor stitched the gang boss' cut, then examined Johnny's torn ear.

Dr. Cuvillie was a lank gray man with a stringy neck; he breathed heavily through his nose. "You're about halfway 'twixt havin' an ear and not," he grunted. Blood was all over Johnny's face. He could feel it gummily between undershirt and skin. When he looked at the lamp, small golden sparks pinwheeled before his eyes. It was the first inkling he had had of faintness. There was a feeling of pressure at the base of his skull.

Cuvillie squinted over his needle. Before starting to sew, he glanced at his patient's face and immediately brought a glass of brandy. "Replace some o' that liquid you've been losing, son."

Johnny held on while his ear was put back together. He lost count of the number of times the needle thrust exquisitely into bunched nerves. He was sweating, and, when Cuvillie threw the needle onto the table, Johnny's arms were stiff from holding onto the chair.

"Guess you can clean yourself up somehow," the doctor said. "I'll take the stitches out in three, four days."

Someone ran up to the car and mounted the steps. It was Babbie, who came into the reek of antiseptics in the car. She wore an old blue robe with her auburn hair in papers; she looked, Johnny thought, like something seen in the middle of an Indian attack, she was that wild-scared.

"Johnny!" she exclaimed. "For the love of heaven. . . ."

She came closer, saw the raggedly patched ear and the blood in which he had dyed himself. She flinched. Her eyes flicked to the doctor and back again. Johnny could see the blood drain away from her lips.

She said, in a whisper: "Doctor, I . . . I think. . . ."

It was Johnny who caught her.

Cuvillie sopped a ball of cotton in ammonia while Johnny laid her on the cot. He passed it back and forth under her nose. "Mighty chicken-hearted, for a railroad woman," he growled.

Her pallor, the dark smudges under her eyes, frightened Johnny. He asked huskily: "You don't suppose . . . I mean, it's not her heart, or anything?"

Cuvillie thought it over. "Not in the medical sense of the word," he grunted.

Johnny hadn't time to figure that one out before Babbie winced and turned from the bite of the fumes. She took a long, tremulous breath. Cuvillie helped her sit up. He handed her the brandy glass.

"It . . . it was such a shock!" she said. Her fingers pressed her temples. "Pop said he only had a little cut. Then I came in and saw him . . . like *that!*" She looked at Johnny, horrified.

Cuvillie folded his arms. He had been a railroad surgeon for fifteen years, with time out to serve with Grant. "How long have you been on the railroad, girl?"

Babbie looked up. "Why . . . all my life."

"Then how is it you pass out at the sight of a little blood?" Cuvillie was apparently going to get to the bottom of this, but there was a sparkle in his eyes.

"A *little* blood!" Babbie stood up and pulled the belt of her robe tighter. She turned her back on the doctor. "I've got coffee brewing," she told Johnny. "Come down for a cup before you go to bed. But for goodness' sake, wash up first!"

Johnny rather liked the turn things had taken. There was a tingling in him when he saw how the color had come back to Babbie's cheeks. He remembered how she had come bursting in, even though she thought it was only a minor cut, and then the way she had worried over his going up to Auburn tonight.

Did those things add up, or didn't they? Even the cold water of the wash trough couldn't cool his blood completely.

Breakfast or midnight snack, Babbie set a tempting table. There was, in addition to coffee, a pan of freshly made doughnuts on the red-and-white gingham cloth. "I made 'em while you were gone," she said. "The women make doughnuts while the men get their heads broken . . . that's the railroad! Johnny, you big lout, do you have to lay every rail and fight every squabble personally on this darned railroad?"

"Line o' duty," said Johnny. The doughnuts were golden brown. Under the tender crust their hearts were light and sweet. *To have a doughnut maker like this in your car!* Johnny thought. His mind was off on a wild tangent; there was a singing in his head. The doctor had said: *Her heart's all right . . . in the medical sense of the word.* Blind! Blind as a bat! All the little clues he had ever had welded themselves together. Now he saw meaning in a so many little memories.

He couldn't help grinning, and Ed remarked: "Wish I felt as gay as you look. But I wonder if we've seen the last of Mister Hedenburg."

"Likely," Johnny said.

Babbie gave him a long, studying glance. Her chin, it seemed, went up a trifle. She promptly stood up. "Well, I don't know about you two, but I'm going to bed. The next time you go out on night patrol, don't expect doughnuts when you get back."

Johnny took six of the doughnuts and made his good nights. He walked on springs to his car. He sat on the cot, unlacing his boots, trying to see the dingy interior as it might be under Babbie's administration. Windows would have to be cut in the walls first, of course, curtains, then, and rugs, and a kitchen installed at one end. And a tub. A woman must get tired of bathing in a copper washtub.

Wise old Cuvillie! Johnny scratched his head. He'd have to bring him up a bottle of something from Sacramento next time he was down. All these months, perhaps, she had really been wanting him to speak. Because he didn't, she got ornery and ran down the railroad and everything it included. But even Ed had said she would be back in a hurry if she ever did leave the iron. She fitted; she belonged. Wishful thinking, maybe, but tomorrow, barring acts of God, he would find out.

V

During the night the rain began. The grade was an ocean of slops when the whistle turned the workmen out in the morning. Broken earth, red as cinnabar, melted into a gumbo that sucked at the laborers' heels. Raindrops, slanting from a gray sky, danced on the yellow puddles. It was late April; this might be the last rain until October.

The supply train came blasting up the grade, and the regular morning circus began. Horses and mules, their backs reeking, struggled through the mire, pulling freight wagons and light iron cars. Foremen brought supplies tallies to Johnny from time to time, where he stood on a flatcar. And again everything was short. There were only twenty kegs of powder in the tin-roofed powder car. It was a mistake someone at the storage yard had made—that was the only way Johnny could figure it. But he would have to wire Rocklin to make sure.

As he started for the telegraph car, one of the telegraphers came down the shoulder to give him a message. Johnny stuffed the flimsy in his pocket and ducked into the Carneys' car. Ed was keeping his promise to eat a leisurely breakfast. He and Babbie were reading the morning mail.

He poured himself coffee and, with a smile at Babbie, sat down to read the telegram. Babbie gave him a quick, careful look and went back to her letter. But Johnny wasn't fooled. He could hardly switch his mind back to business, for all the breathless thoughts in his hand. Then he began to read; the blood rose to his head and seemed to suffocate him. In 300 words, Collis P. Huntington informed him that the always spindly supply line had snapped in the middle. There was no more powder in the storage sheds at Sacramento; there was only a ten-day supply of rails. The Central Pacific had finally stalled.

Ed must have been watching him, for he said: "Now what?"

Johnny took a big swallow of coffee. He read the telegram again. Then he said: "Listen. . . ." He read it. It was a cry of despair and an appeal for help. Someone had been working while the Big Four slept. Hedenburg's store suddenly had the magnitude of a fly that had been annoying them. The real grief had been shaping up in San Francisco harbor. Every steamboat line between Frisco and Sacramento had been organized against the C.P. That hadn't been hard to achieve, Johnny thought; the steamboat men knew their profits would be practically ended when the Central finally laid rails to the harbor. In addition, an unknown party had acquired options on all available dock space. The schooner *Jamaica*, lying at anchor with a quarter of a million dollars' worth of materiel from Baltimore, was unable to unload. Her master had given notice that the supplies would be dumped at Portland, Oregon unless they were taken off before he finished painting and refitting the ship. Huntington said he had done all he could. He now suggested that Superintendent Duff come down himself for a look.

Johnny stood up and flung the balled paper out the door into the mud. "If we had anything but a gang of ex-grocery clerks down there! It's not enough for me to build the damned road. I've got to have a spare-time hobby of pulling supplies out of a silk hat."

"What are you going to do?" Ed asked.

Johnny drew a long sigh, a troubled sigh that ended in a groan. "Go down to the harbor," he said. "What else is there to do? Find out who's got us cornered and how much he wants."

Ed's sunburned face relaxed slightly. "Pretty sure of yourself, aren't you?"

"Why not? It's nothing but a scheme of somebody's to make some easy money. We'll pay him off, if we can't throw a scare into him."

"Maybe," suggested Ed, "the U.P. would like to tie us up for a while, till they can reach Salt Lake City. You couldn't buy General Dodge out."

"We can guess all day," Johnny stated, "but the only way I can know is to go down and smell it out. I'll get a clean shirt and hop the supply train back."

He hesitated, before jumping down. His glance went to Babbie. There was a quiet smile at the corners of her mouth. It was a superior, almost a disdainful smile, as though she knew how it had been with Johnny last night, but also as though she knew that the woman he was already married to, the High Iron, would always throw him a smile at the last minute, this way, and draw him off over the hills. There was nothing he could do but go.

He said: "Well . . . take it easy, you two," and departed.

When the supply train whistled out the flag, Johnny ran down the grade to jump aboard. The little 440 locomotive took up slack with a crash of couplings. Her drivers spun, found the sand, and she started down. It was warm in the cab, where Johnny sat on his valise, but the rain leaped through the openings in wet gusts. He put his gray derby, part of his town rig, under his coat for shelter. He was wet and miserable, but the real misery was inside him.

At Rocklin, division terminal, he transferred to the passenger train, which jolted, swayed, and pitched into the capital in an hour and a half. He had an hour's wait before the packet left for the harbor; he visited the Central Pacific office, over the Huntington and Hopkins hardware store. He found the Big Four sandbagged by their worries.

Huntington reported that the blockade appeared as solid as a brick wall. "Whoever's engineered it," he said, "he's hiding behind the letterhead of the Inland Steamship Company. That's all I was able to find out. The office is on East Street. Just a blind. Look it over, if you want to. And draw on us for up to a thousand, if you need it. We can't last a month without supplies. The payroll will cut us to our knees."

The packet ran out of the storm at Walnut Grove, hauling into San Francisco at dusk. In the murky twilight, fog moved in from the Farallones, dark bars of light breaking it along the horizon. It scuffed across the waterfront and blurred the paper lanterns of Chinatown; it softened the gay, tragic lights of the Barbary Coast.

Johnny went down the landing stage into the chill atmosphere of the Bay City. Despite the dusk, it was only five o'clock. It occurred to him that the Inland Steamship Company might still be open. Accordingly, he took a room near the waterfront and ate a hurried dinner at an oyster shop on Fisherman's Wharf. On the darkening water of the bay, the red and green riding lamps of the fishing fleet bobbed in the mist. Drays cannonaded over the cobbles. Johnny walked until he saw, over an office jostled among a solid row of grimy brick fronts, the sign of the steamship company.

The firm did not, apparently, go in for "front". One lone, elderly clerk stood behind a letterpress in back of a railing. A door behind him warned: **Private.**

Johnny asked: "Boss in?"

"Will I do?" the clerk countered. He did not look up after his first myopic appraisal of the visitor. He had a pouchy, pink-and-freckled face, white hair, and loose under lids like those of a St. Bernard. He placed a sheet of wet muslin between two pages of the copy book, closed it carefully, and slid it in the press.

"It's a business matter," Johnny stalled. "I'm with the Sacramento Poultry Supply Company. We've got an order from a hotel here for a thousand fryers a month. But we can't take their business until we know what it's going to cost us to set those fryers down in the kitchens."

"You could 'a' written and saved the trip." The clerk screwed the press down until it groaned.

"Well, you see," Johnny told him, "I was coming down anyway." He opened the gate in the rail and stepped inside. "If you don't care, I'll just step in and see Mister. . . ."

"No, you don't!" The old man was immediately in his path. "He ain't in. Call around tomorrow, and I'll have the figgers for you."

"Old-timer"—Johnny grinned—"I'm not really with the Sacramento Poultry Supply. I'm a banty rooster myself, and I've got a notion I may find some corn in there."

The veined old hands pushed impotently at him. Johnny stood fast, a big and hard-jawed man in his tight-fitting city clothes, his gray derby down over one eye. "Now, now!" He chuckled as he spun the old man and sat him down. He walked quickly to the office door, and opened it. It was nearly dark inside; there was a single window on the alley. Johnny took a lamp from a wall bracket, entered the office, and set it on the desk.

The drawers were empty. The desk top was bare of all ornament save the lid of a saleratus can, which served as an ashtray. The tray had been used, and, as he looked at it, Johnny became conscious of an aroma. Where—and when—had he known it before? A cigar band lay scorched in the ashes; he examined it, and all at once he knew. An ash—an odor—a red-and-gold cigar band. Sometimes such things are sharper than words to prod the memory. They swept Johnny back to a day in Sacramento just after Mr. Judah's death.

A man named James Daggett had sought him out a week after Judah was buried. Daggett had silver mines in Nevada Territory, about fifty miles from where the road would pass. They called him Silver Jim. Over there across the Sierra Nevadas, they said the mining dollars he owned would make a mountain almost as high as the Sierras themselves. But if the road by-passed the town of Chloride, where Daggett's mines were located, he would take a sharp loss. Other mines of lower-grade ore would boom simply because they were closer to cheap transportation of ore and equipment. Johnny knew this, and Daggett did not make any secret of the fact that he was facing ruin and meant to fight it.

Silver Jim Daggett had showed him a map. It depicted the Central as crossing the summit, not at Donner Pass, but at Johnson's Pass, forty miles south. It would cost little to make this change, he had claimed. And it would set the C.P. right down in his back yard. Since Johnny Duff was the only man who knew where the railroad was supposed to cross the mountains. . . . He explained all these things over cigars and brandy. He was rather proud of the cigars; they were especially made for him in Cuba—rum-soaked. Johnny hadn't cared for them.

Daggett had said: "I like being rich, Johnny. I think you would, too. You should try it sometime."

But Johnny Duff hadn't. And Daggett hadn't liked the way he refused. Johnny had never heard from him since, hadn't thought of him, really, until just now, when he walked in here and smelled one of those miserable rum-soaked cigars, and saw the same florid label.

Very softly, the door was closing behind him. Johnny

reached it in two strides, but it slammed then, and the lock clicked. On reflection, he wasn't sure he wanted to go out that way, anyway. The old man might have summoned the police. Or he might have a gun.

He unlatched the window on a dark and narrow alley, scented with ordure and fish heads. He stepped through and began to walk. He had nearly reached the end of it when he realized he was coming up against a blank wall. He turned and walked back, faster now, toward the other end.

Two men—two shapes, rather—drifted into the mouth of the alley from East Street. At the same time, Johnny heard the window of the steamship office close with a bang. The men up the alley began to walk toward him.

VI

Johnny waited in the middle of the alley. To retreat would only put a wall at his back. He thought wryly of his gun, lying in his valise in the hotel room. A surprise charge, a head-on slam into one of the pair approaching him, began to shape up as his only chance to break out of the *cul-de-sac*. He heard the rear door of the steamship office open. Someone slipped out of the building and stood in the heavy gather of shadows against the wall.

Suddenly the draw cord began to tighten. From three corners of a triangle, they were moving in on him. A swift pulse awoke in him, a throb of desperation. They were all expecting a rush toward the mouth of the alley. That, perhaps, was why his glance reconnoitered the wall at his left.

What he saw held out a hand of encouragement. The ash cans ranked along the wall were tall, whereas the unbroken roof line of the buildings was low. When he moved, it was the man who had come from the steamship office who took his headlong charge. A bludgeon of some kind went up, tardily. Johnny's fingers closed on his wrist, and he forced it back, at the same time driving his fist into a slack belly. The man went down, paralyzed.

Johnny stepped over him, ran a few steps, sprang to the top of an ash barrel, and crouched for the jump. He went up, reaching. The rough fabric of the bricks caught his fingertips. He wriggled, trying to better his hold. A second man, darting in below, swung at his legs with a length of pipe. The muscles of Johnny's right calf cramped agonizingly. He bit his lip; for a moment he was looking out upon a great gulf of blackness into which the pain was drawing him. His leg hung useless.

He saw the man swing again; an urgent despair gave him the power to draw up his left leg and kick, viciously.

The attacker went to his knees, hands over his face. The pipe jangled on the cobblestones.

Johnny chinned himself on the wall, threw a leg over, and sprawled on a roof. He heard a sound that for a second held him rigidly against the roof—the thin *crack* of a small-caliber pistol. That sound blended into the whine of a ball glancing off the brick parapet. Afterward, there was the sound of a man scrambling onto the trash barrels.

Johnny came to his feet and tried to run, but the aching muscle of his leg would provide no better than a dragging limp. The nearest shelter was a raised skylight. As he started for it, he heard one of the trio begin to shout: "Man on the roof! Man on the roof!" It was at once a cover for their own noisy activity and a noose to trap him.

Johnny lay behind the peaked glass tent of the skylight. On East Street he could hear the first random sounds of a crowd taking shape—inquiring voices, boots thudding over the plank wharves. He saw two hands grasp the edge of the roof.

He had an inspiration. He sat up and brought the heel of his hand down on one of the panes. Shards of broken glass jangled into the darkness below. The racket went sharply through all the others. Johnny limped to the low ridge between the individual buildings and dropped behind it just as a head came over the wall. A man scrambled over and, drawing a gun, ran to the skylight. He stood with his back to Johnny, staring downward. Then he ran to the street side and shouted: "He's inside! Block the doors and we've got him!"

He returned, bent over the broken skylight, and tried to peer into the gloom below. He fumbled for a match. He had just lighted one when a sound caused him to turn. The man who had come up on him gave him a gentle push, with just

enough force to thrust him an inch beyond the invisible line
that gravity draws when a man does anything so foolish as to
lean over a broken skylight. It was gravity whose leaden palm
thrust against the middle of his back while, gasping, he
arched himself, drew up on his toes, and reached back with
his clawing hands. As he fell, the scream finally came.

Johnny dragged himself away, limping toward the end of
the roof. A taller building mounted to block him, and it was
here he had to drop again to the alley he had quitted. A glance
showed him a knot of men, one bearing a lantern, clustered
about the rear of a building. He took the six-foot drop hard,
his leg buckling under him. He got up and painfully ran
toward the corner. They were still trying to open the door
when he made the turn.

On the way back to the hotel, Johnny bought a pound of
Epsom salts at a druggist's. These he dissolved in steaming
hot water when he reached his room. The tub was too short
for him; he sat with most of his body above the tub, like a very
long Indian in a very short canoe. His skin was white, all but
his big bronzed hands and his dark face and neck.

For the first time he was able to conjecture about Silver
Jim Daggett's connection with the fracas. Granting that
Daggett's soul would batten on any harm he could do the
Central Pacific, Johnny still could not see what he stood to
profit by the wrecking of the railroad. Revenge, of course, was
always a tasty morsel, but not if it cost Daggett most of his
fortune to achieve it. Steamboat lines did not refuse business
for nothing. It came to Johnny that Daggett was moving some
very heavy machinery with a minimum of noise. Now that
Johnny knew he was in town, he had another lead to follow.
The silver king's home was in Nevada. Therefore he should,
logically, be at a hotel. San Francisco had many hotels, but
only a few good enough for a millionaire.

Johnny's watch said eight-thirty when he finished soaking his leg. He dressed again, put on a clean shirt, and topped it all with the gray derby. The brown-featured, smiling man in the mirror seemed to approve. He was not precisely a vain man, but the notion was there that a man who worked hard for a living cut something of a figure when he came to town. He tried to picture Babbie on his arm, with a parasol and a new bonnet, and he rather liked that idea, too.

At the third hotel he tried, the Marshall, the clerk said: "Yes, sir, we have a Mister Daggett. Mister James Daggett, of Chloride, Nevada. He is *the* Mister Daggett," he added, smiling.

"Will you tell him John Duff wants to see him?"

A bellboy brought word that Silver Jim Daggett would be happy to have Mr. Duff visit him in his suite. Johnny ascended a wide, carpeted stairway and wandered down a corridor.

Down the hall a door opened. A large man with a sagging belly backed out of a room, holding his hat deferentially against his vest. "Yes sir!" he said. "We sure will. We would have this time, only. . . ." Then his head turned, and his myopic eyes found Johnny.

"Mister Daggett," he whispered, "that's him."

Johnny did not slow down. He joined the party. The old clerk from the Inland Steamship Company backed up as Daggett laughed softly.

"It's all right, Harry. Thanks for coming. I'll talk to Mister Duff now."

Johnny prudently looked into the room before he entered. It appeared to be empty. He went inside.

Daggett said: "Sit down, won't you? I rather expected you all week. I notice you're favoring your leg." He smiled, a man of fifty-five who kept his years sternly at bay. There was energy in his movements; his skin was brown and weathered. His hair was dark, brushed through the temples with gray. The shirt under his smoking jacket was pleated white silk; he wore a black string tie.

"Let's put away the fencing foils," Johnny suggested. "I'm favoring my leg, and I reckon a couple of other men are licking some wounds, too. The point is, I found out what I went there to find out . . . that you're the man behind the harbor blockade."

Daggett poured brandy from a cut-glass decanter. He looked into Johnny's eyes as he gave him the glass. "Well," he said, "I'm one of the men, anyway."

"Hedenburg?" Johnny asked suddenly.

Daggett's face told nothing. "Hedenburg? Should I know him?"

Johnny passed it over. "What do you expect to get out of this piracy?"

"Call it piracy if it pleases you," Daggett replied blandly. "I merely took an option on all the Sacramento steamboats to handle my freight. I'm speaking only of railroad supplies, of course."

"Railroad supplies!" Johnny snorted. "Strap-iron rails and ore cars! It's a fraud, and you know it."

"On the contrary," Daggett stated, "I expect to be sending quite a bit of railroad materiel up the old freight road . . . regulation supplies, rails and spikes, ties and powder. I thought you might have heard. I've gone in with some Dutch Flat men on a road of our own."

VII

Johnny was still sitting there in a kind of vacuum when Daggett chuckled: "Go ahead and say it! But it won't do you any good, because I've got more money behind me than Huntington has. This road is more than a threat, Duff. We're going to lay tracks across the Sierras! The main difference between my road and yours is that I'll have supplies to build it with."

Johnny's brain began to function again. "How far do you think you can get," he asked, "when we hold the franchise to build the Pacific railway?"

Daggett lighted a cigar. "The Pacific railway," he said deliberately, "really doesn't concern me. I'm building the Nevada and Oregon. It will run from Virginia City, by way of the Johnson Pass, to Sacramento, and on up to Portland. Probably a branch line to San Francisco. Strangely enough, most of the money for it has been guaranteed by the Dutch Flat men I mentioned. It seems that they have some grievance or other against you. . . ." He smiled.

Johnny did not need a blueprint. Dutch Flat, thirty miles east of end of track, was calling the Central Pacific the "Dutch Flat Swindle". Judah, at one time, had thought of taking the railroad through the lusty gold camp. On the strength of that preliminary line, hotels went up, land boomed, a new stage line was put through from the southern camps. Dutch Flat had never got over the blow of having the stakes finally driven two miles south of Main Street.

"Naturally"—Daggett shrugged—"if we complete our road first, it will kill the Central's reason for existence. So I imagine it will be the Nevada and Oregon that finally connects with the U.P. Johnny," he said suddenly, his eyes animated in the strong, deeply rutted face, "the Big Four are wrecked. But you aren't. I need an engineer, a man who knows the stakes in this country. You're the man. And, by God, I'll pay you more money than you've ever seen, if you'll jump the fence into my pasture."

Johnny stood. His eyes made no lies about how he felt; they were dark with anger at the silver king. For two years he had been standing over this relic of Theodore Judah, daring anyone to meddle with it, and he had not done it by pulling punches. He said: "I'll make you a bet, Daggett. That a year from now nobody will remember the name of the Nevada and Oregon Railroad except some busted stockholders. And that I get those supplies out of the harbor in three days."

Daggett rose as he went to the door. His eyes looked dry and old, and there was a humorless scrape in his voice. "You're a damned young fool, Duff. But you'll be a lot older and wiser if you touch those supplies!"

Johnny walked the foggy streets, angry and upset. He wasn't selling Daggett short. Daggett had millions behind him, his own fortune and the gold money of Dutch Flat. He had a plan that might stand the test of the courts. The idea of building a railroad over 300 or 400 miles of the roughest terrain in the country was fantastic, but it might serve as legal armor from behind which to fight the C.P. If Daggett could keep them tied up long enough, he might gain an advantage they could never overcome, or he might break the company completely. Those supplies had to move, not next month, but now. . . .

Johnny's boast had been made in anger, yet behind it was the skeleton of an idea. One thread of his mind went back to the days he and Theodore Judah had spent in San Francisco while the engineer canvassed every bank, and every lending house in the city for backing. Not a dime of loose money was ever found; it was after this that he moved up to Sacramento and found the Big Four.

Weary, heart-breaking days, but what Johnny was remembering of them was an old ferryboat captain who Judah had almost persuaded to sell out and invest in the Central. He had never even known his last name; everybody called him Captain Harry. Yankee caution had finally kept Captain Harry at the helm of his ferryboat. Yet Johnny recalled how sorely tempted he had been. The fires in Captain Harry were banked, but they were still fires. Johnny walked back to the hotel, wondering if Captain Harry were still tromping the wheel of his ferryboat.

In the morning, Johnny went down to the waterfront and found Captain Harry's Trans-Bay Ferry slip, facing the green, feminine hills of Oakland across a blue reach of water. He paid a quarter and boarded. He passed down the long passenger saloon, which with its walnut pews and stained-glass windows was almost like a church. There was the deep pound of walking-beam engines under the flooring.

He found the captain in the pilot house, reading a red-plush Bible. Captain Harry had not forgotten him. He greeted him warmly. "Well, my boy! Didn't think I'd ever be seeing you again, once those mountains swallowed you."

He had some kind words for Mr. Judah. He had the admiration of one individualist for another. " 'That man,' I told myself, 'will shake California from one end to the other!' " he said. "I wish I could have been in it with you. But you understand . . . ?" He glanced at Johnny. He was a gray-bearded, easy-going giant with fingers the size of sausages, trimly uniformed in blue and brass.

"Sure," Johnny said. He stood at an open window.

A bell jingled. Captain Harry said: "If you'll close the window, John, we'll be starting. That harbor breeze has been honed on icebergs."

The *Marina* nosed out into the bay. In the sapphire embrace of the harbor, ferries turned white shavings from the water, and ships under half canvas glided alongshore. Captain Harry, whose boast was that he had read the Bible eleven times, not skipping the "begats", began to sing a hymn.

**We shall come rejoicing
Bringing in the sheaves! Bringing in the sheaves!**

Johnny decided it was as good a time as any to get his foot in the door. "How would you like to bring in some sheaves of gold, Captain?" he inquired.

"That's a riddle," Captain Harry declared.

"Captain," Johnny said frankly, "I'm in a corner. I'm trying to build that railroad, and somebody is trying to keep me from doing it. That's not according to the Book, is it?"

The captain suggested that he explain. Johnny told him the story. He concluded: "So Jim Daggett has us where all we've got left is a franchise and a payroll. But what would prevent a boat like yours, say, from taking a contract from the Central to carry materiel to Sacramento?"

Captain Harry chuckled. "That's the nicest thing anybody ever said about the old *Marina* . . . that she was fit for the river traffic! But I'm afraid she isn't. She was used for a while on the San Joaquin, but she disgraced herself with her own sluggishness. That's how I got her."

"She could carry light loads, couldn't she?" Johnny insisted. "Captain, I'll see that you make a thousand a month if you'll freight for me!"

Captain Harry's mild blue eyes turned on him. He removed his leather-visored cap and, smoothing down his hair, replaced it. He pondered it. At last he said: "Suppose we see the master of the *Jamaica* tonight about unloading in my slip. Sometimes I've thought I went into dry dock too early, anyway."

VIII

That was the first move in a gambit that brought the *Jamaica* into a ferry slip two nights later. Benches had been removed from the ferryboat and the parquet flooring covered with planks. Tons of iron and a mountain of powder kegs were mounted inside the waiting shed. It took all night and the next morning to unload the schooner, but only four hours to load onto the *Marina* what she could carry. Still, Johnny figured, three or four loads a week would keep the railroad moving until they hit easier going, where the supplies would have to come fast.

He had one more thing to take care of before he returned to camp. He visited a jeweler's and departed poorer by $120, but richer by a modest engagement ring.

Captain Harry hired a river pilot, having only a harbor license himself. At dawn the next day he double-gonged steam into the cylinders, and the overburdened little ex-ferryboat backed out and straightened up for Sacramento. He and Johnny stood at the windows as she plowed up the bay, watching the red disk of the sun come up behind the hills. The boat gained way slowly. Out in the bay, fishing boats were already moving.

After a few minutes Johnny saw the pilot turn to study the boat's wake. He turned back to the wheel. "Boat followin', Cap'n," he said. He was a Roman-nosed young fellow with a brown imperial.

Captain Harry opened a rear window for better vision. From the wheelhouse, the view was a broad one, the lowest deck lying far below, the harbor flecked with whitecaps, open on all sides. A few hundred feet astern, another boat rode

235

their wake. Captain Harry pulled at his chin whiskers.

"Do you reckon we can outrun her?"

The pilot shifted on his high stool. "And us loaded?" he said. "That's the *A. J. Miller* . . . Inland Steamship Company."

So then Johnny knew what they were in for. He watched the other boat eat up their lead until they could see every detail of her white-and-crystal gingerbread superstructure. She was running light, with no passengers to be seen, and only a few crewmen. Her big side-wheels turned strongly, pulling up blue water and pouring back white foam.

"If this was my boat, Captain," said the pilot mildly, "I'd go back. We ain't going to float very long, ever we get stove in."

Johnny stood watching the *A. J. Miller* close in. He felt a lot less gay than he had an hour ago. Captain Harry had the profits, probably, of his whole lifetime in this boat. He said what he had to: "It was a good idea, anyway. But we'd better put her about, Captain. Jim Daggett means business."

The boat lurched gently as the pilot began to spoke off. But the captain hauled the big walnut wheel back. "Did I say anything about going back, mister?" he thundered. "We're still going to Sacramento." He rang ferociously for more steam.

The stub prow thrust a little more ambitiously against the choppy waves. Without effort, the *A. J. Miller* absorbed this slight difference of speed. Then, surprisingly, she began to swing off to starboard, as though making for the Contra Costa shore. They watched her come abreast, far out, then abruptly turn and come back on a course that would bring her into the narrows abreast of the *Marina*.

Captain Harry studied the situation. "She's got right of way, now. If we honor her, she can herd us all over the harbor. If we don't, she'll ram us."

The pilot sat there, sullenly keeping the boat on her course. "I ain't losing my license on your account, Captain," he stated.

The captain's hand pulled him rudely off the stool. "You'll find smellin'-salts in the ladies' lounge, Brown."

The door slammed. Johnny heard the captain mutter: "Sickly, cigarette-suckin', fresh-water sailors! Ten of 'em wouldn't buy one deep-water man!" He took the wheel himself.

Under his collar, Johnny felt the skin roughen. They were coming to the point of the wedge now; the *A. J. Miller* had complete control of the situation.

Then Captain Harry exclaimed: "Thunderation!" He yanked at a whistle pull. The boat's hoarse belly tones went across the water repeatedly. "Distress signal." He grinned. "She's *got* to give way. I may hear from the Commission, but I'll lay odds she won't get past us again if I ever get the lead in the narrows!"

Then Johnny saw steam lift in morning pink puffs from the *A. J. Miller*. She was close enough now that he could see the men at the pilot house windows, and the gingerbread paneling of her side-wheel paddle boxes. The deep pedal notes of her whistle reached them. As Captain Harry listened, the exhilaration left his eyes.

"She . . . ain't giving way," he said. "I believe she intends to ram us."

They watched the riverboat bear closer, her superstructure looming prodigiously over them. She was running with five feet more freeboard than the overloaded *Marina*. That gave her the power to walk up on the ferryboat's deck, sending green water rolling into the boiler room, throwing down her cargo. Johnny thought of those tons of rails beginning to slide.

There was fascination in the way the *A. J. Miller*'s big side-wheel buckets pulled through the water, raising a snowy cataract. The blue of the water, the pink of the sky, and the big steamboat moving between them—it was all very beautiful, but very deadly to any small boat in her way.

Suddenly Johnny straightened. It was a fantastic idea, but so was the situation. He yelled at the captain, as he ran for the door: "Bear off a little! Give me two minutes!"

Down on the freight deck the rousters were standing in an anxious huddle. He put them to work, two men to operate the steam loading boom, and eight others to run out a rail and slide it through a chain crotch line. The loading boom took up the slack. He had the rail swung beyond the guardrail and lowered to water level.

Across them came the shadow of the *A. J. Miller*. She was crowding them off to larboard, her lead secure. Captain Harry hung on the whistle; steam plumed straight up the side of the stack from its brassy mouth. Johnny could see the riverboat's master in the pilot house, far above them, a big, laughing man.

He signaled the men on the loading-boom. "Let 'er go!"

The boom began to swing. The rail, lagging on the crotch line, caught up swiftly, swinging in like a battering ram. Up there in the wheelhouse, the master had stopped laughing, and another face was pressed against the glass for a moment. The rail went into the paddle box like an arrow. The buckets caught the end of it and pointed it at the sky; for a moment the wheel stopped. A paddle tore loose, and the wheel moved again, stutteringly, rolling a few degrees through its circle and halting once more to try to bend the rail.

But it couldn't be done. The paddles swore to that, snapping off like decayed teeth. The pitmans added grinding testimony. Somewhere in the belly of the boat a cylinder head blew off with a shattering report. The *A. J. Miller*'s other engine kept the starboard wheel churning, sending the boat into a slow pinwheel. Her prow struck the *Marina* and slid down her bull rail, then the little ferryboat shook loose and went, pitching and rolling, on up the bay.

The rousters yelled and pounded each other. Johnny ran above and found Captain Harry calmly standing his trick at the big walnut wheel. Looking back, he could see the *A. J. Miller*, motionless now, rocking helplessly on the *Marina*'s wake. San Pablo Bay opened before them. They plowed victoriously toward the narrows.

"I'm not sure, John," Captain Harry said, "that that was according to the Book. But I *did* sound the distress signal. And, by George, it was nip and tuck for a while, wasn't it?"

He began to laugh, his shoulders shaking. "A Sacramento River boat whipped by a ferryboat! They'll laugh the *A. J. Miller*'s captain out of every bar in town. You might call Mister Brown back. I don't think his scruples should bother him now."

Later, as he went by the texas, Johnny heard Captain Harry's voice piously raised in "Old Hundredth". He fancied he also heard the *pop* of a cork.

They reached the Sacramento wharves in time to have the boat unloaded before dark. The Central Pacific storage yard was empty of all but a block-long rank of redwood ties, and a few tons of spikes and fastenings. A line of flats was kicked out on the spur to rush an emergency ration of powder and iron to end of track.

That night Johnny slept on the boat. In the morning he introduced Captain Harry to Collis Huntington, and a contract was drawn up. Huntington agreed to lend whatever was necessary for the acquisition of other boats. The captain did not seem worried about future trouble.

"We're inside the law," he said. "But if Daggett still wants to play rough . . . well, gentlemen, I didn't turn back when the breezes blew off the Horn."

Johnny caught the supply train for end of track an hour later. There was a kind of singing in him. He had met Daggett on his own ground and won the first tilt. Most of all, he had stolen the anonymity that would have been worth so much to the miner who dreamed of a railroad empire. If trouble came again, they would know where to look for the cause.

At Rocklin, another engine was coupled on for the drag up the hill. New locomotives of the John Conness type, 460s, had been ordered, but all the hauling was still done by coupling up locomotives of every wheel arrangement ever known to the California railroads to a combination able to handle the load. They were tough, resplendent little engines, richly endowed with brass—brass steam dome, brass sand boxes, steam chests, and cylinders—but the power in two driving wheels, or even four, was quickly sapped at Barmore Grade, the first pull of the line.

He rode in the cab, where it was warm and a man's clothes wouldn't catch fire from cinders. They boomed across Newcastle trestle and found end of track half a mile beyond. There were springs in Johnny's heels as he legged it up the line toward the camp train. He had some bragging to do to Ed, and he didn't mind if Babbie were around, too. He had the feeling he always had when he was absent from the road, and from her, for a while—that coming-home feeling.

He pounded on the door, and Ed yelled: "Well, don't knock it down, dammit!" Ed was lacing his boots when he entered. The storm had brought a quantity of mud into the car, which Babbie's broom, surprisingly, had not yet molested. The interior was cold, only a small fire crackling in the cook stove. Babbie was, apparently, still in her room.

Johnny straddled a chair. Ed straightened up to look at him. "I don't need to ask if you ate the canary," he grunted. "You've got feathers all over you."

"Got our iron, got our powder!" Johnny declared. "And I got in a couple of Sunday punches, too." He bounced up and told about it while he walked up and down the car, wondering if Babbie were listening behind the door. All at once he stopped. On the cot where Ed slept was piled a lot of gear that he recognized. It was his own. He glanced around; Ed was standing there with a forced smile on his face.

"I took the liberty, Superintendent," he said, "of havin' your damned gear moved over here yesterday. I got to worrying about you catching the scurvy or something in that flea bag of yours."

Johnny was puzzled. Ed's smile seemed to tremble a little; only his mouth took part in the whimsy. His eyes looked haunted.

"Why . . . that's swell," Johnny said. "But what about . . . ?" He jerked his head toward Babbie's door.

"Don't worry about that," Ed said, and his mouth suddenly gave up the attempt to be funny. "You see, Babbie. . . ." He cleared his throat and bent to resume his boot lacing. "Babbie's leaving today, Johnny. For good."

IX

Johnny sat down. It was like a stiff blow over the heart. There were no words in him, nothing but shock.

Babbie's door opened, and she came out. She had her hair up, with a red bandanna knotted Creole-fashion about her head. Her sleeves were rolled to the elbows. "You won't need the alarm clock, will you?" she asked Ed. "As long as there's a whistle in camp, they won't let you oversleep." Then she saw Johnny. "Hello!" she said. "I didn't hear you come in."

"What's this about you leaving?" Johnny asked, with false heartiness.

"Didn't Pop tell you?" She took the clock off the shelf over the stove, and her fingertip discovered grease on the nickel. "Well, do you remember that theatrical outfit that rented a boxcar for a week last winter, when the floods caught them? Garrett's Golden State Entertainers? They stopped overnight the same day you left. Can you believe it? Mister Garrett wants me to sing with them . . . for fifty dollars a week!"

Yes, Johnny could believe it. He could believe anything wonderful of Babbie. And of course there wasn't another girl in California with a voice like hers. But until his heart quieted down, he couldn't accept it. "So you're really going," he said.

"Am I going!" Babbie gave the interior of the car an appraisal that would have been considered good theater almost anywhere. "I'm meeting them at Grass Valley tonight. I'll have a couple of weeks to rehearse before the summer tour of the Lode starts."

Johnny sat with his hands in his pockets; his gaze found its way to the mud and roadside litter beyond the door. Except for a smile he kept pinned to his mouth, he looked as sunk as he felt. "Just for the summer?" he said.

"Not unless they fire me," Babbie declared cheerfully.

"Fifty a week," Ed said in a slow, rough voice. "And I'll eat railroad spikes for breakfast if you aren't back in three months, kissin' the rails! You don't get the iron out of your blood just by changing your address."

"What if you never had it in your blood?" Babbie retorted carelessly.

No one spoke, then. The noises of the construction camp seemed suddenly intensified—the shouting of teamsters down at the creek, the racket from the mess car, a blacksmith's hammer ringing—noises essentially masculine.

"Miss this hullabaloo?" Babbie said. "Miss never getting the dirt out of my house, and having train smoke ruin my wash, and . . . ?"

Ed held up his hand. "The defense rests."

Babbie whirled back into the bedroom, and Johnny had flashes of her moving between dresser and closet and trunk. Ed got up and took his coat off the hook. But just as they were going out, Babbie's voice called after them:

"Oh, Johnny! Will you have them hold the supply train a few minutes? I'll try to be there as soon as they finish unloading."

During the work, Johnny fumbled numbly about. When it was over, he told the engineer to hold the train, and went to get Babbie. And then, from somewhere, there came back to him the certainty he had had the night before he left for San Francisco—that all the time he had been mooning around, she had been waiting for him—that part of her dissatisfaction stemmed from impatience. Well, that was giving himself credit for being pretty much of a lady-killer. But Johnny suddenly knew he was not going to retire that ring to storage without giving it a chance first.

Ed was just leaving the car when he approached. Ed saw him, turned quickly, and walked the other way. Poor old Ed, thought Johnny. It must be as tough for him, in a way, as it was for himself. But maybe he'd have good news for him.

Babbie's trunk was just inside the door. He got it on his back and staggered down to the caboose of the supply train. Then he went back, to find her coming down the steps. "Better let me carry you," he said. "You'll have mud up to your eyeballs."

In his arms she was light and warm. She was quiet, but he sensed an inner disturbance. His arms ached, not with the burden, but with wanting to crush her to him before 3,000 Chinamen and a couple of locomotives. He deposited her on the platform of the crummy. He gave the engineer the highball.

Babbie reached her hand down to him, her eyes suddenly moist. "Johnny, you've been grand. . . ."

Johnny swung onto the platform as the couplings crashed down the line to the caboose, and the train slowly started. He looked into the caboose. It was empty. He turned and took possession of her hands. Her eyes were puzzled.

"If you're wondering if I've gone crazy," he said, "you're right. I've been a little crazy ever since you and Ed came to the job."

Her eyes searched his face. He had never seen her so serious. And then she gave a little laugh, a laugh with reproof in it. "Johnny Duff," she said, "you aren't going to propose!"

Johnny fished the ring out of his watch pocket. "I've carried this thing two hundred miles. And at that, I almost didn't get to use it." He felt his grin slipping. He couldn't be gay about it. "Babbie, you know what I'm trying to say . . . I'd have said it months ago, only . . . well, I didn't think there was any use until that night after I got mussed up at Hedenburg's. What I'm trying to say is. . . ."

The caboose, to have its say in the matter, gave a lurch that banged them together. It was the easiest thing in the world for Johnny to bring her into his arms. He had his arm around her waist, slender and supple as a willow branch; he had his hand behind her head, his fingers in her hair, and his lips were on hers. She did not resist; he thought a tremble went through her. Then she pushed him away, a little bit breathlessly.

"Why, Johnny, I'm surprised!" she scolded. "And you a married man!"

Johnny stared.

"Well, if you aren't married," Babbie conceded, "you're as good as married. You've already got a fiancée, and her name is Railroad. A girl might as well be married to a switch engine as to a man in love with the iron."

The platform under Johnny was tottering. Things were not working out. He said desperately: "Maybe I let Cuvillie fool me. But I thought you were pretty worried that night. . . ."

"Of course I was worried," Babbie said. "Why not? You're the kind a girl likes to worry about. Nice, and quiet, and . . . well, *almost* good-looking. A girl could be more than just worried about you, too, but you see, Johnny, I've been careful. I knew what it would come to if I ever did let myself become interested. Because with men like you and Pop, there's no compromise."

It meant everything, the question Johnny was going to ask, and Johnny's eyes were grave. "Would there have to be a compromise? Don't you think things might look different to you, if . . . ?"

"I don't think," Babbie said gently, "that the road could ever look any different to me. I'm all through with shanty cars, and melted butter in the summer, and frozen potatoes in the winter. I'm going to be civilized. I'm going to wear slippers, instead of brogans. I'm going to see flowers in my front yard instead of piles of ties." She squeezed his hand. "Johnny, can't you see why I want them? Because every woman has a right to the kind of life she wants. And mine isn't here."

The hell of it was that Johnny could. And Babbie knew it. Her eyes told him that. She folded his fingers over the ring. "If we'd met anywhere but on the railroad," she said. "But we didn't, darling. So there's nothing to argue about, is there?"

Johnny put the ring in his pocket. "You talk better sense than any girl I ever knew," he admitted. "But it's the first time I've ever wished a girl would talk as crazy as I've been!" He said: "Good luck, Babbie. We'll be looking for you once in a while."

The train was limping over unsettled track. From the bottom step, he jumped onto the neat apron of new ballast. He waved, and turned, and under the cold gray ceiling of mist started up the tracks. . . .

He got through those first few days as a man gets through anything he has to. He groped, searching in his work for a foundation for his spirit, and not finding it. What he could never get out of his head, what kept him eternally out of step, was the idea that he had somehow muffed it. If he could have accepted it, could have believed what she had said about not letting herself become interested, it might have been easier. But he kept thinking: *It's a test. She's making me decide between her and the road.*

Well, hadn't he decided? He couldn't give up the iron. That was as sure now as it had ever been. Yet somehow hope kept the place for him, like a slip of paper in a book he intended to reopen sometime. But if it were a test, he soon realized it was a real one. By the end of spring, she had not come back. Two months of the ninety days Ed had given her were two-thirds gone. They had letters from Downieville, from You Bet, from Nevada City. She was thrilled about her work. Mr. Garrett promised to take her to San Francisco when the troupe went back for the winter season. But not a word about the railroad. In his heart, Johnny began at last to doubt.

But with the road things began to pick up. Captain Harry bought another boat and hired a tough crew to man it. Supplies were moving again. And yet Johnny could never forget Silver Jim Daggett. He never shook the feeling that a fuse was burning somewhere.

With sweat, black powder, and more sweat, the powder gang finally blasted through Bloomer Hill to release the logjam of materiel piling up behind it. The grading camp was already far ahead of the main work camp. Now Johnny whipped his tie-and-rail crews through the cut.

Summer heat was upon them. The white laborers grew dark and gaunt. The Chinese worked on as cheerfully as ever, stopping frequently to take sips of lukewarm tea from kegs along the right of way. Johnny thanked the gods for them. They were peaceable and hard-working, healthier than the white workers because they did not try to live on a diet of starches. Their little cooking pots were filled with dried oysters, cuttlefish, bamboo sprouts, and seaweed.

In July the railroad made contact with the stage road at Auburn, beside the ashes of Hedenburg's store. Now at last they had punched a hole to tap the rich traffic of the gold fields. From all the towns and camps of the district, miners and their freight poured down the stage road to the temporary station at Auburn, to finish the trip into Sacramento in parlor cars.

A few days later they had word from the marshal at Auburn, that Tim McKewen had broken jail. The trouble at

Bloomer Cut seemed so far behind that at first the name had no meaning for Johnny. Then he remembered the telegrapher who had been a party to the dynamiting in which two workmen had died. McKewen had made his escape just two weeks before he was to hang. Johnny was vaguely disturbed, but the following week he had enough grief to make him forget McKewen.

All at once they were in the mountains, and everything that had gone before seemed like a pleasant dream that would not come again. The scarps soared breathtakingly before them; pine forests and manzanita thickets deepened. Wood-cutters went ahead to hack a path through tangles of red-and-green manzanita. They opened an aisle a tall man could not see over. Their bucksaws and axes sang in the pine and fir woods.

These were mountains to keep lamps burning half the night in the engineering car. Granite studded the blood-red piles of earth that went up to rock-fanged ridges. Dry Creek Valley, Clipper Gap, Wildcat Summit—they fought these battles and won them. Behind end of track was a gigantic rubbish of deserted sawmills and the trash of broken camps.

Then one day Digory Huling came down from the camp at Bear River Gap, where the first tunnel of the route was being blasted through 500 feet of gray rock. He was almost in tears.

"Them chinks, Mester Duff!" he wailed. "Hit's fair driving me to my grave! Buggered drills by the case. They'll drill a two-foot 'ole and try to set a charge! I'll stand up fer 'em in the open air, but hin a tunnel they're worthless."

Johnny went up to the camp with him. He knew Digory was right; hard-rock men was what they needed for the tunnels, but Huntington insisted they could not afford a crew of experienced miners.

They reached Bear River Gap in an hour, a high notch in one of the flinty ridges north of the American River. It was far too lofty for tracks to be laid through it.

Judah had specified a 500-foot tunnel as the only solution. Digory had a crew at each side of the ridge, working toward a meeting at the center. Johnny called together the men who spoke English. To them, he outlined a plan by which a man might earn up to a half dollar a day in extra pay; he added that, as another feature of the plan, they would pay for time lost retrieving broken drills. But the half dollar got them. They went back to work.

Digory took his crew to the north tunnel. Johnny decided to stay today and watch the result of his plan. He gave the men time to have drilled a six-foot hole twice. Then he went past the gang of muckers, chattering among empty powder kegs at the adit of the tunnel to see how the charge was being set. Two Chinese were rolling powder in newspapers for insertion into the breast hole. Johnny tested the hole with the tamper. It was about three feet deep.

He put them back to work: two men to doublejack, one to relieve the man on the sledge. They had been singlejacking before, work and rest, work and rest. Now the hole went twice as fast.

He set the charge himself. The muckers were still seated at the mouth of the tunnel, smoking and talking. "Clear those men out," he told one of the workmen.

Without warning, one of the muckers leaped from the keg on which he had been sitting. Johnny did not understand the words he screamed, but he did know the language of smoke and flame, which were emanating from the keg he had been sitting on. In a kind of paralysis, he saw the muckers scramble from the tunnel. He heard the pressure in the keg build up to a hiss.

X

Johnny looked into the haggish face of terror. He stood there, watching a geyser of flame mount to the ceiling, hearing the rush of imprisoned gases. The keg had not apparently been empty, after all. A spark from one of the pipes had ignited the powder. It was 100 feet from where he stood to the adit. It was an inch to death.

A dense cloud of smoke blotted out the daylight. It swirled toward him, a bright fog shot through with flame. He began to run. He fell, cutting his hands and knees on the stones. He went on in a scrambling crawl until he realized what he was doing and got to his feet again.

The pressure in the keg was now a screaming force that tried every seam. The smoke, choking him with its sulphurous hands, enclosed him. He flung himself past the searing heat of the powder keg. He fell on the ground, and a small pajama-clad shape darted out to drag him from the tunnel.

They ran up the hillside into the pines, waiting for the blast that might destroy the work of many days. Johnny dropped, his head hanging forward and his arms splayed back to support him, getting his breath. The air was hot, but it was clean, and bright and free.

Smoke continued to billow from the tunnel, but the blast did not come. At last they knew that the heat had burst the top from the keg and allowed the powder to burn without exploding. But Johnny was still trembling.

He hunted up Digory. "You can hop the stage any time you want," he declared, "and bring back a crew of Cousin Jacks. I'll fight it out with Huntington when the payroll goes

250

in. These would-be powder-monkeys are going back to the tie gang."

He went back to camp. Ed, working out the alignment of a curve while track layers waited, laughed when he saw him, black with smoke.

"Somebody give you a trick cigar?"

"Somebody gave me a trick powder gang." Johnny told him what had taken place. Then his attention was caught by a clerk approaching with a yellow telegraph flimsy, and he waited. But the man handed the message to Ed.

"Just came in, Mister Carney."

Ed's brows pulled in as he read it. "Now, what the hell!"

"Funny one, ain't it?" the clerk agreed. "Johnson said he thought the tap was familiar, but he couldn't place it. No station letters, either."

Ed hesitated a moment, then shoved it into his pocket. "All right. Thanks." Then he glanced at Johnny and walked slowly toward the camp train. He handed him the message. Johnny read it.

Some things is worth more than railroads, Carney. If you got anything particular you don't want to lose, better find another job.

Ed was growling: "Somebody must have tapped the line somewhere. What the hell do you suppose it means?"

Johnny's mind was away ahead, in an ugly country that frightened him. *If you got anything particular you don't want to lose.* . . . He was thinking about Babbie, singing in the rough towns of the Mother Lode, where anything might happen. It might mean nothing, but again. . . .

He said: "Remember Tim McKewen? He was a telegrapher. And Johnson thought the hand was familiar."

Ed's lips clamped together for a moment. "Yes, but why? What would it buy him? Or do you suppose somebody else . . . ?"

"That's what I was wondering." Johnny was asking himself if Silver Jim Daggett had somehow acquired McKewen. The Irishman was enough of a drunk to do anything for a little money. But somehow he couldn't believe that even a pirate of finance like Daggett would resort to such measures as this to cripple a competitor. Yet Daggett must know that the loss of Ed Carney, the best mountain engineer in the country, would hit the Central Pacific hard.

All at once it came to him that the answers to all his questions might be within riding distance. If McKewen had sent the message between here and Auburn, he must have left tracks somewhere.

"I suppose," Ed remarked, "they think they can scare me out by threatening to put a slug in me. Hell! If I thought my life was worth a dime, I wouldn't be building railroads for a living."

Johnny stared at him. Could he really be that simple? Did he think the gun was pointed at him, rather than at Babbie? So much the better if he did. And Johnny fostered the illusion by saying: "I reckon that's it, Ed. You'd better send it down to the marshal, anyway, just to keep him posted."

He went to the wash trough, sluiced away the powder smudges and dirt, and a few minutes later jogged out of camp with his rifle in the boot.

He followed the line of cross-arm poles beside the newly laid track. The sun was hot against his face, slanting toward the rugged western horizon. In this country there was only a brief twilight; the sun went down, and darkness flowed in. He gave himself two hours of trailing before sunset. He had gone about three miles when he noticed a suspicious congress of boot prints at the base of one of the poles on the bank of a ravine.

Looking up, he could see where the wire had been scraped to provide a good connection for another wire. It was from here, then, that the message had been dispatched. On this spot, McKewen or some other telegrapher had knelt to tap out the message with a portable key.

Finding the horse tracks was not hard. They started below the grade and followed a zigzag path to the bed of a dry stream, then struck roughly southeast. It was rough, brushy riding. He crossed a couple of low gaps and, at last lifted to a high notch, saw the broad gorge of the American River south of him. The terrain was suddenly familiar. He turned to squint northward.

Three miles away, over the tumbled hills, he saw the dust haze of end of track. He was following a course at an angle of about twenty degrees to that of the railroad.

The trail took him down to the gorge of the river. Presently he lost the sun. Coolness flowed down the mountainside, and darkness began to gather in the many side ravines. On rises, he stopped occasionally to study the trail. Far ahead, abruptly, he saw dust. He put the horse to a lope, but the turnings of the trail gave up no glimpse of a rider.

The vast lonely cañon of the American was strongly in his memory. He knew every landmark before it came in sight. Giant piles of stones, taken from the river by miners working the river gravel ten years ago, stood like monuments of an ancient race. Ahead, mounting a precipitous half mile from the riverbed to the sky by a series of bluffs, was a black granite buttress Judah had nicknamed Cape Horn. It followed the curve of the American for a half mile, a rugged, inhospitable block of stone.

Johnny remembered how for months they had fought

against the fact that tracks must be spiked in some fashion to the broken face of the Cape, a thin thread of steel 1,500 feet above the river. But at last Judah was forced to accept it as part of the route. There was no other passage that did not lead into a blind alley. It would be the toughest part of the entire route, he had prophesied.

Johnny rode beneath the bluff, tensely alert. The foot of it was immersed in twilight, the timbered cap ruddy with the last glory of the sun. He brought the bit back, suddenly, to sit listening. A scrape of shod hoofs came from only a few hundred yards ahead. A horse that, by the sounds, was moving fast.

The buckskin could travel when called upon. Johnny spurred it to a lope, his carbine warding off the slap of willow branches. The trail cut to the left, between two great boulders, and it was here that a lash of gun flame from a brush thicket sent a ball whistling down the trail.

XI

The bullet exploded against the boulder at Johnny's right. It screamed across the trail and caromed again from the other rock. For a second the pass was a place of wild echoes and the expansive thunder of the gun. The horse began to pitch. Johnny blew both stirrups. He landed, sitting. He scrambled up swiftly and made a lunge for a trailing rein. He got it in his left hand and fired the carbine with his right as the stallion began to drag him. It was purely a defensive shot. But a moment later he heard the other rider strike on up the trail.

He was forced to drop the gun to hold the horse. After he got it under control, he began to work back to where the gun lay in the dirt. It seemed as though he had not breathed since the shot came. He picked up the carbine, shoved a new paper cartridge into the chamber, a cap over the nipple, and waited. Above him, a horse ran brokenly up the switchback trail that swung from the American, with Cape Horn behind, to ascend Robber's Ravine.

He remounted. He had his choice, now, of riding into another ambuscade or of turning back. He didn't like suicide patrols any better than any other man. But the prize ahead was worth some risk, and the thought that, if the man got away, it might eventually mean danger to Babbie, sent him stiffly up the trail. His hands felt clumsy, the stock of the gun unfamiliar. He went at a walk, so that he could tell by sound the instant the other horse stopped.

But the horse did not stop until, far above, Johnny saw a hoof spark where the trail topped onto the mesa. Just for a moment he had the vision of a man humped across the withers of a tired horse, looking back, and he cautiously held his own horse, until the cut-out picture against the rusty-green sky, just merging into night, disappeared.

He rode another half mile, the trail breaking sharply back and forth as it carried him to the same spot where he had last seen the other rider. Now he dismounted and left the horse tied to a manzanita. He went ahead on foot.

In the middle of the trail, he stopped. He wondered if he had got twisted somehow and circled back to camp. For below him, on the sloping tableland, glowed the flames of a dozen supper fires. By the piles of materiel, it was unmistakably a railroad camp.

He was too shocked to move. Here, less than ten miles from end of track, was another camp—another end of track—pointing *west!* Building to meet the Central Pacific!

Overhead, the sky was black, frosty stars beginning to prick through the velvet. He could see nothing but what was delineated by the glow of the campfires. He reckoned, by Central Pacific standards, that this number of group messes indicated about 400 men. Not a large camp. But how in the name of railroading had it been brought this close without their knowing it? What about the blasting?

He had to look at the raw ends of the rails out there on the flat, risk or not. He started ahead. He could hear men talking and laughing. He smelled wood smoke and coffee on the air. Suddenly the trail came into a wide, smooth path, free of boulders: the grade. A second look showed him it could not possibly be. The ground here was lower than that on both sides of it. Not far ahead, however, the low mole of a true grade began.

Then he knew. The old Dutch Flat-Johnson Pass freight road was being converted into some kind of a railroad—the Lord knew how! If he could see the rails they were using, he might be able to understand how it was being done. So he went on, step by step, until he saw ties ranked evenly before him, and another fifty feet beyond, the end of the day's track. He knelt to examine it. It was narrow gauge—hardly wider than a mine railway.

Johnny slowly straightened up, understanding it all now. A cheap, jerrybuilt line was being laid down with no idea of ever running a locomotive over it. A railroad built for the sole purpose of getting a prior claim on Cape Horn!

Then, from the weary day's end murmur of the camp, a nearer voice went up like a skyrocket: "Ben! By God . . . if that don't look like. . . ."

A pile of ties had half hidden a tent twenty-five feet to his right. He saw two men standing at the flap of it. One of them snapped a rifle to his shoulder. The other, drawing a revolver, ran toward him where he stood rigidly in the middle of the grade.

Johnny fired at the first man and broke for the brush.

XII

What had been a lazy, day's end murmur over the camp died completely. Then the air hummed with startled men springing from the fires, as the reaction from the shot took hold. Men shouted questioningly into the darkness. A few moved uncertainly toward Hedenburg's tent.

Johnny figured it was about 300 yards to his horse. Whether or not he reached it before someone sent a shot down the path was doubtful. It was a chance he could not take. He hit the brush.

This was one of the sections where the manzanita grew so thickly a horseman could not get three feet off the trail. A man afoot could bull through the mesh of polished red branches if he were willing to leave some of his hide hanging on every third twig. He could crawl, rend the fragrant latticework with his bare hands, force openings with his arms over his head. This was how Johnny started into the brush. He had a dozen deep scratches before he had gone twenty feet. The misguided energy of the camp was being channeled toward him by the shouts of big Ben Hedenburg. There was no confusing the sutler's voice with any other in California. It was deep as the booming of a drum, as imperative as artillery. Johnny found no paradox in his presence. The link between him and Silver Jim Daggett was as natural as it had been invisible. Daggett had been the prime mover behind Hedenburg's store. And Johnny was asking himself if Daggett and Hedenburg were giving protection to Tim McKewen in return for value received?

His plan was to swing into Robber's Ravine, to strike the

258

streambed and work back to the horse. The very fury of the pursuit was the best weapon he had, for the hounds were making ten times the noise of the hare. When he stopped, he heard men forcing through the thicket behind him and at both sides. He had a clutch of apprehension. It was time to bear off to the left, to the ravine, but if he veered that way just now, there was every chance he would run into one or more of the hunters. Yet if he went much deeper into the thicket, he would be hopelessly lost. He decided to cut for the ravine and take his chances.

Sounds behind him melted into the general uproar of the search, but those between him and the ravine became suddenly imminent. He crashed ahead a few feet and listened, moved on again, and again listened. He was moving to a junction with one of the searchers, yet to try to hang back would place him in jeopardy from the rear. In this dry jungle he was slowly being caught in a noose.

Suddenly he was conscious of the crashing of brush at his left. A moment later the manzanita stirred and a burly shape shoved through. Johnny waited. The man had a revolver in one hand, and with the other he wrenched back the last branch separating them. Johnny leaped on him.

He had the man's gun wrist solidly in his grip. He swung the barrel of the carbine against the round-domed hat and felt it strike the man's skull. He slapped his palm over the slack mouth, but only a sound like a snore came as the man went down. Johnny stepped across him and struck out for the ravine.

The confusion of yells and snapping brush faded. Under his feet the ground began to tilt. Then the manzanita thinned, and he was sliding down a rough bank serried with rain gullies. Part way down, he swung left, downcañon, running and sliding until he emerged into the main trail. It was only another 100 yards to his horse, but, as he ran toward it, he heard men coming over the crest.

He saw their bodies come into profile in the notch. He snapped the carbine to his shoulder; the shot hammered the ground near them. They fell back, fighting each other to get the crest of the hill between themselves and the gunman they could not see.

Johnny ran on, vaulted to the saddle, and wheeled down the trail. He kept the animal at a lope until the trail flattened out beside the river. Then he stopped, listening. But over the whispering of the river he heard no sounds of pursuit.

He jogged along, reloading the carbine, thinking about Daggett and Hedenburg, and about Tim McKewen, who was a crack brass pounder, but whose key said all the wrong things. There was nothing he could hang on Daggett except the crime of harboring a criminal, but that would be enough, if he could prove it. It meant searching the Nevada and Oregon camp in the morning for McKewen. He looked forward to that.

He hoped Daggett's outfit would try to shield him, for it would be a lever by which the Big Four's lawyers might be able to pry Daggett loose from his hold on the Horn. Unless some strategic weapon were put into Johnny's hands soon, it was obvious that the fight ahead would be won by the man who could throw the most men into the battle.

Ed was already worrying when Johnny reached camp. Johnny ate lightly, talking it out with him. It was, Ed declared warmly, their best break in months. If they could find McKewen in camp, they would finally have legal ammunition for their guns.

Very early they started for the Nevada and Oregon camp. They took six riding bosses with them. This time Johnny followed the mesa road, instead of dropping down into the cañon of the American as he had the night before. It was the half-graded trail the railroad itself would follow.

Between Bear River Gap and the Horn, farmers had done much of the grading for them. The grade flanked orchards and small farms, ran along easy hillsides and jumped many small ravines by fills. It marched through the raw new village of Colfax that had sprung up on the promise of railroad trade; it teetered along the edge of Rice's Ravine for a half mile, and then went into the tightest turn of the route, a full half turn across the cañon, striking the other side to double back along a steep hillside that became more and more precipitous until, suddenly breaking back, it terminated in the dominating cap of granite called Cape Horn.

Here the grade camp was stalled, while engineers made final tests of the type of geologic structure they were about to tackle. Johnny cut left from the grade onto the mesa, detouring around the Horn. They struck the freight road.

After a mile they sighted the Nevada and Oregon camp. In the hot and dusty morning, redolent of heated brush, they rode on into the full clamor of the work.

Ties had been bucked to end of track and beyond; rail setters were laying down iron to a riding boss' cadence. In the daylight, the whole thing looked more like a railroad than it had the night before. It differed chiefly from the Central in being narrow gauge. Johnny was surprised to see, flanked by stacks of materiel in the dingy city of tents, a panting work engine.

The riding foreman spotted them and came from the welter of workmen to them. Even before he reached them, Johnny knew it was Ben Hedenburg. The tall sutler raised a hand as he pulled up. He had a grin for Johnny. "Been a long time, Duff," he remarked. "I heard you're building a railroad, too, over there."

Hedenburg's eyes were the only semblance of coolness about him, pale gray, with heavy, dark brows. His brown face was streaked with sweat, rutting the dust, and his buckskin shirt showed dark patches around the armpits, and a damp margin rising from his belt. He was an essentially ugly man, yet Johnny saw a crude magnificence about him, the physical impressiveness of the Horn itself.

Johnny ignored his thrust. He demanded bluntly: "Where's McKewen?"

"McKewen?" Hedenburg repeated, and then he smiled. "Duff," he said, "it seems like I can't get far enough away that you don't come a-manhunting. What makes you think I've got McKewen?"

"I had an idea," Johnny told him, "that he was one of the boys whacking the brush for me last night."

Hedenburg leaned on the broad Mexican horn of his saddle. "You didn't have to be so damned cagey last night." He chuckled. "What do you expect when you come sneaking in on your belly? After McKewen told me who you were, I had the boys hold their fire. I still wanted to know what the hell you were doing."

"You couldn't guess, when you saw McKewen?"

Hedenburg gave him a slow, studying glance. "If you're here about Tim," he declared, "you'd better talk to Daggett. He's in the crummy."

They watched him ride back to where freight wagons were taking loads from the supply train.

Ed and Johnny glanced at each other. Daggett—up here! Impatiently Johnny put his horse through the work gangs, to draw rein at the platform of the caboose. Daggett appeared at the rail after a moment. He was in shirt sleeves, a cigar in his mouth, and a derby on the back of his head. All the signs of the mining king were gone—the diamond stickpin and the

$300 suits—and yet he was still Silver Jim Daggett, the man who bragged that he worked hell out of his miners and made them love it. He wore laced boots and work clothes, and his jaws had not seen a razor in several days. His air was as confident, as commanding as ever.

"Light down, boys," he invited. "There's whiskey in the car, and nothing but sun out here."

Johnny put his business shortly: "Have you got Tim McKewen?"

Daggett tapped his cigar against the brake wheel. He looked at them as he drew on it. "He's inside," he said.

It startled Johnny, but not enough to keep him from swinging down and mounting the steps of the caboose. Ed followed, after a word to the others. The rear portion of the car was fitted as an office. There was a desk, a letterpress, chairs. Beyond a partition, ranks of bunks in a windowless corridor could be seen. Daggett took a bottle and three crockery cups out of a cupboard.

"Ben sent word down last night that he'd caught him," he said. "I came up from Randall on the supply train."

Ed snorted. "You mean you can run a train on these streaks of rust?"

Daggett set the bottle down. "Excuse the California crockery, gentlemen. McKewen's in the bunk room."

Johnny entered the gloomy, sweat-and-tobacco-steeped sleeping section. None of the bunks was made, but in one of them a man lay huddled. Even though he knew McKewen must be tied, Johnny nevertheless felt a small shiver of apprehension as he went toward this man who had once cheated a hang rope, who had been desperate enough last night to attempt another murder to make good his escape.

He prodded him with the barrel of his Colt. "We're taking you back, mister."

McKewen did not turn over. Johnny waited, and then, wondering if the man were gagged, he reached down and touched his face. His hand recoiled. Tim McKewen was as cold as stone.

XIII

Johnny went back and took up the drink Daggett had poured. He drank it in one tilt. "Was that a joke?" he asked. "He's dead as a mackerel."

Daggett shrugged. "Does it matter? The posters read 'Dead or Alive'. He wanted Ben to hide him again after you made your break. Ben told him to go to hell. He already lost one saloon trying to shield that mick. He tried to throw down on Ben, and Ben let him have it." He poured Johnny another drink. His hand was rock-steady.

It chilled Johnny a little, for he knew Daggett had used McKewen as he would have used any other property he owned, discarding it as soon as it was useless to him. "What about the telegram?" he asked, watching Daggett's eyes as he put the question.

Daggett regarded him steadily. "Talking to you," he said, "is like playing poker. What's it going to cost me to get you to turn that card over?"

The cold vanity of his manner began to get under Johnny's hide. "I'm going to turn over a lot of cards in the next few weeks," he snapped, "and they're going to cost you exactly what you've put into your road. You made a brag once about some supplies in San Francisco Bay. I stuffed that one down your throat, and I'm going to do the same thing with another."

"Is there a law against building a railroad?" Daggett asked.

"Let's not talk about laws. We're making our own. Our lawyers could chew it over for three years, but, by the time they were through, one of us would have a railroad and one would have a fortune in rust. You can build from here to Alaska if it pleases you, Daggett. But don't try to build around the Horn. That's C.P. property."

"As a matter of fact," said Jim Daggett, "that's just where I am going to build. It's the only possible route, and I'm taking it."

"And when you get through with it," Ed stated, "we'll move those rails a little farther apart and take them into the family."

Suddenly Daggett smiled. "We're talking like schoolboys, aren't we? If I wanted to boast, I could tell you that I've got half of Dutch Flat ready to back me up, that I can write a bigger check than a lot of banks can cover, and that I've already got blueprints for what I'm going to do to Cape Horn. Nothing makes more noise than the rustle of a dollar bill. And I'm going to rustle a million of them right under your nose . . . cash!" He pointed a finger at Johnny. "You can take this down to Huntington, mister. Jim Daggett will put up a million in gold for fifty-one percent of his stock . . . tomorrow, next week, any time!"

Johnny was unimpressed. "We've laid out two and a half million already," he told Daggett. "The surest way to cover that investment is to keep on talking like a schoolboy. If you don't think I mean what I've said, just keep on following the stakes to Cape Horn."

He went past Ed, the violent leaven of fury in him. Ed followed him, looking somehow let-down.

Jim Daggett was on the platform of the caboose as they mounted. When they wheeled past him, he said pleasantly: "Then I'll see you on Cape Horn, boys. So long."

If Johnny Duff had not been convinced of it before, he was now persuaded that Daggett meant to stand up against anything the Big Four could throw at him. Perhaps in the beginning it had been bluff; by tying up their supplies, he had hoped to buy into the company and force a route change. Now the picture was darkening. The privilege of pressure was his. He could force them to take the initiative or stall them indefinitely. He could rally scores of miners to his standard—men who had money in his fight. Johnny, because he hadn't the wages to pay a complete crew of white men, counted a few dozen experienced railroaders, forty Cousin Jacks, and his army of Chinese who knew and cared about no more of fighting than they found in a brisk game of fan-tan.

There was only one way to break the Nevada and Oregon's blockade—to strike before it was finished. He thought about it all the way back. When they reached camp, he had mapped what he knew would be the last campaign of the war. Theodore Judah had said it would take months to build across the Horn. Johnny Duff was going to try to do it in weeks.

End of track was only a quarter mile short of the Bear River Gap tunnel. Johnny moved Digory and half his Cornishmen from the almost completed tunnel up to the Horn. He amassed a working force of 400 men, wired Auburn to double the daily powder ration, and put every freight wagon in camp to hauling the tools of road making over the gap and on to the grade camp at Cape Horn. Ed was not enthusiastic about the possibility of crossing the Horn with even a foot trail before Jim Daggett reached it. "All he needs is a ledge a hundred feet long, and we're licked."

Test holes were shot. Digory brought back the good word that the bluff might give less trouble than they had expected. The black granite formation broke easily into blocks and ledges. Johnny hastily made up a dozen gangs to work ahead of the main camp. From the cliff top he had them lowered in bos'n's chairs down the precipitous face of the cliff. Hanging there like spiders, they drilled and tamped and set off charges that could not otherwise have been reached in days.

Through that week the roar of black powder went out over the vast cañon of the American River; dust and rock spouted to the sky, and, when it settled, muckers swarmed in and shoveled the débris over the cliff. Ed, growing thin and brown and tired, laid track through Bear River Gap tunnel, and in four days brought the iron on to the end of the grade.

Ed's temper wasn't improving any with the heat and tension. He didn't like the way the alignment engineers were tackling a brow of granite that shoved out fifteen feet beyond the cliff face. He complained to Johnny while the Cousin Jacks set a charge.

"Daggett be damned! We've got to run trains on this outfit someday. They're undercutting my lines to where we'll have to jack the rails up on stilts. Nothing's going to run on this road but a train with rubber couplings."

Then suddenly Johnny's glance, caught by a flash of color down the line, transmitted the incredible intelligence that they were about to have a lady visitor. His heart squeezed down and then seemed to swell until it filled his whole chest, for what woman in California but Babbie could walk through those sweating work gangs with the grace and pride of a girl entering a ballroom?

A foreman named Clancy walked with her, red-faced and self-conscious. He said—"Somebody to see you, Mister Carney."—bobbed his head to Babbie, and disappeared.

Ed turned quickly. Like Johnny, he couldn't do anything but stare. Was this the girl who had come to womanhood in the rough school of the railroad? This girl with a silk parasol over her shoulder, with a blue gown fitted to a miraculous waist and the breathtaking swell of her bosom? It was Babbie's smile and laugh—that was sure.

"Well, you two! Aren't you going to ask me to come in and set a spell?"

Ed had her in his arms, his cheek against hers, crushing her until she gasped. With a grin, he released her and looked at her. "You're no daughter of the iron!" he declared. "For shame! Splurgin' about looking like a bit of Dresden china!"

"Cornstarch and curlers," Babbie said, "can make the ugly duckling look like a peacock." And she made a little self-conscious gesture of touching her hair. It was more than that, Johnny thought hazily. Modiste and hairdresser had had their part in the transformation, but the real glory was still Babbie's. The little things—the tilt of her chin, the sparkle of her eyes—these were the things you meant when you said Babbie; the silk parasol, the fancy hair-do were fluff.

"It took a flood," he recalled, "to bring Garrett's Golden State Entertainers to us before. What act of God do we thank for this?"

"You can thank the fact that we're playing Dutch Flat tomorrow night." Babbie smiled. "The stage is waiting for me over at the road. Naturally I couldn't go by without stopping." She looked at him with sudden, almost flattering candor. "You're brown as an Indian, Johnny. You're even beginning to look like a railroad man."

"According to Huntington," said Johnny, "the resemblance ends right there." He reached to take her parasol with one hand and examine it minutely. "You know," he told Ed, "if we fitted the boys out with these things, we might be able to keep a crew."

"Laugh all you want," Babbie defended. "But I can't sing 'The Lass with the Delicate Air' and not look the part." Off in the distance a stage horn blared twice. "Somebody's getting restless," Babbie said. "I wish I could have let you know we were coming up here, but it was pretty sudden. I'll see you both at the show, won't I?"

She did not wait for an answer. She pecked Ed on the cheek and squeezed Johnny's hand at the same time, and the next moment, except for a tiny trace of perfume in the warm air, it was just as though she had been a daydream he had had.

They were slow to get back to reality. Johnny was still breathless and tingling. He had thought a protective coating was forming around the ache in him, like an oyster with a grain of sand. But what he was carrying around in his heart did not feel like a pearl, but a chunk of rusty iron. At last he knew how far Babbie had come since she had left the road. She had the luxuries she had always yearned for. She was being paid to do the thing she liked best. Johnny Duff sighed, and felt as forgotten as the caboose at the end of a forty-car string.

Finally Ed broke the spell by hitching up his pants. "Well, this ain't getting any spikes pounded," he growled.

Digory came up with a roll of fuse over his shoulder. " 'Old your 'ats!" he said tersely. He stood, eyes squinted, as they awaited the shot.

The blast came, a deep, slow jolt through the hill. Smoke and dust burst from the cliff, a gray cloud for the breeze to turn and tear. Ragged blocks of granite tumbled slowly through the long, twisting fall to the river. A section boss brought a clean-up gang forward. Johnny and Ed followed the rattling carts.

The black powder had torn out a good chunk of rock. Barrows and carts began transporting the rubble to the cliff edge. Ed spoke to Digory.

"Let's have the next one right alongside that. A few more of those will bring us back in line."

Digory looked up. Slowly his jaw loosened.

Johnny's gaze was on Digory's face, so that the first warning he had of disaster was when the Cornishman started back involuntarily. He saw his features twist, and then the yell came: "Look out! The whole domned cliff's a-comin' down!"

The countenance of the cliff, as Johnny glanced aloft, was altering. Cracks appeared; dust pattered down in rivulets. The whole terrifying mass was slowly toppling forward.

Suddenly men were screaming, stumbling, running. A boulder landed with jarring force in the middle of the grade. Johnny saw a Chinese blindly roll his wheelbarrow off the cliff, fight for balance, and fall, shrieking.

XIV

In that instant, with the scream of the workman still in the air, he was able to stand there and look about him. He was the only man on the ground who did not appear to have a plan. Some ran a race with the rockslide, betting they could move 100 feet in three seconds, but most of them crowded against the face of the cut, hands warding off the shale that rattled down upon them.

Just before the cliff was obscured in swirling veils of dust, one thing became clear. There was only one place on the ledge that would not, in five seconds, be covered with broken rock, and that was the boot hole left by the blast.

Ed was gone, vanished somewhere. Johnny scrambled through the race of rock fragments ricocheting from the foot of the bank. The boot hole was a shallow cave about as deep as a saucer. He threw himself against the wall, flattening to its contour. He heard the mass of the slide roar down upon the roadbed and the men still trying to get clear of it. A thick, choking dust shut him in. Rocks were pelting him, but they were only the inner cataract of the slide. The voice of the avalanche was something he felt in his belly, a jarring roar that shook him.

Suddenly it was over. A few more small boulders thudded onto the talus of wrecked granite. Then silence and horror claimed the field.

Almost the first thing Johnny heard when he climbed out and began searching along the wall, where men the cliff had protected were beginning to move, was Ed's voice: "This proves it, kid. The Lord meant us for railroad men."

Ed, with Digory and four others, was pinned against the

cliff by rubble up to his knees. But unlike the rest, the accident had marked him. His left arm hung awkwardly; blood was on him. His shirt was ripped away from a white, mangled shoulder, but he stood there patiently, as if afraid to try to move.

There were sounds of swearing, and down the tracks came Doc Cuvillie. He stopped to curse a gang of frightened Chinese; they stirred themselves and followed with shovels and crowbars.

Most of the large boulders had spilled over the cliff. In an hour the job of digging out was finished. Four of the men did not need Cuvillie's diagnosis to draw blankets instead of bandages. Of seven others, most had severe injuries. Ed was lucky; his collar bone was broken, and he had a bad cut on the shoulder, but he would be able to walk the grade without assistance.

Cuvillie, convinced that every accident on the job happened mainly to inconvenience him personally, sourly gave Ed his orders.

"Bed for a week. No work for ten days. And if I catch you riding a horse before a month, you can damn' well doctor yourself." He stamped out.

Ed closed his eyes. Cuvillie's drugs had not quite obliterated the pain. "Fill me a pipe, Johnny," he murmured.

Johnny loaded his pipe and lighted it. Ed drew on the warm smoke. "Listen," he said, "if Babbie hears about this, somebody around here is going to have his ears cut off. You're still going up there, but you aren't going to tell her about the cave-in. Got that?"

"She's not a kid, Ed," Johnny grunted. "Any alibi I give her will be wasted breath."

Ed puffed on the pipe. "Tell her," he said, "that I had to go to Sacramento on business. That's logical, ain't it?"

"About as logical as that you overate and didn't feel like making the ride."

"Just the same," Ed insisted, "you're going to try. She's having the time of her life. If she quit to take care of me, they might not take her back. How do you think I'd feel if. . . ." He made an impatient gesture with the pipe, and then bit down on the stem of it.

Johnny stood up. "OK, old-timer. I'll say my piece, but don't blame me if I come back with her trunk behind the saddle."

So it was Johnny who rode into Dutch Flat at sundown the following day. The town was a raw-boned settlement of hastily constructed frame buildings and a few red-brick structures thrown along crooked hillside streets. Summer dust was a foot deep. The miners breathed it with the air; they ate it with their food.

Placards posted before Odd Fellows' Hall advertised the entertainment. There was already a line, although it was an hour before the show was to start. Johnny had a steak at a short-order house, and walked down to the hall fifteen minutes before curtain time.

The theater was full of Nevada and Oregon workers, brought over in wagons for the entertainment. Johnny's glance picked out big Ben Hedenburg. He had ceased to worry about Tim McKewen's threat, however, now that McKewen was dead. He did not think that Daggett, if the idea had been his, would care to pursue it further.

A piano began to work through the raucous audience noises. The split curtain jerked open a few feet, and a lank, hungry-looking individual in a brown frock coat and buff trousers appeared. He stood there with a stovepipe hat held carelessly in his hand.

In a stagey baritone he introduced himself and his

troupe—Walter Garrett, no less, who hoped their poor offerings would please. The curtains parted, and a long minstrel act got under way. But none of the jokes alleviated the queasiness of Johnny's stomach.

Then a new poster was placed on the tripod: **Miss Barbara Bly. Ballads Old and New.**

Johnny felt as though he had evaporated, all but his eyes and his pulse. Miss Bly was attired in a gown of robin's-egg blue, from which a sprinkling of sequins threw back the glare of coal-oil footlights. Her accompanist sat at a weathered piano, the same lean, lank-haired man who had opened the show.

Miss Bly sang in a light voice, a golden voice, an unspoiled voice. She sang easily, but never with great volume, so that the house was hushed to every note. Someone called for "Annie Laurie", and a lump came into Johnny's throat. She used to sing it in the evenings, when wood smoke made the early darkness fragrant, and all the harsh sounds of railroading were stilled. The song carried him back; it was a sharp wrench to hear her voice die away. She sang two more numbers, and then a couple of black-face comedians came on. But for Johnny the show was over.

Afterward, he went backstage. Babbie let him into her dressing room, modestly leaving the door open. Seated before a cracked mirror, she removed the stage make-up that had almost shocked Johnny when he saw her up close. He felt a little backwash of relief as she wiped the last of it off and applied just a suspicion of color to her lips and cheeks.

"You were great, Babbie," he told her. "Some change from singing for a couple of hundred rust-eaters, isn't it?"

"It's a change, all right. I'm not sure it's so much better." She arranged her gown carefully in the top of the trunk. "The main difference is that I get paid for it. But when they pay, they get the idea, sometimes, that they've bought the right to make cat-calls, too."

The mere notion of it whipped the blood hotly to Johnny's head. "Anybody make any cat-calls tonight?"

Babbie smiled. "Thanks just the same, Johnny. I don't need a champion, really. I just stop singing and stare at them, and they stop. Anyway, it's a great life for a tumbleweed. I haven't slept three nights in the same town since I left the railroad." Suddenly she straightened from the trunk. "Where in the world is Pop? Didn't he come up?"

Johnny didn't trust his eyes. He began stuffing tobacco into his pipe. "Ed sent his best. Danged if he didn't get a wire to go to Sacramento this morning."

Babbie's eyes continued to search his face. She came over and took him by the ears so that he had to look at her. "Pop's sick!" she said.

Johnny sighed. "I told him it was no use trying to alibi for him. The fact is, we had a little rock slide just after you left. Nothing to get excited about. Only he had a collar bone broken, and he'll have to take it easy for a few days."

Babbie closed her eyes; two tears squeezed through. "Poor Pop! Every time it's something . . . a broken arm or a twisted ankle . . . just so he won't forget he's working on a railroad." She added: "Can you get a wagon to take me and my trunk over?"

"That," Johnny declared, "is just what I'm *not* going to do. Ed's all right! He made me lie for him, because he knew you'd throw over your job and come down to cry over the body. Cuvillie's going to let him get up in a week, anyway.

"Then who's going to do for him while his shoulder's still out of whack?"

Johnny held her hands. "Can't you see it, Babbie? The last thing he wants is for you to come back to the iron, feeling the way you do. Give him a break. You'll only make him feel like an old woman."

Babbie's chin lifted. "You talk such a good case I wonder whether it's you or Pop that's afraid I'll come back. . . ."

"It's both of us," Johnny said grimly. "I'm still trying to stay on the iron standard. And having you around scrambles my values."

She said something strange then. She said, on a kind of sigh: "That's nice, Johnny. That's like having a poem dedicated to you. You're somebody special, even if you are a railroad man. Maybe, if I could scramble your values completely, we'd both be happier . . . but right now I want you to carry my trunk out and get a wagon."

She pushed him out of the room. Johnny's mind was wildly pulling petals as he went in search of a horse and wagon. When he came back, he heard her talking with Walter Garrett in the back of the hall. Apparently there was some unpleasantness over her leaving.

"I don't know why we had to come down here, anyway!" Garrett was storming. "There weren't enough towns where we were? We had to travel seventy-five miles just to play this misbegotten offscraping of the Mother Lode!"

"I just thought," Babbie said quietly, "that we'd have some good houses over here."

Garrett said slyly: "And perhaps you just thought you might see your young friend of the railroad, eh?"

"What young friend . . . Mister Garrett?" Babbie asked.

"*What* young friend! Young woman, when someone your age subscribes to all the Sacramento newspapers to see how many miles of track a certain railroad has laid each week, it is a safe guess that she is not particularly interested in traffic receipts."

"It happens," Babbie declared sharply, "that my father is

building the railroad. Or at least helping." She added: "I'll try to join you at Nevada City next week. If I'm not there, you'd better not wait."

Walter Garrett declaimed in his heaviest stage voice: "Be assured, Miss Carney, we shall not!"

XV

Johnny moved his gear from the chief engineer's car back to his musty boxcar. It was not entirely a happy transaction, exchanging the bright if rumpled shanty car for the windowless gloom of his own quarters, but in his own heart there burned a small lamp that had almost gone out. He had built up quite a case for himself. Maybe she wouldn't leave again. Maybe, if she stayed around long enough, the ring he had bought in San Francisco would be disinterred from its velvet casket.

But in the morning, when the yellow sun sliced every furtive shred of romanticism from the camp, he realized how puny was the evidence on which his case had been built: a girl's subscribing to a newspaper! Maybe she liked to read the ads. His common sense dismissed the case for lack of evidence.

He was busy all morning. At noon he dropped in on Ed. The car was foggy with dust. Babbie, her hair up in a bandanna, sleeves to her elbows, was making war with broom and dustpan. The magic odors of mulligan stew were in the air. Johnny did not cavil when Babbie said casually: "You might as well stay for dinner. You may set the table, if you want."

After dinner he talked to Ed. "I'm riding up to get a line on Daggett," he said. "Take your eyes off him for five minutes, and he's putting a frog down your neck."

Babbie removed her apron. "I'll go with you," she announced. "I want to see just what makes this Cape Horn proposition so tough."

At the corral, Johnny saddled his horse and selected a

279

pony for Babbie. She ran down the path presently in denim pants with turned-up cuffs, and a plaid shirt. In the rude glare of the sunlight, Johnny saw that the months away from the road had stolen her tan. But in a way, it made her all the prettier. There was certainly nothing wrong, to his mind, with gray eyes and red lips set off by fair skin.

They followed the work road along the curving cap of the cliff. A summer day haze softened the sharpness of objects at the bottom of the cañon. Babbie stopped once and pointed down. "How are you going to cross that side ravine?"

"A bridge, temporarily," Johnny told her. "Then we'll fill with rock."

After they started on, she said: "It seems as though you ought to be working on it, then. You'll catch up and have to wait on the B and B outfit."

"Maybe you're right," Johnny said. But when he glanced at her with a shade of amusement, she was looking straight ahead.

From a hogback they could see that the Nevada and Oregon had brought its rails over the crest of the mesa. A trestle was being thrown up to bridge Robber's Ravine. At the near end, timbers were being set in the hillside that, a mile farther on, swung into Cape Horn. Babbie scanned it through his binoculars. She did not comment when she returned them.

Halfway back, she declared suddenly: "You know you can't do it, don't you?"

Johnny stared at her. "If you mean shut him out," he retorted, "we can, and we're going to."

Her eyes regarded him coolly. "You can build across Cape Horn, Johnny, because you can do anything you really set out to. I wouldn't call it genius, exactly. It seems to have more to do with butting your head against the bricks until they fall.

But you're going to fight Jim Daggett pretty soon . . . not a mountain. And I don't see any blueprints for *that* fight."

"What do you want . . . the Horse Marines?"

"Daggett is exactly the same kind you are . . . that's the trouble. He's about as easy to reason with as a badger. His answer to your refusal to cut him in on the Central was to stop you cold. And I don't see that you've offered him much of an answer."

"I'll do my debating the next time we meet."

"Sure," Babbie sniffed, "you'll steamroller right over him. But the fact is that he has five hundred white workmen to your hundred and fifty. And don't expect the Chinese to go to war for you."

"We'll bore that tunnel when we come to it," Johnny declared grumpily.

Babbie gave him an amused glance. She had maneuvered him into a corner, and she knew it. It was something Johnny hadn't let himself worry about, but nevertheless it had been there at the back of his mind, fretting him. He could conceive of only one kind of argument with Daggett next time—a head-on collision. There was a prize-fighter's axiom to the effect that a good big man could always lick a good little man. Johnny Duff knew that when time was called for this showdown fight, he was the one who would come out of the little man's corner.

The stubborn fiber of the Horn gave them a few feet a day. They could scheme and plan, but when a charge was shot, no amount of oil burned in the engineering cars would make the boot hole any larger. Behind end of track mounted a vast pile of materiel. The moral rot of inactivity invaded the boarding cars. Liquor was being smuggled in; gambling became the heaviest work that ninety percent of the men indulged in.

Fights were constant. Every check showed another dozen white workers missing, as the quartz and hydraulic mines drew off disgusted workmen.

But there was work now only for the powder men and a handful of muckers. For a while Johnny kept the others busy clearing brush and stacking supplies. Then these jobs petered out, and there was nothing to do but pay them to vegetate.

Often, now, they could hear the blasting from Daggett's camp. In a week he was attacking Cape Horn itself. The trail his graders cut was barely wide enough even for his narrow-gauge track, but it was wide enough to establish a claim. Between the two sweating armies of railroad workers there now lay a quarter mile of granite.

Among the engineers and foremen there was little talk. They knew what was ahead, and Johnny knew they were trying to decide whether or not to stick. But of his worries, this was the least. If they were worth the name of railroad men, they would stay with the road to which they had sworn allegiance. So Johnny did not worry. But one morning he had a rude surprise from the Chinese side of the camp.

You could be around Orientals for years and never quite understand them. Language itself threw a smoke screen around them. It was staggering to stare across the tracks that morning and discover the long aisles of gray canvas tents deserted. . . .

A riding boss brought the first word. Not a man of his gang had shown up! When he rode over to hunt them, he discovered only a few score Chinese drifting around. 1,500 workmen had deserted during the night! Johnny rounded up the others and grilled them. An interpreter told the story.

A big man with a black beard had appeared the night before from the Nevada and Oregon camp, telling a story of $50 a month wages—pay whether a man was sick or well, short hours, easy work, and money could be drawn every night, if a man desired. During the night, silently, they packed their small belongings and departed. The ones who stayed with the Central were either old, sick, or lazy, content with their $35 as long as they did not have to work for it.

In a sort of mental paralysis, Johnny walked back and told Ed and Babbie.

"There goes our railroad," Ed groaned.

Johnny was thinking away back, remembering a man who had entrusted a dream to him. He had tried to keep that dream bright, but somehow the tarnish had come, and now you could hardly see the dream for the blunders he had made. Where had he failed? He did not know. He had failed only in not being equal to the trust.

There was not even the satisfaction of thinking that the road would still be built, even if the C.P. didn't build it. Jim Daggett was a schemer, not a builder. He would build for what there was in it for him, and in the road he planned to construct, across the impossible Johnson Pass route, there was only ruin.

Babbie had deserted her dishes. "Well, what's the answer?" she demanded.

Johnny looked at her, not resentfully, but wearily. "You make a guess. I've been guessing wrong ever since Judah died."

She looked astounded. "You're not giving up!"

"All I know about railroad building," said Johnny, "is that you keep on laying ties until you connect somewhere, and somebody tells you you're finished. As long as I've got my Cousin Jacks, I'm still in the railroad business."

For a girl who hated railroading, Babbie Carney betrayed violent agitation. She walked back to the sink and dried another dish, and then threw the towel down. "I don't know why you can't hike over there and hire them back! You can *promise* sixty a month, can't you, even if the Big Four don't approve it?"

"But we can't pay them every night the way Daggett can," Ed pointed out.

"But for a week or two! That's all it will be, isn't it?"

Johnny shook his head. "Even for a week."

Babbie turned away without answering.

Johnny left. He heard her voice through the window: "This place is like a graveyard. I wish somebody'd set off a charge or something. . . ."

Presently she came after him. "I thought you might saddle a horse for me," she said. "I'll go crazy sitting around here, if I don't get away for a while."

They walked to the horse corral. "You can always go back to Garrett," Johnny remarked. "Come to think of it, your time's about up with him anyway, isn't it?

"I'm through with Garrett. Traveling around like that is fun for a while, but I'll go down to San Francisco when I'm ready to go back. And Pop isn't really able to do for himself yet, anyway."

Johnny cut out a pony for her. Babbie walked over to a tool shed, and, just as he was finishing, she returned with a shovel and an iron skillet. She colored under his frowning stare.

"Well, I might as well be panning gravel as doing nothing," she defended. "The miners say you can still make five dollars a day almost anywhere with a shovel and a pan. It's only an hour down to the river."

Johnny watched her ride off, with an uneasy feeling that he had been given, if not an alibi, at least a half-truth.

The day lagged. The few remaining Chinese were put to work mucking. The white men, all of them specialists, lay in the shade, smoked in the cars, drifted off toward Colfax to the saloons. It was mid-afternoon when Babbie came back, but, when she returned, there was not a man in camp who did not know about it.

They could hear the horse running up the grade, and then, as she pulled in, the cry went up and down the line.

"Gold, Johnny! Gold! The river's full of it! I panned that much in an hour!" She held up a small bottle that had once held vanilla extract, but which was now a quarter full of what, even at a glance, was obviously coarse gold.

XVI

The sleepy boarding cars began to disgorge wild-eyed Irishmen. The sixty or seventy Chinese still in camp ran insanely about, hunting shovels and pans, screaming the news. In five minutes a trail of blue-pajamaed workmen was streaming up over the hill toward the river trail.

Cornishmen were running back to learn what had happened. At the tool sheds, white workers fought over picks and shovels. And Johnny Duff caught the bottle of gold dust Babbie tossed him and ran his fingers through his hair. He looked at it, then he frowned and stared at her.

The gold was about two-thirds sand. The color was too coppery to be pure gold.

Then he felt Babbie's grip on his arm. "Stop them, Johnny!" she cried. "Let the Chinese go, but stop the white men! With a gun if you have to . . . !"

Johnny was too sandbagged to move.

"Don't you see?" Babbie whispered. "I filed some old jewelry up and mixed it with sand. We had to steal Daggett's men somehow! Those men will pass within a quarter of a mile of the Nevada and Oregon camp on the way to the river. Daggett won't have a dozen men by tonight. But we've got to see that *we* do!"

Johnny was looking at Babbie, but he was seeing through her, and beyond her. He was seeing a chance to regain what he had thought was lost, and he knew that Babbie had given it to him.

He caught her with an arm about her waist; he felt her body yield. But in this moment there was nothing to say, nothing to do but hold her tightly, her face against his neck, and not ask himself how much of what he saw in her eyes was true, but to accept it.

The urgency of the moment brought him back. He released her, and, as he hesitated, she pushed him toward the boarding cars. "Go build that railroad, Johnny!" she said.

Johnny did not fool himself that anything but force would stop these men who were on their way, so they thought, to riches. The first man to reach the corral, shovels at shoulders and pots, pans, and skillets banging, found him seated on the large stone beside the gate. "What's the hurry, boys?" he asked mildly.

Clancy, the rail foreman, eyed his carbine. They all stopped behind him. Clancy growled: "There's enough for all of us, Super'ntendent. But if we don't highball it, them chinks is going to stake out everything in sight."

Johnny shook his head. "The truth of it, Clancy, is that there isn't enough for any of us. That was a mean trick of Miss Carney's. But I'll defend the intention." He threw the bottle at Clancy's feet. "That's the gold she panned, boys."

Clancy stared at him, picked up the bottle, and poured the contents on his palm. His thumb and forefinger tested it. Then he gaped at the others. "Sand and filin's!" he grunted. "And not more'n ten-carat filin's at that. Duff," he said grimly, "I hope there's a good reason for this. It'd be the first time I ever quit a construction job if there ain't."

Then Johnny told them—them and the others beginning to collect about the corral. He told about Babbie's trick, and then he began to talk railroad—and there was nobody in California, now that Judah was dead, who could talk railroad like Johnny Duff. When he got through, when his dreams and his heartbreaks were reflected in the sentimental Irish faces, he drew himself up.

"So that's how it is, boys. Jim Daggett has lost the first hand in six months. You can help me rake in the blue chips if you're interested in saving the best damned railroad in the nation . . . and earning fifty dollars' bonus per man!"

Clancy glanced around at the others, and no heads shook. They shifted and cleared their throats, but in the awkward way of inarticulate men they waited for someone else to do the talking. Thus it fell upon Clancy to accept.

"It's plain what they'll be sayin'," he declared. "The Irish built the U.P., and the Chinese built the Central. But we're your men, Mister Duff."

It was decided to wait until dark.

As dusk merged into the big star-frosted mountain night, Johnny found himself in a fit of nerves. All the diffused forces of the last two years had suddenly become focused upon the hour ahead. He sat in the pallid filter of camp light coming through his door, wiping his carbine with a dry rag. Daggett might fight, or he might not. But Johnny was going prepared.

Someone approached the car. Ed said: "It's about time, Johnny!"

Johnny stood up. "Kind of rushed, aren't you, for somebody that's not going?"

"Who says I ain't? Clancy's saddling my horse right now."

"Babbie'll scalp you!"

"Don't let her fool you." Ed chuckled. "She sent me! I was a few months off on my guess, but she's back to stay. Maybe she don't know it yet, but she's been rearranging furniture and washin' curtains like a new bride. When she ain't doing that, she's standing in the door sniffin' the smoke like it was night-bloomin' jasmine!"

They walked down to the corral. Most of the horses were under saddle. The pipe smoke of half a hundred rust-eaters came to them from where the workmen sat on the hillside, waiting with pick helves, crowbars, and scantlings. Digory was on hand with his Cousin Jacks.

In the darkness the *creak* of twenty saddles was a warm and strong commotion. The men without horses made a great, hearty racket as they strung into line behind the riders, joking and swearing and throwing their weapons onto their shoulders. If he'd ever needed a testimonial that he was in the right trade, Johnny thought, he had it now. It was in the downright way these men accepted the fact that they would fight for him, simply because they were needed. When they hired their bodies to a railroad, they didn't lock their loyalty in a vault.

By the mesa trail it was a half mile to the Nevada and Oregon camp. The tents and stockpiles had been brought forward to the north side of Robber's Ravine. Just what he had expected, Johnny did not know, but the silence was what struck him as they drew near the camp. A yellow slice of moon gave just enough light to show the gaunt trestle bridging the ravine. They reached the tracks and peered down the converging streaks of iron to the camp 200 yards ahead, on the hillside. Not a pinprick of light showed.

He swung down. The others followed suit. They started cautiously ahead. Out of the darkness came the shapes of tie piles and long ranks of rails. A city of tents ascended the slope into darkness, but there were no supper fires tonight, no sounds of gabbling Chinese taking their evening meal.

Up the line a string of flatcars lay along the curve behind a narrow-gauge engine with its vast diamond stack, and, as they advanced, the soft glow of the firebox surged softly against the ballast. Something about it all was not right. The supply train should not be here at all, at night—with the piles of ties still unloaded.

Johnny turned back. He said: "Have your men start

tearing up rails, Clancy. We'll see what can be done with a few tons of powder."

Then, like the throb of a war drum, rifle fire broke from the flatcars.

The volley was shattering—a concerted crash of musketry that tore the silence raggedly, a hail of balled lead that funneled upon the small group on the tracks. Winking spurts of fire stuttered from the close-stacked ties, running the full length of the train.

For an instant Johnny's army was stricken with paralysis. Then with one motive the whole group broke, running, crawling to shelter. For most of them, that meant the brush. Others piled over the bank into the ravine. Johnny and Ed hit the brush. The fire kept up for half a minute, raking up and down the right of way, as, one after another, the flatcars came into action.

Through loops in the thick walls of ties, the Dutch Flat men, probably all the workmen Daggett had been able to save, laid down a fire that kept the unarmed Central Pacific men on the ground. Then the shooting stopped. They could hear a man groaning nearby.

Ed stood at Johnny's elbow. "How's it read now?" he asked.

Johnny clutched the carbine so tightly his knuckles ached. He knew he had not more than a dozen men with guns, and every one of those flatcars was a blockhouse to be stormed and taken.

Suddenly the flare from the firebox brightened. The locomotive puffed windily, and began to back down the tracks toward them, caboose first. Ed said hurriedly: "Mister, I don't know just what we thought we were going to do, but we're going to get the hell out of here!"

"No!" Johnny said it without knowing what he could offer

them, beyond the chance to be cut to pieces by Daggett's mobile fortresses. But he knew that he had been granted one night in which to achieve what he had failed to do in two years, and he was not throwing it away.

"They've got us, Johnny!" Ed argued. "It won't buy anything to have the boys hunted down like jack rabbits. Let's get out of here."

Johnny found it then—found it the way he had discovered escape from the alley that night in San Francisco. It was as though, maybe, Mr. Judah hadn't deserted his railroad after all, but was standing behind Johnny, whispering in his ear. And what he was talking about was so simple he chuckled. "Take charge of the platoon, corporal!" he said. "When that hog goes by, there isn't going to be much shooting done!"

He crowded out of the brush. In the darkness he ran up the line toward the train. Someone saw him, and a rifle roared. He heard the ball strike the ground behind him. A couple of guns farther up the line took up the hunt, but the cars were joggling too much for accuracy. Johnny had his eye on a pile of ties 100 feet ahead. The caboose of the train was almost even with it.

Before he won the safety of the stacked timbers, the shots were coming at him too closely for comfort. He got the ties between him and the tracks then. He moved to the far end of the stack and watched the caboose move past, then the slow procession of flats. He could see into the cab of the locomotive as it neared him. The fire door was open, and someone was throwing in chunk wood. The engineer was silhouetted at the door.

At the last second, Johnny walked to the track and caught the grab irons. He went into the cab with his carbine preceding him. The engineer was unarmed, but Johnny was in a hurry and in no mood to take chances. He planted a boot in the man's belly and watched him reel backward out the door. He took time to horse the throttle wide open. The fireman realized, as the drivers spun, what was going on. He whirled from the fire door. There was a gun stuck under his belt, and he drew it as he turned, and in the same instant Johnny knew it was Ben Hedenburg.

XVII

He shouted a warning, but Hedenburg's thumb was on the hammer of the Colt, and a savagery like madness was in the man's eyes. Johnny fired. Hedenburg faltered, but the hammer fell. The ball shattered the glass behind Johnny's head. Johnny closed with him, and knew again the horror he had known the night he was forced to shoot Kearns, in that musty little room in Hedenburg's saloon. For Hedenburg's body was loose and unresponding; he swayed against Johnny, beard rough against his face. Johnny twisted the gun out of his hand and thrust him away. Hedenburg backed off, teetering on the platform for a moment. Then one foot dropped down the step, throwing him off balance; he went down, his hands clutching flaccidly at the greasy wooden floor. All at once he sprawled away into the darkness.

The locomotive's drivers slipped on the new rails. Johnny shot her some sand. The cars began to gather speed. When they passed the brush where the men were hiding, the speed was a good twenty miles an hour. Under the wheels the track was rough, mined with blind sags that tried every bolt. Johnny heard shouts beyond the tender. He pulled down a tier of wood and began to heave it into the firebox.

The solid *click* of the rails altered. They boomed across the Robber's Ravine trestle and pounded out upon the mesa. There was a mile of nearly straight track, and then the long, winding fall to the cañon of the American River began. The little 404 was clicking off more knots than a narrow-gauge locomotive was ever designed to. Couplings yanked; the floor under Johnny's feet bounded. It was about time, he decided, to bail out. He found a maul in the tool box under the engineer's seat and put the throttle out of commission.

He heard wood sliding down the tender. He pivoted, and stopped dead. He had almost forgotten Silver Jim Daggett in the last few hectic minutes. But it was the Nevadan who stood on the buffer between the cars, fighting the sway. In the flare of the fire, his face was harshly shadowed, the channels that bracketed his mouth deeper than ever, his eyes older, narrow and dull. He carried a long-barreled Navy Colt in his hand.

Johnny's stomach muscles cramped under the scrutiny of that round black eye, for his carbine was empty, and it was a long reach to his revolver. He stood there, awaiting the impact of the slug. Instead, he heard Daggett's voice, over the clatter of the trucks:

"I've never killed a man before, Duff. But I will tonight, unless you throw down that gun and back out!"

Johnny dropped the gun and took a step back. He felt the Johnson bar prod his shoulder blades. Daggett came into the cab, and Johnny grinned. "I've been thinking it over, Daggett. Maybe I'll take that job you offered me, after all."

The grim line of Daggett's mouth said it wasn't funny. He made a quick gesture with the revolver. "I'm telling you to jump. I mean *now!*"

Johnny thought of a lot of things—of Babbie, of the heart-warming bustle of camp on a frosty morning, when the steam from the supply train was as pink as striped candy, of the masculine smells of wood smoke and freshly-graded earth—all things he loved, and didn't want to lose, but the next ten seconds might take them from him forever because what Daggett was asking was not what he intended to do.

Daggett's face contorted as Johnny continued to stand there; he was at the extreme of his nervous endurance. The gun barrel trembled.

Johnny's shoulder moved against the Johnson bar. A lot of things happened as the drivers tried to go into reverse. Wood thudded down in the tender. Daggett sprawled backward and sat down. Johnny was hurled across the car, where he struck the wall and fell. He was up again, scrambling after Daggett. Daggett, lying in the tumbled blocks of wood, fired as he came on. The bullet tugged at Johnny's coat.

In a battle like this, there were no such things as ethics. Johnny's boot connected with Daggett's jaw. The mining man fell back. Johnny took his gun and swung back to the controls, as Daggett fumbled about, half-conscious. Heavily he horsed the Johnson-bar over. The locomotive ceased shuddering and settled down to a gallop. With the maul, Johnny locked it permanently in place.

For a few seconds he stood on the step, looking for a soft spot in the dark blur of brush and rocks. He gave up, took a deep breath, and stepped into the rushing darkness. He took three bounding strides, and the ground slapped him.

He lay there only a few seconds. He came up groggy. There was blood and gravel all down one side of his face and arm. He could hear the train rushing down the grade, hanging blindly to the jerrybuilt track.

It seemed much later that the sounds changed. There was a tearing crash, and then for an instant there was no sound at all. Flame burst from the mountainside, cascaded down the steep banks toward the river. The sound of the wreck was a far-away thunder that built to a climax, and then subsided.

In the cañon of the American River, there was silence.

It was a four-mile hike back to camp. Before he had covered a mile, he saw a flush of light along the mesa. The turns of the track brought him to where he could see the flames. The trestle at Robber's Ravine was on fire. Farther along, stacks of ties were going up. Presently a rush of flame sheeted up the barren hillside, and Johnny knew the tents were gone. When the workmen came back tomorrow, they would come back to desolation. There would be a lot of contrite and sheepish rust-eaters hunting work in a day or two. . . .

He was thankful when the rattle of shod hoofs came down the hill to him. Ed and four other men came along, riding high and hunting trouble. They wheeled when they saw Johnny. But he called out to them, and Ed spurred to his side. He mounted behind Ed, and they started back.

No one had to ask questions. They all knew that what they had come to do had been done. It was not the kind of thing that made a man want to brag, but probably their minds were all running the way Ed's was when he said, sniffing the weather: "I reckon we can count on another two months before frost. It might be a good idea if we established a camp at Donner Pass and got things under way there. These slow-ups look like hell on a report."

In the chief engineer's car, lamps burned yellow behind the windows. The door opened, and Babbie stood silhou-etted with a hand to her cheek. A lump came into Johnny's throat. She was so courageous, so fine, so far above what any railroad man could offer. Once he had said there could be no compromise with his work, but tonight he knew there must be.

They went into the heart-warming atmosphere of frying doughnuts. Johnny had no opportunity to speak until Ed ducked out to see if he could rustle up whiskey rations for some men who had earned them. Then, reaching across the gingham-covered table, Johnny captured her hands.

"I've still got that ring," he said.

Babbie's eyes caught the golden luster of the lamps. She said: "You won't have it long, darling."

"Babbie," Johnny said, "I know the road is no place for a woman. But if you could stand it six months out of the year, I'd take a job in town the other six."

Babbie came around and sat on his lap. She held his face in her hands and kissed him lightly on the mouth. "Don't you know yet," she said, "that Pop was only an excuse for me to come back? In the first place, there's no fun in singing to anybody but you and Pop, anyway. And besides . . . well, all you have to do to appreciate a thing is to do without it for a while. I don't ever want to be out of the sound of a train whistle again as long as I live. I'll take the dust and melted butter if I have to, but there's rust in my heart . . . and it's wonderful!"

High in the Sierra Nevadas, where the magnificent shoulders of the Donner Pass hold up the sky, there is a tie siding called simply Barbara Bly. It is all that remains of the girl who sang to the mining camps of the Mother Lode.

But Babbie Duff was with the Central Pacific when the ties stepped down the mountains into Nevada, crossed the desert to Salt Lake City—just a few days before the Union Pacific would have made it, and on to Panorama Point, where the East and West were finally fused. There were some real railroad men on the U.P., God rest them, but there weren't two Theodore Judahs in the country to leave their memories as an inspiration.

Probably there weren't two homes like Babbie's, either. It had wheels, of course. It had windows—lots of them. It had rugs, and a bathtub that folded into a closet, and other things even a city woman wouldn't have sniffed at. It wasn't long before the big bedroom had to be cut up into two rooms, and that wasn't the end of it, either. Before the Duff family was all tallied in, a second car traveled with Johnny and Babbie when they were out on a job.

It got so the Brotherhood didn't say a certain railroad was built by John Duff. A hoghead would declare cheerfully: "You don't have to worry about the grades on that road, mister. It was built, by God, by the Duffs!"

About the Author

Frank Bonham in a career that spanned five decades achieved excellence as a noted author of young adult fiction and detective and mystery fiction, as well as making significant contributions to Western fiction. By 1941 his fiction was already headlining Street and Smith's *Western Story* and by the end of the decade his Western novels were being serialized in *The Saturday Evening Post*. His first Western, *Lost Stage Valley* (1948), was purchased as the basis for the motion picture, *Stage to Tucson* (Columbia, 1951) with Rod Cameron as Grif Holbrook and Sally Eilers as Annie Benson. "I have tried to avoid," Bonham once confessed, "the conventional cowboy story, but I think it was probably a mistake. That is like trying to avoid crime in writing a mystery book. I just happened to be more interested in stagecoaching, mining, railroading. . . ." Yet, notwithstanding, it is precisely the interesting—and by comparison with the majority of Western novels—exotic backgrounds of Bonham's novels that give them an added dimension. He was highly knowledgeable in the technical aspects of transportation and communication in the 19th-Century American West. In introducing these backgrounds into his narratives, especially when combined with his firm grasp of idiomatic Spanish spoken by many of his Mexican characters, his stories and novels are elevated to a higher plane in which the historical sense of the period is always very much in the forefront. This historical aspect of his Western fiction early drew accolades from reviewers so that on one occasion the *Long Beach Press Telegram* predicted that "when the time comes to find an author who can best fill the gap in Western fiction left by Ernest Haycox, it may be that Frank

Bonham will serve well." Among his best Western novels are *Snaketrack* (1952), *Night Raid* (1954), *The Feud at Spanish Ford* (1954), and *Last Stage West* (1959). *Dakota Man* will be his next **Five Star Western**.

About the Editor

Bill Pronzini was born in Petaluma, California. His earliest Western fiction was published under his own name and a variety of pseudonyms in *Zane Grey Western Magazine*. Among his most notable Western novels are *Starvation Camp* (1984) and *Firewind* (1989). He is also the editor of numerous Western story collections, including *Under the Burning Sun: Western Stories* (Five Star Westerns, 1997) by H. A. DeRosso, *Renegade River: Western Stories* (Five Star Westerns, 1998) by Giff Cheshire, and *Tracks in the Sand* by H. A. DeRosso (Five Star Westerns, 2001). His own Western story collection, *All the Long Years* (Five Star Westerns, 2001), was followed by *Burgade's Crossing* (Five Star Westerns, 2003) and *Quincannon's Game* (Five Star Westerns, 2005). His next **Five Star Western** will be *Coyote and Quarter Moon*.